THE RUIN OF A RAKE

Also by Cat Sebastian

The Soldier's Scoundrel
The Lawrence Browne Affair

THE RUIN
OF A RAKE

CAT SEBASTIAN

AVON IMPULSE
An Imprint of HarperCollins Publishers

An excerpt from *The Soldier's Scoundrel* copyright © 2016 by Cat Sebastian.

An excerpt from *The Lawrence Browne Affair* copyright © 2017 by Cat Sebastian.

THE RUIN OF A RAKE. Copyright © 2017 by Cat Sebastian. All rights reserved. Printed in the United States of America. No part of this book may be used or reproduced in any manner whatsoever without written permission except in the case of brief quotations embodied in critical articles and reviews. For information, address HarperCollins Publishers, 195 Broadway, New York, NY 10007.

Digital Edition JULY 2017 ISBN: 978-0-06-264252-3

Print Edition ISBN: 978-0-06-264253-0

Cover art by Fredericka Ribes

Avon Impulse and the Avon Impulse logo are registered trademarks of HarperCollins Publishers in the United States of America.

Avon and HarperCollins are registered trademarks of HarperCollins Publishers in the United States of America and other countries.

FIRST EDITION

17 18 19 20 21   HDC   10 9 8 7 6 5 4 3 2 1

For everyone who tries to live in the space between.

ACKNOWLEDGMENTS

Many thanks to my editor, Elle Keck, who helped reassemble this story into something much better than I had envisioned, and also for her limitless support and enthusiasm.

I'm grateful to Michele Howe, who checked this manuscript for Americanisms and anachronisms (any that remain in the text are only there due to my own bad judgment). Margrethe Martin has been an invaluable friend as well as a sounding board for stubborn plot issues and source of scientific background.

CHAPTER ONE

London, 1817

Julian pursed his lips as he gazed at the symmetrical brick façade of his sister's house. It was every bit as bad as he had feared. He could hear the racket from the street, for God's sake. He pulled the brim of his hat lower on his forehead, as if concealing his face would go any distance toward mitigating the damage done by his sister having turned her house into a veritable brothel. Right in the middle of Mayfair, and at eleven in the morning, when the entire *ton* was on hand to bear witness to her degradation, no less. Say what one wanted about Eleanor—and at this moment Julian could only imagine what was being said—but she did not do things by halves.

As he climbed the steps to her door, the low rumble of masculine voices drifted from an open second story window. Somebody was playing a pianoforte—badly—and a lady was singing out of key.

No, not a lady. Julian suppressed a sigh. Whoever these

women were in his sister's house, they were not ladies. No lady in her right mind would consort with the sort of men Eleanor had been entertaining lately. Every young buck with a taste for vice had made his way to her house over these last weeks, along with their mistresses or courtesans or whatever one was meant to call them. And the worst of them, the blackguard who had started Eleanor on her path to becoming a byword for scandal, was Lord Courtenay.

A shiver trickled down Julian's spine at the thought of encountering the man, and he could not decide whether it was from simple, honest loathing or something much, much worse.

The door swung open before Julian had raised his hand to the knocker.

"Mr. Medlock, thank goodness." The look of abject relief on the face of Eleanor's butler might have struck Julian as vaguely inappropriate under any other circumstance. But considering the tableau that presented itself in Eleanor's vestibule, the butler's informality hardly registered.

Propped against the elegantly papered wall, a man in full evening dress snored peacefully, a bottle of brandy cradled in his arms and a swath of bright crimson silk draped across his leg. A lady's gown, Julian gathered. The original wearer of the garment was, mercifully, not present.

"I came as soon as I received your message." Julian had not been best pleased to receive a letter from his sister's butler, of all people, begging that he return to London ahead of schedule. Having secured a coveted invitation to a very promising house party, he was loath to leave early in order to evict a set of bohemians and reprobates from his sister's house.

"The cook is threatening to quit, sir," said the butler. Tilbury, a man of over fifty who had been with Eleanor since she and Julian had arrived in England, had gray circles under his eyes. No doubt the revels had interrupted his sleep. "And I've already sent all but the—ah—hardiest of the housemaids to the country. It wouldn't do for them to be imposed upon. I'd never forgive myself."

Julian nodded. "You were quite right to send for me. Where is my sister?" Several unmatched slippers were scattered along the stairs that led toward the drawing room and bedchambers. He gritted his teeth.

"Lady Standish is in her study, sir."

Julian's eyebrows shot up. "Her study," he repeated. Eleanor was hosting an orgy—really, there was no use in pretending it was anything else—but ducked out to conduct an experiment. Truly, the experiments were bad enough, but Julian had always managed to conceal their existence. But to combine scientific pursuits with actual orgies struck Julian as excessive in all directions.

"You," he said, nudging the sleeping man with the toe of his boot. He was not climbing over drunken bodies, not today, not any day. "Wake up." The man opened his eyes with what seemed a great deal of effort. "Who are you? No, never mind, I can't be bothered to care." The man wasn't any older than Julian himself, certainly not yet five and twenty, but Julian felt as old as time and as irritable as a school mistress compared to this specimen of self-indulgence. "Get up, restore that gown to its owner, and be gone before I decide to let your father know what you've been up to." As so often happened when Julian ordered people about, this fellow complied.

Julian made his way to Eleanor's study, and found her furiously scribbling at her writing table, a mass of wires and tubes arranged before her. She didn't look up at the sound of the door opening, nor when he pointedly closed it behind him. Eleanor, once she was busy working, was utterly unreachable. She had been like this since they were children. He felt a rush of affection for her despite how much trouble she was causing him.

"Eleanor?" Nothing. He stooped to gather an empty wine bottle and a few abandoned goblets, letting them clink noisily together as he deposited them onto a table. Still no response. "Nora?" It almost physically hurt to say his childhood name for her when things felt so awkward and strained between them.

"It won't work," came a low drawl. "I've been sitting here these past two hours and I haven't gotten a response."

Banishing any evidence of surprise from his countenance, Julian turned to see Lord Courtenay himself sprawled in a low chair in a shadowy corner. There oughtn't to have been any shadows in the middle of the day in a bright room, but trust Lord Courtenay to find one to lurk in.

Julian quickly schooled his face into some semblance of indifference. No, that was a reach; his face was simply not going to let him pretend indifference to Courtenay. He doubted whether anyone had ever shared space with Lord Courtenay without being very much aware of that fact. And it wasn't only his preposterous good looks that made him so . . . noticeable.

The man served as a sort of magnet for other people's attention, and Julian hated himself for being one of those people. As far as he could tell, the man's entire problem was that people paid a good deal too much attention to him. But one could hardly help it, not when he looked like *that*.

Even in the improbable shadows of Eleanor's south-facing study, Julian could properly appreciate Courtenay's famous profile, from the aquiline perfection of his nose to the tousled waves of his overlong coal black hair. Portraitists had fallen over themselves to capture the strong lines of his features in ink and charcoal and oil paints. Rumor had it that the artist of the most famous portrait, the one that had hung in Mrs. Olmstead's drawing room for years after their affair, had actually paid Courtenay for the privilege of painting him, as if he were a common artist's model and not a peer of the realm.

Standing a few scant yards from him, breathing in the scent of the noxious cigarillo Courtenay held in one languid hand, Julian had to scramble to think of anything suitable to say. An insult would do the trick. He was rummaging through his brain to come up with a cutting remark, when a moan sounded from one of the bedchambers upstairs. Julian winced in embarrassment.

"Somebody knows how to start the day," Courtenay murmured, his voice somehow even more obscene than the sound overhead.

"It is nearly midday," Julian snapped, as if the time were what mattered. "The day is not starting here, nor anywhere else in England. Some of us have been up and about for hours."

Courtenay held his gaze for a moment, his green eyes heavy with boredom. "My apologies," he drawled. "I stand corrected. I ought to have said that somebody likes having his cock sucked." He paused and glanced upwards, as if meditating on the soft sounds coming from upstairs. "At least it sounds like cocksucking. No sign of the pounding"—here he rhythmically slapped his hand against the arm of his chair—"that you'd expect to hear with any actual f—"

"Enough!" Julian felt warmth spread through his body—anger and lust all tangled together the way they so often were where Courtenay was concerned, damn it. One of his first memories of London was seeing one of Courtenay's portraits hanging on the wall of a salon to which he had somehow managed to get invited. There it had hung, as if daring Julian to look, to stare, to throw away his tenuous claim to respectability and give himself over to pleasures the portrait seemed to hint at. He had assured himself that in person, the man's eyes couldn't be quite so striking, that surely the passage of time would have done something to soften the perfection of his features. But when Julian finally met Courtenay this winter, he found the man every bit as appallingly attractive as that portrait. It had taken a heroic effort to behave with some semblance of decorum. And for all that, Courtenay hadn't even seemed to notice him, had scarcely so much as looked Julian's way. Not that Julian wanted to be noticed, or anything so vulgar as that. It was simply that after six years spent trying not to lust after a man, it was a bit levelling to have not so much as a glance thrown in one's general direction.

Perhaps it was the coarseness of Courtenay's language

and not Julian's angry outburst that finally got Eleanor's attention, but she finally looked up from her writing with an expression of consternation.

"What are you doing here, Julian?" She had the nerve to sound put out by her brother's presence. "I wasn't expecting you back until after Easter."

There was a time when she would have been glad to see him. Only last year she had pleadingly renewed her offer that he make his home with her instead of keeping his own lodgings. He desperately tried not to think of that now. "That much is evident, my dear. This isn't the sort of entertainment to which I'm accustomed."

Oh, he sounded so peevish, so priggish, but he reassured himself that he had the moral high ground. "I came because I had word that your servants were all about to give notice. If they had aspired to work in a brothel, they likely would have arranged their lives somewhat differently."

Eleanor rose to her feet. Julian didn't know whether to be amused or gratified that she was wearing utterly correct morning attire. It was the striped muslin ensemble they had picked out together—which was to say Julian chose it for her when she showed no interest in refreshing her wardrobe for the season. He noted that at some point in the past several weeks she had stopped wearing a cap. Courtenay's doing, Julian supposed. A lock of her sand-colored hair, identical to Julian's own, tumbled onto her shoulder, and he resisted the urge to reach out and pin it back up.

"You'll not come into my house and talk like that." Eleanor's fists were balled at her sides, dots of pink on her pale cheeks. Julian would never get used to how pale his sister was in England, after a childhood spent under the tropical sun. Nevertheless, she looked extremely well, and the most tiresome part of Julian's nature bitterly wondered if that was what taking a lover had done for his sister.

"Perhaps we could have this conversation elsewhere," he suggested through gritted teeth.

Her eyes narrowed. "Yes, there's something I've been meaning to tell you."

Julian was aware of Courtenay looking back and forth between them like a spectator at a tennis match, when the light shifted and Julian could make out the title of the book Courtenay had open on one long leg.

The Brigand Prince of Salerno.

Left alone in the parlor, Courtenay eyed his empty glass. He very much wanted to fill it with some of that Bordeaux Eleanor had lying about, drain it, then repeat the process several times over in rapid succession. But he knew with a certainty born of vast experience that drunkenness wasn't going to make anything better. He'd only have a rotten headache and still be no closer to fixing his shambles of a life.

It was abundantly clear that he ought not to have come back to England. There was nothing for him here—only sneering prigs like Eleanor's brother. And the usual debt, ostracism, and the sort of scandal that had seemed thrilling at twenty but now, at a few years past thirty, was tedious. He was no longer amused by scandalizing society. But that ship had sailed long ago: London society had made up its mind to be scandalized by him, and he could hardly blame them. He seemed to drift into infamy without the slightest effort, and rumors of his extravagance and his exploits had traveled back to England long before he did.

The sodding *Brigand Prince* was the final straw. It had been published weeks after his return to England, and whoever had written it had drawn a perfect portrait of him. He knew this because he had been told so by several gleeful acquaintances. Every detail was precisely correct, from the length of his hair to the drawling manner of his speech to the way he tied his cravat—sloppily, he had always thought—but the villain of *The Brigand Prince* spent hours berating his valet before the looking glass, so that was what Courtenay was believed to do. All the rest of Don Lorenzo's misdeeds were attributed to Courtenay as well. He didn't bother correcting anyone. The novel had only proven what everybody had believed all along.

Courtenay was effectively stranded in London, a city populated by people who thought him a monster. He had spent the last of his money getting here, and his affairs were in too much confusion for him to figure out when, if ever, he could expect his coffers to be replenished. He had no family to speak of; his sister was dead and his nephew far away, and it was nobody's fault but his own.

Instead of refilling his glass, he tossed his cigarillo into the fire and rose to his feet. The cook would need to be attended to first. He didn't consider himself a man of many talents, but years living abroad with a tight income and a spendthrift sister had given him a background in household diplomacy. No matter what, one maintained peace with the cook and trusted her to negotiate treaties with the rest of the staff. But before reaching the kitchen stairs, he heard footsteps in the foyer. He turned to find a girl struggling into her cloak, while the footman stood awkwardly by, his hands hovering midair.

"Good God, man, she's a tart, not a leper," he hissed into the footman's ear. "Not to mention she's her ladyship's guest." That last bit was something of an overstatement. She was one of the girls Norton had produced midway through last night's revelries. Norton and the rest of his assembled merry makers were nowhere to be seen; the house had fallen silent upon Medlock's arrival and had resumed its usual air of serene, chilly silence. This girl was likely the last to leave. Courtenay took the cloak from the footman and held it out for her to step into.

"Thank you, m'lord," the girl said, flashing a crooked smile over her shoulder. Christ, but when had tarts gotten so young? Courtenay suddenly felt like a lecherous old roué. "Pleasant change of pace not to get pawed at, if you know what I mean," she added.

Courtenay raised an eyebrow. "I trust young Norton knew how to behave himself."

"If you're asking whether he and his friend paid me, then aye, they did."

That wasn't what Courtenay was asking, but he hardly knew how to ask what he really needed to know. English was a terrible language for this sort of nuance. Add that to the running tally of grievances against the motherland. He reached a hand into his coat pocket, and was almost surprised to feel his fingertips brush against the cool solidity of a coin. A crown. Far too much if Norton had already paid, but unspeakably paltry if they had mistreated her. Either way, he could ill afford it. He handed it over to the girl anyway. At another time, another place, Courtenay would have tossed it to her with a wink and a smile and an open invitation, but now he pressed it into her palm.

She closed her ungloved fingers around his own. "I'm at the opera if you want to call on me after a show. Ask for Nan." Her fingers were warm and contained the promise of hours spent not alone.

He pulled his hand away.

Courtenay leaned against the door frame, watching the girl descend to the street. He felt nothing more than a kindly, avuncular interest in her. How demoralizing.

After a decade of debauching himself most comprehensively, he found that he couldn't quite muster up the appropriate enthusiasm for any of his old pleasures. London seemed haunted—by ghosts of dead friends, of bad decisions, of good times that now were tainted by the knowledge of what came later. He couldn't enjoy himself properly with the ghosts whispering in his ear, reminding him of the price of pleasure. It was a sin and a shame to let a talent go to waste, and Courtenay had once had a genius for depravity.

Courtenay pushed himself off the doorframe and headed back into Eleanor's house, patting the pocket where he kept the miniature portrait of his nephew.

CHAPTER TWO

Julian glanced around the disused parlor Eleanor had led him to. "We haven't disrupted any fornication, have we?" he asked dryly.

"Enough, Julian. Enough. Things got out of hand with some of my guests last night, but that's none of your business," she said primly. She tilted her chin up, just the way he had taught her. She looked like a duchess, but her eyes were furious. Julian was about to respond that it was far more than one night, but Eleanor cut him off. "No, don't you dare argue with me. I'm a grown woman—a married woman—and if I choose to behave abominably it's no concern of yours."

Julian wanted to say that if she indeed chose to behave abominably, she had gotten off to a rollicking start. Instead he paced over to the hearth and started poking at the fire. "We had a bargain," he said without turning around. *We were friends*, was what he wanted to say. *We were allies, until Courtenay interfered.*

"I held up my end of the bargain. I married well." She

broke off into an anxious laugh. "So well, my husband has kept the diameter of the globe between us in order to let me spend my fortune in peace. There's no reason I shouldn't live out the rest of my days doing precisely as I please."

He never knew what to say when Eleanor alluded to her marriage. That brought them too close to discussing the actual terms of their bargain, and Julian wasn't certain he was equal to that. "What about me?" he asked. Damn the plaintive note that had crept into his voice.

"What *about* you, Julian? Everyone considers you the consummate gentleman." Julian was not certain whether he only imagined a trace of irony on *considers*. "You don't need my cooperation anymore."

He would always need her. "So you've decided to become a demondaine," he retorted, because it was easier to be rude than it was to be honest about how abandoned he felt, how much he wished everything could go back to the way it had been a few months ago. "I came this morning because Tilbury sent word that your servants were giving notice and your household was in shambles."

"You can see for yourself that isn't the case. Tilbury exaggerates. But if you're so eager to be helpful, then there's a favor you could do for me."

Julian wanted to leap at the chance to be useful, to be busy, to be at all relevant to Eleanor. "Anything," he said.

"It's Courtenay—"

"No."

Eleanor sighed. "*The Brigand Prince* has been the final nail in the coffin of his reputation."

"I should have thought that Courtenay's reputation was long dead and buried. Well beyond the point of coffins and nails."

"You know how it is when people see a thing in print. They take it as the word of God."

"The book doesn't exactly specify that it's about Courtenay," Julian said, focusing his attention on the swirling pattern of the carpet. While he didn't quite like the idea of people believing all the nonsense in that silly novel, seeing Courtenay in Eleanor's study this morning, in disordered evening dress and rumpled hair, and having *quite* clearly spent the night, he felt that the man deserved everything that was coming to him.

"It hardly needs to, and you know it. The trouble is that Lord Radnor read *The Brigand Prince* and now won't let Courtenay see his nephew."

"Radnor is one of your friends. Surely you can persuade him to your way of thinking," Julian said doubtfully. "I can't see that there's much I can do about it."

"I'm very cross with him, but he only wants to keep Simon safe from what he thinks is a corrupting influence."

"I daresay Radnor has the right of it. If I had a nephew, I wouldn't want him anywhere near Courtenay either."

"Well, you're not in any danger of getting a nephew, are you?" Eleanor was nearly shouting, and when Julian gestured for her to lower her voice, she only got louder. "Courtenay has been a friend to me." Julian resisted the urge to respond that the two of them seemed *very* friendly indeed. "He practically raised that child. And now he can't even visit him.

You're always looking to interfere with things that aren't your concern. Why can't this be one of them? Why can't you fix things for Courtenay?"

It was becoming increasingly clear to Julian that Eleanor was beside herself. He desperately wanted to suggest to her that she leave London and spend a few weeks at some quiet seaside resort that catered to overwrought gentlewomen. But he knew his sister far too well to make so disastrous a suggestion. "I'm afraid I can't—"

"Yes, you can," she interrupted. "You're invited everywhere, you're acquainted with everyone. Bring him about with you. Let people see that he's harmless."

Julian nearly reared back in astonishment. "Bring him about with me," he repeated in tones of incredulity. "Like a pet monkey or a parrot?"

"Let him borrow some of your respectability. Let a bit of your polish rub off on him."

Julian wanted to protest that this wasn't how respectability worked. He had spent years acquiring the shine of gentility that one usually had to be born with. But the truth was that he had helped himself to other people's respectability—he had finagled invitations and then gradually insinuated himself into higher and higher social circles. He had borrowed and stolen and finally hoarded up respectability until now he had more than he knew what to do with.

"What, do you expect me to get him vouchers to Almack's? Nothing doing, Eleanor."

She appeared to seriously be considering the question. "No, perhaps not Almack's—"

"Not anywhere. I've worked too hard to throw my good name away by spending time with the likes of Lord Courtenay. You have your title even if you choose to consort with every rake and scoundrel in Christendom." Without his good name, Julian was a merchant from the colonies, a man with tastes that wouldn't bear looking into. Eleanor knew this. And she was asking him anyway.

"For me, Julian," Eleanor said, and now she was almost begging.

"A bit rich to ask me to parade your lover around town. Bad *ton*, Eleanor."

"He's not my lover," she sniffed, "but I thank you for your concern for my virtue, brother."

"I don't give a damn about your virtue. I care about whether you're happy." And it was true, he realized. He'd rather his sister not be the subject of malicious gossip, but more than that he was worried about her. "Dash it, Eleanor. What am I supposed to think with all this going on?" He gestured vaguely to indicate the house and its inhabitants. "You've, ah, had a bit of a turnabout in the past few months."

She had a smudge of ink on her jaw, and he wanted to wipe it away, the way he used to when they were young and ambitious. "Courtenay and his friends are amusing. They sing and play charades and tell droll stories. They fall in love and fall out of love and when I'm near them I feel alive. You won't begrudge me that, will you?"

When she put it like that, he wouldn't begrudge her anything. She was his older sister, his best friend, his accomplice, and more than anything he wanted to make things right with her. He wanted things to go back to the way they used to be, the way they were supposed to be, but if that wasn't possible he'd settle for whatever she was offering. She had the upper hand in this negotiation.

If helping her lover, or whoever Courtenay was to her, was what she required, then he would agree. "All right," he conceded. "I'll help him."

Before Courtenay reached the kitchen stairs, a door swung open. It was Eleanor's dull brother, a prim sort of fellow who always looked at Courtenay as if he were a fly in the pudding. Courtenay knew the type well: stuffy, smug, and terribly concerned about what everybody else thought about him.

Courtenay didn't have the patience for this. He wanted to settle things with Eleanor's cook, get some sleep, and . . . well, that was as far as his planning took him. Surely Medlock had someplace else to be. His club. A middling tailor. Some kind of chapel. Whatever normal gentlemen did with their time, and which Courtenay had never bothered with—and had never been asked to participate in.

"Come in here." Medlock gestured imperiously to an open door. "Please," he added, and somehow made it sound like an insult.

Everything about Medlock seemed calculatedly bland: neither handsome nor ugly, neither tall nor short, neither dark nor fair. His hair fell in the sad territory between brown and blond, his shrewd eyes were an unremarkable gray brown. His features were sharp, except for his mouth, which had a hint of incongruous softness when it wasn't twisted into a grimace of irritation.

Courtenay followed him, expecting to find Eleanor within. But the room was empty. "Alone at last," he murmured suggestively, because it was amusing to watch Medlock get flustered and annoyed. He leaned in close and raised an insinuating eyebrow. "Be sure to turn the key in the—"

"Save your breath. I'll pretend you're saying the foulest things imaginable and you can rest assured that I'm revolted," Medlock said. "We'll save ourselves a good deal of trouble."

Courtenay had no intention of doing that. He much preferred to keep Medlock in a lather. Otherwise the plumpness of those lips might give him ideas, and Julian Medlock— straitlaced, officious, and Eleanor's brother—was the last human on earth about whom he wished to have ideas. "Anything else you'd like to fantasize about with me, Mr. Medlock?" Really, it was too easy. What the fellow needed was a good hard rogering. Courtenay would lay four to one odds on that being precisely the sort of thing Medlock fancied, not that Courtenay was going to do a damned thing about it. At least not in England. Being pilloried would do nothing to help his present state. There were plenty of law-abiding ways for him to slake his lust, thank God.

"Eleanor wants me to take you about," Medlock said in a rush, the words all bleeding into one another.

"Pardon?"

"My sister has asked me to bring you about with me." He spoke the words as if they tasted bad. "Go riding in the park, that sort of thing."

Courtenay took a full step backwards, as if Medlock were ill with some contagion. "Why the devil would I want to do a thing like that?"

Medlock—no hint of softness in his mouth now, thank God—answered from behind gritted teeth. "She is under the impression, misguided though it may be, that if I lend you my countenance, you could achieve a small margin of respectability."

His countenance? Had Courtenay ever heard anything so pompous? "Good God. Am I supposed to want that?" He scanned the room for the brandy bottle and found it on the mantelpiece. His hand had closed around its neck before he had quite made up his mind to have a drink.

"Yes. Because," Medlock went on, in the exasperated manner of one speaking to a foreigner or a child, "Lord Radnor might grant you permission to see your nephew if you weren't entirely a social pariah."

At the mention of his nephew, Courtenay released his grip on the bottle. It had been months since he had seen Simon. When he had first arrived in England, things had looked promising enough—he had taken Simon to Astley's, then to Tattersall's. It had almost been like old times. But then Simon had returned with Radnor to the arse end of Cornwall and that blasted book had come out. Radnor's secretary sent Courtenay an infuriatingly proper letter suggesting that Courtenay take himself as far away from Simon as humanly possible until the scandal died down. It was heavily implied that the scandal would die down at some point coincidental with Courtenay's death.

Courtenay had no recourse, either legal or moral. He had given up the matter as a lost cause and tried not to think about Simon—with the predictable result that any towheaded child he caught a glimpse of reminded him of his nephew. Now that Medlock was presenting him with an actual plan to bring Simon back into his life, Courtenay was ready to agree to nearly anything.

"And you think that spending time with you would rehabilitate my reputation. Because everyone is so fond of you. Everyone likes you so very much."

Courtenay was simply trying to follow Eleanor's logic. She was the genius, he a mere acolyte. It would have been helpful if she had kept him apprised of her intentions, however brilliant and convoluted, before involving her self-righteous brother. But for whatever reason, Medlock took offense. His spine visibly stiffened and his chin tilted up.

"It doesn't matter in the least bit whether anybody likes me," Medlock said, in about as sniffy a voice as Courtenay had ever heard from a grown man. "What matters is that they respect me."

Courtenay was about to tell Medlock where he could shove his respectability when a kitten tumbled off a nearby table and onto Medlock's boot.

Medlock made a noise somewhere in between a squeak and a cough. "Don't scratch that boot. Naughty!" Medlock was wriggling in a way that Courtenay might have found highly interesting under other circumstances. "Oh dear, and there's another one under the settee."

"There are six," Courtenay said blandly.

"Six!" Medlock looked scandalized. Courtenay had no idea there was a limit to the number of cats a decent person could acquire. But Medlock seemed like the type of person who would have up-to-date information about this sort of thing, so Courtenay was prepared to defer to his greater knowledge.

"This is Eleanor's cat room."

Medlock blinked. "Her—oh, never mind." He looked like he dearly wished to express himself on the topic of cat rooms. "Where in heaven's name have they all come from?" he asked, finally grabbing the kitten by the scruff of its neck and holding it aloft.

"Well," Courtenay said, glad to have the chance to reclaim the upper hand, "they do come about in the usual way. A mother cat and a—"

"Stop!" Medlock looked both mortified and furious. Evidently even allusions to feline fornication were enough to discompose him. Courtenay would keep that in mind.

Courtenay reached for the kitten that Medlock was presently dangling from his fingertips. "They don't mean any harm by it," he went on, as if oblivious to Medlock's consternation. "It's just in their nature." As he took hold of the animal, his fingers brushed Medlock's, and he knew he didn't imagine the frisson of awareness that passed over Medlock's face.

"They . . . what? Oh, never mind." Medlock seemed to recover himself. "Meet me tomorrow night at the opera."

He left before Courtenay could object to these plans.

All Courtenay knew was that if he were going to spend time with Medlock, he'd need to do his best to keep the man cranky and irritated. Otherwise he might start getting ideas, and once Courtenay started getting ideas, it was only a matter of time before he acted on them. And from there, everything would go to hell, because that's what it tended to do. He'd lose the only real friend he had in this blasted country and throw away his last remaining chance to see Simon. No, he really needed to keep Julian Medlock at arm's length.

Chapter Three

"You've heard about my sister, I suppose?" Julian took a nonchalant sip of tea while keeping his gaze fixed on Lady Montbray's face.

Julian would never get over the strangely illicit thrill of being granted access to the drawing rooms of people like Lady Montbray, people who had titles and pedigrees stretching back centuries and money from vague sources that nobody ever mentioned.

It felt like an accomplishment but also—and surely this said no favorable things about Julian's character—deliciously fraudulent, even though the drawing room belonged to somebody he had called a friend for years. Well, perhaps not a friend. He wasn't entirely certain that he had friends, apart from Eleanor, and even that seemed doubtful these days. Friendship and rampant social climbing did not mix. Or more to the point, friendship and Julian did not mix: he was cold and guarded, composed of layers upon layers of secrets, each painted over with a polite lie. That was the way he liked it: he preferred the smooth, sleek varnish of falsehood to the unpleasant truths beneath. He didn't want to think about the torpor of helpless days confined indoors, nor about sisters with troubling new appetites for vice. Why the devil would he invite a person into his life to get a closer look at precisely the things he avoided dwelling on? That was what friends were, people who could look at one's inner nastiness the way Eleanor looked at pond scum under her microscope. No thank you.

He smoothed his hand down his waistcoat—dove-gray silk embellished with only the most tasteful suggestion of a stripe—and waited for Lady Montbray's response.

Lady Montbray looked momentarily as if she might deny any knowledge of Eleanor's recent foray into disrepute. When she spoke, she looked at Julian with the shrewdness of a card player trying to understand why an opponent had put down an unexpected hand. "I had always thought that if Lady Standish wished to disgrace herself," she said slowly, "she'd do it by wearing trousers in public or setting fire to her house during one of her scientific misadventures. I certainly hadn't expected *Lord Courtenay* to figure into it."

Julian sighed with unfeigned relief. A lesser person might have made him explain the entire mess in excruciating, incriminating detail. "I knew you'd understand. Nobody could have expected Courtenay to be in England, much less to have taken up with Eleanor."

"I take it they are . . ." She decorously let her voice trail off into polite vagueness.

"It hardly matters." No answer Julian gave would stop

gossip from circulating, and besides, one never looked more ridiculous than when protesting that salacious gossip was untrue. It spoilt everyone's fun.

Lady Montbray's deceptively innocent eyes grew bright with suppressed mirth. "I should think it matters a good deal to her. Is he as handsome as his portraits?"

Courtenay had left England when Lady Montbray was still in the schoolroom. She and Julian had both had their first London season six years ago: she as the wealthy and marriageable daughter of an earl and he as the heir to a shipping fortune and brother to a newly married peeress. Neither of them had met Courtenay before his exile, but the stories of his misdeeds had been whispered by ladies behind fans and celebrated by gentlemen in smoky clubs.

"I daresay he is," Julian acknowledged. He was assailed by the image of Courtenay sprawled in the chair in Eleanor's study. Handsome hardly covered it. Julian felt about Courtenay's looks the way radicals thought about money: that it was deeply unfair and problematic for one person to possess such a disproportionate share. "His hair is shockingly long. Almost to his shoulders." It was almost as if he *wanted* everyone to know he didn't hold himself to decent standards.

"I understand that he's in with a rather artistic set," Lady Montbray offered. "Louisa Norton's youngest son, I believe."

He nodded grimly. "And now Eleanor wants me to rehabilitate Courtenay's reputation. I told her it wouldn't be possible, of course."

She glanced at him over the rim of her teacup. "I should think not."

That was not precisely the reaction he had hoped for, even though it echoed his own doubts. He took another sip of tea. "I'll give it my best, though. Eleanor dearly wants this."

A shadow crossed her face. "I see." After all, she knew about misbehaving siblings. Her brother had been entangled in some or another sordidness—gambling away his fortune and consorting with low company, Julian gathered, although it had all been nicely hushed up—that led to the man not being widely received by people of quality, and instead living in a quiet sort of way. "But what's in it for you?"

He nearly flinched. "It's not like you to be so mercenary."

"But it is like you, Mr. Medlock."

"Touché." He felt his cheeks start to flame. These days, most people didn't refer to his origins, at least not to his face.

"That wasn't an aspersion on your parentage, only a statement of fact. You aren't one to hold your good name cheap, sister or no sister."

Medlock felt some of the tension drain from his shoulders. "Well, if I can clear Courtenay's name a bit, then that will stop Eleanor from being tarnished by association, which in turn will help me." He hesitated. "I do have a proposition that might interest you."

"Do you, now?" A fine blonde eyebrow slanted upwards.

"Are you planning to attend the opera tomorrow?" When she didn't immediately respond, he added, "I promise to make it worth your while."

She hesitated. "What would I wear? None of my opera gowns are in mourning colors." She was supposed to be in her last months of mourning for the late Lord Montbray, but never had Julian seen a lady make such a halfhearted observation of mourning conventions. Today she wore a rose muslin day gown, not a stitch of black on her, nor even gray or lavender. Not that he could blame her; the late Lord Montbray hadn't merited much in the way of mourning if half of what one heard about him had been true.

And that was just the devil of it. Lady Montbray had been delighted when her old sot of a husband had decamped for foreign shores, and likely even happier when he broke his neck. When Julian and Eleanor had left India and established themselves in London, Julian had expected Eleanor's husband to follow. But when he didn't, Eleanor hadn't seemed too cut up about it, so Julian assumed she was one of the many ladies who were only too glad when their husbands made themselves scarce. Julian realized now that he had been wrong. Eleanor was unhappy, and likely regretted ever having come to England and wished Julian at the devil. It had been six years, though, six years of not talking about her happiness or her marriage or what she wanted, and he couldn't simply waltz up to her and ask her whether he had ruined her life. But it had also been six years of improving health for Julian, six years of gradually getting used to the idea that he wasn't going to die anytime soon, and six years of the sneaking suspicion that Eleanor had paid the price for his life. No, he couldn't talk to her about this. It was always best not to ask questions if one didn't want to know the answer, best not to acknowledge problems that had no solutions.

"You have your white silk," he said, glad to have a problem he could solve. "That's perfectly proper."

"And you'll escort me? I take it that's your proposition? That's good of you, Julian, but—"

"No. I'm going with Lord Courtenay."

"Goodness," she breathed. "I'll be sure to polish off my opera glasses so I can watch the entire *ton* go into a frenzy. And so I can get a good look at the man himself. But, Mr. Medlock, are you quite certain this is a good idea?" Concern flickered across her face. "I'd hate to see Lord Courtenay embroil you in any kind of scandal."

At the thought of the sort of scandals that Courtenay usually found himself embroiled in, a wave of heat washed over Julian's body. Embarrassment but also something much more dangerous. "I'm quite certain it's a terrible idea," he admitted. But he wasn't only talking about his good name being sullied. He also thought of the way Courtenay's voice was an insinuating purr, the way he had leaned toward Julian in Eleanor's parlor.

A terrible idea, indeed.

"**W**hat's this about, Eleanor?"

Courtenay had found her walking in the garden, where the first green shoots were emerging in a flower bed.

"The crocuses are late," she answered. "They ought already to be in bloom."

It had done nothing but snow, rain, and otherwise precipitate since he arrived in England a few months earlier. If the crocuses never bloomed he'd hardly be surprised. He would be glad to return to warmer climes, which he supposed he'd do if Radnor continued to succeed in keeping Simon from him. "True. But I was speaking of your brother. He'd rather eat glass than be seen with me, and yet he's going with me to the opera, in plain view of God and everyone. Did you blackmail him?"

He had meant this last remark as a joke, something to smooth the furrow from her brow. But she stiffened, wrapping her shawl more tightly around her shoulders. "It was *not* blackmail, whatever he might have said."

Courtenay took this to mean that she had most certainly blackmailed her brother. She was slightly ruthless—that was part of what he liked about her, after all—so he wasn't surprised to discover a Machiavellian streak. The only thing that surprised him was that Medlock had any secrets worth keeping. Perhaps he had worn the wrong waistcoat or forgotten Sir Somebody's name or committed some equally boring infraction.

"Whatever it was, thank you," he said. He wasn't accustomed to receiving favors, especially from people who had outright refused to share his bed, as Eleanor had done. "I don't like my odds of success, but thank you."

She looked up at him sharply now. "Radnor isn't a monster, you know. He may yet come around."

He shook his head. "But—"

"Give it a few weeks," Eleanor said. "Things could work out for you. They don't always, not for everyone." There was a sorrowful note in her voice that made him want to take her by the hand, but she smiled with false brightness, forestalling any sympathy. "But they could for you."

Courtenay wasn't interested in discussing the shipwreck that was his future. "That bonnet is fetching. Blue becomes you. Is it new?"

"Flatterer." She looked away, turning her attention to the weak shoots of green in the loamy flower bed. "That's another reason you ought to let Julian try to help you. It'll give him something to do other than buy me things. If he sends me so much as another parasol, I swear I'll set it on fire. He's bought me four dinner gowns in the last month. Four!"

Courtenay was surprised to learn that Medlock, who seemed a tight-fisted sort, bought his sister's clothing. Eleanor was always dressed expensively, even lavishly. He had thought it a sweet, vain streak in his new friend, the care she took in selecting her attire while never seeming to notice what she was wearing.

Eleanor had been one of the first people he had met after arriving in England. She had been staying with Radnor at his godforsaken shambles of a house in Cornwall, doing something involving electricity.

He had promptly tried to seduce her. Unsuccessfully.

She had been amused by his attempt, as if it had never occurred to her that anyone would want to get her into his bed. Courtenay felt nothing but contempt for her absent husband, the fool. To abscond to the Orient, or the Antipodes, or wherever the fellow was when one had a wife like Eleanor seemed the height of idiocy.

They had fallen into an easy friendship, the sort of camaraderie that usually took years to establish. He had more or less followed her to London like a duckling after its mother. He hadn't anywhere else to be, so he hired a set of rooms that wouldn't put him too badly out of pocket. He frequented the sort of coffeehouses where artists and other clever people congregated, but he found himself most often at Eleanor's house. Even after he spelled out to her the damage his friendship would cause her reputation, she had waved away his concern. "What, will I ruin my prospects?" And then she had laughed bitterly.

Over the past few months, Courtenay had come to understand that Eleanor—despite being sufficiently rich and utterly brilliant—was sad. Whatever was causing her sorrow, she wouldn't talk about it, but Courtenay had formed his own opinions. Courtenay understood very well what it was like to have old troubles that lodged like a splinter in one's brain.

"Give your frocks away," he said blithely. "Found a charity to clothe fallen women." He fell into the habit of talking nonsense to take her mind off her troubles. It was what he did.

"Ha! I doubt fallen women would have any interest in the sort of gown Julian fancies. Everything is correct, from the number of ruffles to the exact cut of the neckline. It would be an insult to fallen women to subject them to such boring frocks."

"They're very becoming," he said, "in a sedate sort of way." And it was true, but now that he knew the gowns weren't Eleanor's own choice, he could see the hand of the man who had chosen them. It was as if Medlock had an equation to solve, and the answer was a cornflower blue promenade gown with three flounces and a matching pelisse. Everything studiedly correct, painstakingly proper.

Then he remembered the fullness of the man's lips, and the way he his eyes had flared at Courtenay's coarseness. Perhaps not so proper after all.

"Come here." He unknotted the ribbons of her bonnet and retied them in a bow under one ear. Much more fashionable that way. "There we go." He took her by the shoulders, holding her at arm's length to admire his handiwork. She scowled at him but didn't retie the bow. Dropping his hands to his sides, he said, "I spoke with the cook. She won't give notice." He had begun by complimenting the cook's pastry, comparing it favorably with the efforts of the chefs he had employed in Italy and France. "It seems that she had a row with your butler and each of them said a good many regrettable things."

She shook her head. "I wasn't worried about that."

"I know, my dear, but I was." He was fond of her, and she seemed on the precipice of something . . . irrevocable. He didn't know precisely what, but he knew what someone looked like before they made a bad decision. He knew it very well indeed. "I'm not doing you any favors by spending so much time here."

Eleanor crouched to poke at one of the emerging bits of green, the edge of her shawl dragging in the dirt. "We've been through this," she said, steel in her voice. And so they had. Courtenay had no intention of reembarking on a subject that was tiresome to them both. The world was filled with enough tiresomeness without deliberately adding to it.

Courtenay only wished she sounded happier in saying so. It would all be well and good if Eleanor actually enjoyed consorting with disreputable artists and rogues such as had congregated here last night. But she had regarded the party like a spectator at a play: she wasn't enjoying herself so much as staving off boredom. Or worse.

He bent forward and kissed her cheek. "Let's go inside and have some tea."

They went in arm in arm, Eleanor lost in her silent troubles and Courtenay considering how long he could in good conscience let Eleanor associate with him.

Perhaps it was just as well Radnor wouldn't let Simon anywhere near him. Courtenay knew by now the havoc he wreaked on everyone close to him. There was a grave in an Italian churchyard testifying to that. Yes, Isabella had made her own choices, but Courtenay was her elder brother and ought to have known better. He had spent a decade doing whatever pleased him—going where he wanted, spending what he wished, bedding who he desired. Now his fortune was gone, his sister dead, his nephew lost, and Courtenay had come to think of himself as an agent of destruction. Even when he meant well, ruin followed in his wake like vultures after a hunt.

CHAPTER FOUR

Julian was starting to fear that bringing Courtenay to the opera had been a tactical error. For one, Courtenay seemed to take up twice the space of any normal man. It wasn't his size—indeed, Julian found himself repeatedly confirming that Courtenay was not much larger than he was himself—a bit broader in the shoulders and perhaps an inch or two taller, but he was hardly a giant. No, Courtenay simply arranged his body with no regard for anyone who was forced to share space with him. Instead of sitting on the chair like a normal person, he positively sprawled, propping one of his long legs on the empty seat before him and stretching an arm along the back of the empty seat to his side.

They had the entire box to themselves, but Julian was acutely aware of all the places where their bodies almost—but not quite—touched. Every breath brought him into acute danger of one of his limbs meeting one of Courtenay's. And that was a fate he ardently hoped would not come to pass, for reasons he chose not to dwell on.

It was all he could do to keep his attention on the opera. Actually, that wasn't true, because he had no idea what had happened thus far beyond the usual foreign singing, and it was nearly the interval.

And then there was the matter of Courtenay's reading material. To have brought any book whatsoever to the opera was eccentric at best. But Courtenay, somehow managing to lounge decadently in the stiff-backed chair as if he were reading in bed, for God's sake, had brought the blasted *Brigand Prince*. Why bring any book at all, unless it was to demonstrate how bored he was with his company? As if his posture alone didn't communicate that fact quite sufficiently.

Occasionally, for whatever purpose, Courtenay would read a passage aloud.

"Listen to this, Medlock." Courtenay lowered his voice so as not to be heard by anyone in a neighboring box. This was, ostensibly, polite, but the raspy quiet of his voice, combined with the darkness, suggested an intimacy Julian did not want to think of. "Don Lorenzo has caught Agatha traipsing through the haunted abbey. Do you think they'll finally take one another's clothes off?"

Julian nearly protested that it wasn't an abbey (it was a monastery), it wasn't haunted (the eerie noises came from imprisoned monks, not specters), and this was hardly the sort of book in which the characters took off one another's clothing (more's the pity). But he reflected that a highly specific knowledge of the contents of *The Brigand Prince* was not something Julian Medlock ought to know in his capacity as a gentleman.

Instead, without looking at Courtenay, he murmured, "Is that so?" in the same polite tone one would use with someone who was tiresomely complaining about a toothache. They did not need to be friends. They did not even need to be *friendly*. All Julian needed to do was indicate to the world that Lord Courtenay was a person a respectable gentleman could be seen with.

And seen they were. For the entire performance, Julian had been acutely aware of glances darted their way, opera glasses aimed towards them. "You might try sitting up straight," he hissed. "Please recall that we're here to create the illusion that you're not an unfit companion for an impressionable child."

Instead Courtenay slid his chair into the shadowy recesses of the box, and then proceeded to cross his ankles on the seat before him, adopting a posture that signified contempt for the entire enterprise: the opera, society in general, and Julian in particular. The least he could do was pretend to be grateful for Julian's efforts. Julian didn't know what his sister saw in the man. But it didn't matter. He was discharging his obligation to Eleanor, and then it would be over.

"Agatha's frightened," Courtenay said. He still hadn't looked up from the book, which Julian might have found flattering under other circumstances. "But not nearly as frightened as she ought to be, if you ask my opinion. Lorenzo—that's me, you know—grabs her by the wrists—"

Julian could not let that go by. "My understanding is that people popularly assume Lorenzo to be modeled—physically, at least—after you, but unless you've spent time manhandling maidens in monasteries, you can't properly say that Lorenzo *is* you."

"Who's to say that I haven't? I can't recall doing anything untoward in a—you're quite right, it's a monastery, not an abbey. How clever of you to remember." Julian cringed at his slipup. "But I can't pretend to remember every last one of my sins. Since you've read the novel, let me ask you who you think Agatha is? Norton is certain that she's supposed to be Mrs. Castleton's oldest daughter, but I've never laid eyes on the girl, much less seduced her, so it seems an odd thing to have us pawing at one another in Italy."

"Agatha certainly doesn't paw anybody," Julian said. Courtenay—he meant Lorenzo, dash it—was the only one who could properly be said to paw.

"Oh, yes she does," Courtenay said, flipping through the pages. *"Agatha gripped Don Lorenzo's cloak. 'Give me my locket,' she cried, twisting the heavy velvet in her small, white hands, until Don Lorenzo had no choice but to bend towards her, or otherwise risk tearing the valuable fabric."*

That was a grossly out of context passage. "That's hardly pawing," Julian hissed, indignant on poor Agatha's behalf. "She needs the locket to prove that she's the prince's rightful heir. And he's trying to abscond with it, so of course she wants to stop him." Before he could think better of it, he had shifted over and taken a new seat beside Courtenay. "Give me that." He took the book from Courtenay's hands and closed it firmly.

"But she goes on holding his cloak for three pages. Lorenzo doesn't make the slightest move to get away," Courtenay murmured. "He just lets himself get pulled to and fro by a slip of a girl." He was silent for a moment, and Julian dared to hope that this topic was closed. "That's what I don't understand. How did the author know?"

Julian tried to focus on the foreign lady who was singing onstage, but he could not let that remark pass. "Know what?"

"That it's precisely the sort of thing I like."

"Velvet cloaks? Jewel theft? Depriving decent people of their birthrights?"

A low chuckle. "No, the manhandling."

A spasm of lust jolted through Julian's body and settled in the neighborhood of his cock. He tried to keep his attention on the stage, not on the image of Courtenay engaged in anything resembling manhandling.

"You like to intimidate women," he managed. "How unsurprising."

"Good God no, I mean it the other way around. That's why I think it has to be one of my former lovers who wrote it."

"The other way around," Julian echoed.

"Being manhandled. Having the manhandling done to me. Not that I mind it either way, to be frank."

Julian knew he ought not to pursue this line of conversation. The less said about Courtenay's bedroom preferences the faster his obviously *insane* prick might recover. And the less said about this infernal novel, the better. But his traitorous cock, which had woken up at the word *manhandling*, had ideas of its own. "And so you think one of your conquests wrote this novel?"

For the first time, Courtenay turned to face Julian. Julian

could feel the man's gaze on him, even as he forced himself to attend to the stage, to his own shaking hands gripping the arms of the chair, and his stupid, stupid prick. "One of my . . . What an odd way to put it."

"It was written by a gentleman," he heard himself say, and hoped Courtenay didn't notice his hoarseness. "It says so, right on the frontispiece. *By A Gentleman*." He knew Courtenay got up to all manners of mischief, but somehow it had never occurred to him that Courtenay fancied men. Julian's prick had never paid closer attention to a conversation.

"I daresay you'd have a point if none of my lovers had been gentlemen, but—"

Julian lost the rest of the sentence to the sound of blood rushing in his ears.

Manhandling. Julian dragged his thoughts away from that word, that concept, that sudden and startling *want. Gentlemen.* A wave of awareness traveled through his body, and he had to force himself to remember that he was at the opera. He was only sitting beside this infamous reprobate as a favor to his sister, not to gratify his own suddenly deranged prick.

He was here as a favor to *Eleanor*, who was this man's *lover.* What in heaven's name had come over him, and why in hell could his cock not understand that this was *wrong*?

He ought to have known better than to trust himself anywhere near Courtenay.

They could say what they wanted about Courtenay's mental faculties but he knew a cockstand when he saw one, and

Medlock most certainly had one. Well, to be fair, it didn't take much intelligence to figure it out: there it was, an erection, plain as day, straining against the fabric of Medlock's breeches, even though he tried to cover it with the novel.

And he looked none too pleased about it. Courtenay had a moment of fellow feeling for the man. Misplaced desires were a plague. Nor was Courtenay a stranger to being the recipient of unwanted lust. Nobody wanted to want a man such as he. Or, rather, plenty of people wanted him, but only for a couple of tumbles, a feather in one's cap, a story to tell later on.

If Courtenay were any kind of decent human being, he might have pretended not to notice Medlock's state.

But Courtenay was not decent, and sometimes being a reprobate had its advantages.

After confirming that they were safely in the shadows and out of view of the rest of the opera-goers, he took his feet off the seat where he had propped them—really, he may have gone too far in trying to bait Medlock—and hooked an ankle around the leg of Medlock's chair, tugging him into the dark privacy of the corner.

"What do you think you're doing?" Medlock whispered, but he didn't stand and go back to the seat he had occupied earlier.

Courtenay took the book out of Medlock's lap, letting it slide unceremoniously to the floor. Then he traced a single finger down the length of Medlock's erection. "Impressive," he said, and was conscious that this was the first compliment he had ever paid Medlock.

Medlock's only response was an inarticulate growl.

Courtenay liked that. Hadn't taken Medlock for the growling type. What he liked even more was that Medlock still didn't move away, or even so much as swat Courtenay's hand. Instead his fingers were wrapped tightly around the arms of his chair.

Courtenay drew his finger back up the rigid line of Medlock's cock, lingering at the tip.

This wouldn't be the first time Courtenay had gotten up to no good at the opera. Nor even the second. It wouldn't be the first time he had dallied with a person he wasn't terribly fond of, nor the first time he had turned lust into a kind of revenge.

There was, objectively speaking, nothing new here.

So when he cupped Medlock's cock, and Medlock responded by pressing ever so slightly into his palm, and letting go of the chair not to push Courtenay away, but to fling a hand over his mouth, muffling an oath, Courtenay really shouldn't have felt anything beyond the predictable stirring in his breeches. Workaday lust, nothing to worry about.

He certainly shouldn't have taken hold of Medlock's fussily knotted cravat and pulled him close for a hungry kiss.

But that's what he did anyway.

It was a savage collision of lips and it was Courtenay doing all the kissing, but Medlock brought his hand to rest on Courtenay's shoulder and that really oughtn't to have made a difference but it did. He wouldn't have guessed that Medlock tasted like chocolate, would have thought he tasted like very correct after-dinner port or maybe tooth powder. But Courtenay had always felt that kissing and groping and flat-out fucking were perfectly good ways to get to know somebody.

Not that he wanted to get to know Medlock.

But still, now he knew the man drank chocolate and that felt disconcertingly relevant.

He had Medlock half out of his chair and onto his lap when he drew one of those soft lips into his mouth. Christ, but those lips belonged on somebody else. Somebody Courtenay actually liked. Medlock, prim and stuffy, ought to have a stingy little mouth.

When Medlock pulled away—Courtenay knew he would before they got to anything more interesting than kissing—he wiped that incongruous mouth with the back of his hand.

"What the devil is *wrong* with you?" Medlock was safely back in his own chair now. "Are you mad?"

"It's an open question. I prefer to think I'm indolent and hedonistic but you can draw your own conclusions."

"We're in public. For God's sake, do you think being exposed as a"—he lowered his voice from a whisper to something even quieter—"sodomite will help your cause?"

It didn't escape Courtenay's notice that Medlock objected to the location rather than the activity. "I'll be sure to find a more private place next time."

"There won't be a next time." Even in the shadowy dimness, Courtenay could see Medlock's eyes go wide with outrage at the suggestion. "I don't know what came over me. I must be coming down with something." He looked most gratifyingly flustered.

"Interesting illness that gives one a hard cock," Courtenay mused, letting his gaze drift to the placket of Medlock's breeches. "You seem to have recovered, though."

"I think I hate you."

"I *know* you hate me." And it was true. The expression in Medlock's eyes was, if not total hatred, then at least scorn. No matter. Courtenay was used to it. He told himself that Medlock's contempt didn't matter, and the twisting feeling in his gut was a mere coincidence. "I don't know what Eleanor sees in you." He suddenly looked stricken. "Oh my God. Eleanor."

The fellow most definitely thought Eleanor and Courtenay were lovers. Courtenay could have put his mind at ease, but bugger that. Let the man tear himself up a bit. Let him get a taste of what it was like to be on the wrong side of the rules.

Chapter Five

<hr>

All eyes were on them as they made their way to Lady Montbray's box during the interval. Julian didn't like it one bit. He preferred to hover unobjectionably in the background. As always, he used absolute propriety as both sword and shield. Nobody could suspect him of lax ethics or any human frailty when he was the most correct person in the room. He could hardly suspect it of himself. He nodded and bowed to acquaintances and reassured himself that whatever madness had come over him earlier was a temporary aberration rather than a decline into moral turpitude. Courtenay must bring about that sort of reaction. There was no other explanation.

Courtenay looked . . . perfectly fine, actually. Julian had half expected the man to show up in a purple waistcoat or other sartorial abomination but instead he wore a perfectly unremarkable and quite well tailored black coat. Really, he was dressed more decently than Julian could have expected. He almost looked like a normal aristocrat rather than the infernal scapegrace he was. It was strange that he had taken care to arrange himself so properly, when he clearly couldn't care any less about propriety in all other facets of his life.

The only blot on Courtenay's appearance—apart from the tragedy that was his hair—was his cravat. The man's valet must be blind or demented. However, it looked no different than it had when they entered the opera earlier that evening, even though it must have come askew during that ill-advised kiss. Perhaps that was why he tied it in such a sloppy manner—so nobody would be any the wiser if he indulged his lascivious inclinations. Perhaps he kissed and fondled men every night and women every morning and hosted a mixed orgy every afternoon. Perhaps their embrace had been as unremarkable for Courtenay as a regularly scheduled meal.

Not so for Julian. He preferred discreet liaisons, conducted with gentlemen who understood the value of moderation. There was no unbridled passion, thank God, but rather a straightforward and healthy fulfillment of a need.

He did not, in other words, get his cock stroked by his sister's paramour with hundreds of potential onlookers.

As they approached Lady Montbray's box, Julian patted his cravat to make sure it bore no traces of his indiscretion.

"It's perfectly fine," Courtenay said. Julian hadn't even realized the man was watching him and felt a prickle of belated awareness course through his body.

They found Lady Montbray alone with her companion. Julian was pleased to see that Lady Montbray had on the white silk gown he had advised her to wear, very correct and becoming. She also had a profusion of feathers in her hair, which might perhaps have been vulgar in anyone lacking her pedigree, wealth, and beauty. Rich aristocrats who looked like Dutch dolls could put whatever they wanted in their hair, he supposed. Everybody else had to cleave closely to every rule and regulation or be branded an upstart vulgarian. *Not one of us, dear.*

That made it all the more galling that Courtenay had thrown that privilege away. He had been born to wealth, inherited a title, and was as good-looking as it was possible for a human being to be, as much as it irked Julian to admit it. But he had—if gossip was to be believed—gambled away half his fortune and spent the other half on women. He had behaved so outrageously that even his title wasn't enough to redeem him.

If Julian had half the status Courtenay was born with—an entry in Debrett's, a coat of arms—he'd be the prime minister by now, for God's sake. Instead his sole accomplishment was being here, a gentleman so polished and pristine his very humanity was concealed beneath layers of glossy refinement. That had been his goal when he and Eleanor had arrived in London; his eighteen-year-old self had even thought being received by the highest rungs on the ladder of society would be a sort of gift for Eleanor, a present to thank her for having come with him. Perhaps he had been naïve.

He shook that thought off and performed the necessary introductions while Lady Montbray looked at Courtenay as if he were a lion in a zoo. Really, she wasn't even bothering to conceal her shocked curiosity. Perhaps Julian had gone a step too far in bringing Courtenay to her. But at the beginning of the interval she had waved her fan ever so slightly at him, from her box to his.

One didn't get where Julian was without being able to smooth over some minor awkwardness. He did what one always did in these situations, which was to make a stock remark about how one hoped one's acquaintances enjoyed the rest of the evening, and then beat a hasty retreat. But before he could manage the thing, Courtenay had pulled up a chair next to Lady Montbray's companion and drawn her into conversation.

"Oh dear," he muttered. Miss Sutherland looked openly irritated. She was a thin, rather plain woman who Julian suspected of bluestocking tendencies, and she had not come to the opera to be assailed by rakehells.

"Mr. Medlock," Lady Montbray whispered. "I was hoping you'd bring him to me. I've been dreadfully bored and meeting an infamous character was precisely what I needed."

That gave Julian an idea. "Do you think anyone else will share that sentiment?" He could launch Courtenay into society as a novelty, perhaps. That would be better than nothing.

At that moment, a pair of ladies Julian only vaguely recognized entered Lady Montbray's box, took one look at Courtenay, and turned wordlessly on their heels to leave.

"Perhaps not," he said.

"But look. He's made a conquest of Anne. I hadn't thought her at all the type to be charmed by a rogue."

Anne Sutherland was an impoverished relation of Lady Montbray's late husband and had taken up residence with Lady Montbray some years earlier. She had a habit of looking at one as if she knew precisely what one was about, which made Julian slightly wary of her. But her earlier annoyance was quite gone, and now she was regarding Courtenay as if he were a clever child who had brought her a posy. They were talking about the book Miss Sutherland had open in her lap. How the devil had he managed to encounter the only two people on earth who read at the opera?

"Nobody's safe," Julian said bitterly.

Lady Montbray raised an eyebrow. "I think Anne is quite safe."

"That's what you say now." In truth, Julian would have thought a mousy bluestocking like Miss Sutherland to be the last person on earth to draw Courtenay's attentions. But looking at her now, she didn't seem in the least bit drab. She looked lively and engaged. And when Courtenay reached into his coat pocket and produced that infernal novel, she actually laughed. He had never heard her laugh. He had hardly ever heard her speak, come to think of it. Whatever mysterious quality of Courtenay's made one behave like a feral animal had the result of making Miss Sutherland positively blossom. He wasn't flirting with her—it wasn't anything as pointed as that—but it was as if he was bringing the best part of her out into the light.

She wasn't half crawling into Courtenay's lap, though, so perhaps she was made of stronger stuff than Julian, damn it.

"You *must* read it," he was saying. He was *recommending* it? Julian was horror stricken. The last thing he needed was for anyone else to read that blasted book and associate it with Courtenay.

"We'd best be getting back," he announced.

Courtenay bent over Miss Sutherland's hand, and instead

of kissing the air above it, he turned her hand and kissed her palm. Good God. And she *laughed* at this impertinence, as if he had told the funniest witticism. "Thank you for the conversation," he said to Miss Sutherland. "I don't meet many people who share my taste in poetry."

"I could say the same to you," she said.

His departure from Lady Montbray was more formal, thank heavens. Julian took hold of Courtenay's sleeve and all but dragged him away.

"**W**hat were you doing with Miss Sutherland?" Medlock said once they had gotten back to their box. "You can't possibly have hoped to get under her skirts."

Courtenay regarded him in bewilderment. "Do you think that's the only interest I have in people? You talk to women and as far as I've observed, you haven't any interest in getting under their skirts."

They were now seated in the respectable center of the box, amply lit, so Courtenay could see the blush that rose to Medlock's cheeks. Pretty, a part of him thought. The part in his breeches, naturally.

"I like brilliance," Courtenay explained. "I can't resist it. I like clever people."

"You must have run in devilish clever company, Courtenay," Medlock quipped. "Must have run into geniuses everywhere you went."

"I don't just mean fucking them, Medlock." He watched the blush rise in Medlock's cheeks again. "How old are you?"

"Four and twenty."

He acted much older, and it was strange to realize that he was scarcely older than Norton's opera girl. "That explains it."

"Explains what?" He sounded affronted.

"I forget what it's like to be young enough to think you have answers."

"It's not about thinking I have the answers. My desires are well regulated. I have self-control." And yet, the blush had returned to his cheeks and he shifted in his seat in a way that made Courtenay wonder if his prick knew about this program of well-regulated desires.

"You need a good hard rogering."

Medlock looked like he was trying to purse his lips but couldn't quite manage it. Oh, he was trying his damnedest to hate this conversation, but he couldn't help himself. "And I suppose you're volunteering?"

Well, *of course*, he was volunteering. But it wouldn't do to say so. Medlock had rebuffed his advances earlier, and Courtenay wasn't in the habit of trying to argue his way into other people's beds. "I do apologize for that earlier assault on your person, Medlock," he said with exaggerated politeness. "I ought to know better than to inconvenience Eleanor by debauching her brother."

He heard Medlock suck in a breath. He was irritated. Good.

Courtenay decided to take pity on the fellow. "Look, you don't need to do this," he said. "We'll tell Eleanor you tried your best to make me respectable but it didn't take."

Medlock made a noise that might have been a snort in

a less correct gentleman. "If you think it's that simple, you don't know my sister."

"She's . . . tenacious."

"Tenacious doesn't cover it. And she's . . ." a whisper of pain flickered across his face ". . . not herself lately."

It went unsaid that Eleanor's association with Courtenay constituted this great departure from her usual behavior. Courtenay might have been hurt if he hadn't already developed a convenient callous over that part of his heart.

But Courtenay wouldn't let that casual aspersion on Eleanor's character go unanswered. "A lucky few people have desires that map onto what the world expects of them." He spoke slowly, giving Medlock time to reflect on how little he belonged in that group. "For the rest of us, it's like holding down a balloon."

"A balloon?" There was a hefty dose of scorn in Medlock's voice, but Courtenay had plenty of practice ignoring worse.

"Before they launch a hot-air balloon," he said, all patience, "it's tethered to the earth with the thickest ropes you've ever seen." Eleanor had taken him to a see a balloon launch the previous month. He had at first thought it simply an expensive form of suicide, but then watching the colorful orb coast into the sky, he thought he understood. "The thing is made of nothing but wicker and silk and air, but it's straining these ropes to the breaking point trying to float away." And then once it was released from its tethers, the balloon went anywhere it damned well pleased until it fell out of the sky, more or less. He felt that his metaphor stood.

"And you're telling me that Eleanor's *desires*"—he said

the word with an audible cringe, like one might say *sewage* or *lice*—"are similarly strained."

"We aren't lovers and we never have been." Was it his imagination or did Medlock look relieved in a way that had nothing to do with his sister's virtue? "But desire isn't always about fucking." He enjoyed the shiver of distaste, or whatever it was, that went through Medlock's lean frame at the sound of that word. "Has it occurred to you that your sister's intellectual pursuits depend on her husband's absence? All those natural philosophers she corresponds with assume she's managing her husband's business interests while he's away. If they are ever reunited, that would all be over for her." He paused, not sure whether to go on. "However, she may have other wants that require a husband's more immediate presence."

"I see." Medlock's mouth was a tight line. "And she has confided these secret desires"—another moue of distaste—"to you."

"No, Medlock, she has not. But I can read between the lines." It was a wonder that Medlock hadn't. "I had a sister of my own, you know."

"From what I understand, your sister had little in common with mine."

He meant that Isabella had been a hellion, whereas Eleanor was a paragon. "My sister made a marriage that was founded more on practicality than on affection." He paused, letting Medlock decide whether there was a parallel. "Later, she found the marriage to be unsatisfactory."

"That, I believe, is when she ran off with the Italian."

He hadn't been Italian, but that was hardly the point. "She left her husband, taking Simon with her." Simon had been little more than a baby, Isabella hardly more than a child herself. Courtenay had followed them on the next boat, not to bring her back, but to make sure that wherever she went she had a friend.

"And then she died."

"Six years later she became ill and died. Even the strictest moralizer would hardly attribute her death to her behavior."

Medlock's hesitation indicated that he might not agree with those hypothetical moralizers. "I hardly see what this has to do with Eleanor."

"You may not, but I do. I'd hate to see your sister as sad as mine was. Not everyone is cut out to be an outcast." Isabella hadn't been. Eleanor certainly wasn't. Even Courtenay had his moments of doubt.

"Is that a threat?"

Courtenay abandoned his pretense of bored lounging. "For God's sake, man! Listen to yourself. No, I'm not threatening your sister's virtue or her happiness. I'm trying to say that when I leave, you'll need to be there for her, regardless of what she chooses."

"When you leave?" It was a terrible habit Medlock had, this repetition of phrases with only the barest hint of a question mark to give the pretense of civil discourse. "I thought you meant to stay in England to be near to your nephew? Why the devil are we doing this, if you only plan to leave?"

"*If* I leave, then. Which is what I'll need to do if you fail in your efforts to change Radnor's mind."

"Nonsense. I won't fail." He spoke with a degree of confidence Courtenay would have found galling if it weren't his fate—and Simon's—that Medlock was so confident about.

"It'll take more than a visit to the opera."

The barest pause, the hesitation of a man before throwing a coin into the center of a card table. "I'll get you an invitation to the Preston ball."

It took Courtenay a moment to realize who and what Medlock was referring to. "No, Medlock, you most certainly will not." Lord Preston was Chancellor of the Exchequer; Lady Preston was one of those ladies who secretly ruled all of London society. If Courtenay were on fire in the middle of their ballroom, they wouldn't stop the ball to douse the flames.

"Oh, yes I will." There was a steely resolve in the man's voice that made Courtenay almost believe him.

Julian didn't know exactly why he was about to do this, but he was absolutely determined that he would.

Partly because he wanted to prove Courtenay wrong. That was understandable, he told himself.

Partly because he wanted to make things right with Eleanor. Even if this only constituted the tiniest sliver of his motivations, it was enough to justify his actions. Surely that was the way these things worked, one pure motive washing away the fatuity of his third reason, which wasn't even a reason at all, but rather a confusion of lust.

Julian couldn't remember when he had started to fantasize

about Courtenay. It was years before meeting him. He knew of Courtenay from rumors and gossip; even though he disapproved on principle of everything Courtenay had done to deserve his notoriety, he found his speculations about Courtenay taking a decidedly unwholesome turn. The idea of a man whose only compass was his pleasure drew Julian in like the sweet scent wafting from a bakery. Meeting him had only made it worse; now he could hardly shut his eyes at night without an unbidden fantasy. And while he knew that spending time around the man would only make things worse, he wanted more. Now his self-recriminations about his uncontrolled lust would be tangled up in Courtenay's own words about pleasure and tethered balloons and manhandling, which took him right back to tethers in a less metaphorical sense, God help him. His mind was refusing to behave in the linear, well-regulated fashion he expected of himself.

They left the opera a few minutes late, after the bulk of the crowd had dwindled but the lobby was far from empty, and Julian could be certain of orchestrating the scene he had in mind.

They passed a handful of people on the stairs. Mr. Fitzwilliam—no, he wouldn't do. Mrs. Anderson, Sir Francis Legerton . . . and then he saw Lord John Ramsay, the youngest son of a duke. He was snobbish and rude and exactly what Julian needed. Best of all, Julian had never liked him and had no qualms about throwing him to the wolves.

"Lord John," Julian said affably. They belonged to the same club and, as two of London's short supply of eligible bachelors, had been at many dinner parties together. "I daresay you haven't had a chance to see Lord Courtenay since he returned from France." Truth be told, Julian wasn't entirely certain where Courtenay had returned from, but it hardly mattered. He was telling people France from now on. "Lord John Ramsay, allow me to present Lord Courtenay."

Lord John looked precisely as aghast as Julian had hoped. "I . . . good evening, Medlock," he said, his voice full of reproach. And then he walked away.

Perfect.

"What the devil are you up to?" Courtenay asked under his breath. "If that was one of the Duke of Linfield's sons then you're barking up the wrong tree. I went to school with one of that lot. All sermonizing and hellfire." He paused. "I think you'd get along damned well with them."

Well, that was an insult if Medlock had ever heard one. "As you can tell, I certainly do not. Now be quiet, because I need to talk to this fellow." It was Lucius Barry but it could have been nearly anyone for this part of his scheme.

"I say, Barry. Just had the oddest thing happen. Have you talked to Ramsay recently? I think somebody ought to check on him. We were leaving Lady Montbray's box"—this was a lie, but only a little one—"and Ramsay gave me the cut. He couldn't possibly have meant to. Oh, I say, have you met Lord Courtenay?" He performed the necessary introductions between a dazed Barry and a slightly alarmed-looking Courtenay. "He's devilish good friends with Eleanor, you know. Science and all that. But really, I do think somebody ought to check on poor Ramsay in case—" he glanced furtively around him and lowered his voice—"in case he's gone as barmy as his uncle was." Julian knew nothing of Lord John Ramsay's uncles, barmy or otherwise, but the Duke of Linfield had relations all over the kingdom, and it stood to reason that at least one of them had to be somewhat off.

He watched in suspense as Barry performed the required calculation: snub Julian and Courtenay and therefore align himself with the possibly demented and widely disliked Lord John, or go along with what Julian—proper, affable Julian Medlock, whom nobody quite disliked and everybody always was glad enough to see—was suggesting, which was to accept Courtenay as an acquaintance.

"I daresay Ramsay ate something that didn't agree with him," Barry finally said, including Courtenay in his remark. Julian wanted to congratulate him on hitting on so diplomatic a response. "Good to see you again, Courtenay. I think you were a year behind me at Oxford."

To Julian's delight, their conversation had been overheard by several passersby.

Ten minutes later they were on the street. "How much of that was planned?" Courtenay asked.

"That was why we went to the opera." Julian tried not to look triumphant. But really, he had done well, and was glad Courtenay knew it.

"The rest of it—visiting your friend and getting trussed up in my best coat, that was all stage craft." He suddenly looked aghast. "I sat through that for nothing?"

"Well, we could hardly have only shown up at the end," Julian pointed out.

"What you just did in there . . ." Courtenay shook his

head. "That was some combination of snake charming and verbal acrobatics."

Yes! Julian wanted to shout. That's precisely what it was. It was a damned hard trick and of necessity not exactly the sort of accomplishment one could share with the world. He shrugged with as much nonchalance as he could muster and said, "Well, that should do it. Send me any invitations you receive and I'll decide which to accept."

It was only later that he realized he now had no choice but to foist Courtenay on society, regardless of whether Courtenay wanted it. Because now his own reputation—and Eleanor's—would hinge on Courtenay's success. But also because now he had a purpose, something to do with himself. It felt like a gift, like a relief, and he'd be damned if he didn't succeed.

CHAPTER SIX

There *was* rather an excessive number of cats in Eleanor's parlor. Every time Courtenay visited, there seemed to be an increase.

"Eleanor." When she didn't look up from the letter she was writing, he rose and gently removed the kitten who had nestled into her shoulder.

"Hmm? Oh, are you still here, Courtenay?"

Hardly flattering, but that was Eleanor for you. "Afraid so. These aren't all the mouser's kittens, are they? Have you been taking in cats off the street?"

She didn't meet his eye. "Perhaps one or two."

He sat on the edge of her desk, looking down at her. "Eleanor, my dear, you'll have every tomcat in London howling at your door."

"It's my house, and if I want it to be floor-to-ceiling cats, that's what I'll have."

As far as the law was concerned, the house was not hers but her husband's and they both knew it. "What you mean is that Standish can come and stop you if he doesn't want his house turned into a menagerie."

Well, that got Eleanor's attention. "I'm not talking about that," she snapped. Courtenay ought to have known better: Eleanor wouldn't tolerate any mention of her marriage. And then, in her usual distracted tone, she said, "It's hardly a menagerie if it's only one species of animal. Besides, I like them. They're sweet." She idly stroked a kitten who was trying to get inside an empty teacup. "Do you know, before the mouser had her kittens, I hadn't touched another living thing in months?"

He knew this was her roundabout way of alluding to her marriage. "I, ah, offered to help out with that."

She laughed, and he was glad to see the forlorn expression drop from her face, however briefly. "That's not the same thing," she said, scooping the kitten up and burying her face in its fur.

"I should damned well hope not," he said, feigning affront. But he took her hand and held it, and she squeezed his in return before pulling away.

"What I mean is . . . well, never mind." She didn't need to spell out what it was she wanted, and how a fling with a scoundrel wasn't even close to the mark.

He picked up a paperweight from her desk. It wasn't a proper paperweight at all, but rather a very peculiar rock. It fit perfectly in his palm, however, and when turned over revealed a core of the most incongruous lavender sparkly bits. Eleanor had called it a geode, and when he had asked her where she got it, had only said *a friend*.

"I daresay the cats go some distance toward vexing your brother, which seems to be a new hobby of yours."

"Julian? Heavens, no. He's always been fond of animals, the dirtier the better." He noticed that she didn't deny going out of her way to irritate her brother.

"Impossible." He passed the rock from palm to palm, running his fingers over the rough surface and letting the crystals bounce flecks of colored light across the insipidly pretty flowered wallpaper. He wondered if Medlock had chosen it. "Only last week I saw him nearly have an apoplexy when a cat threatened to scratch his boots."

She furrowed her brows. "He has gotten finicky. But in India he was forever rescuing three legged dogs and birds with broken wings. Once he kept a mongoose in the library for a fortnight."

"Why the devil didn't anyone stop him?" Courtenay didn't like this new picture of Medlock. The youth who had rescued animals might have grown into somebody Courtenay might actually have liked. He much preferred thinking of Medlock as he currently was, stiff collar and stiff posture.

And a stiff cock, he recalled. No, damn it. He would not let his mind wander in that direction.

"Well, I was fond of the little beast."

"Your brother or the mongoose?"

She threw a wadded-up piece of paper at his head. "The mongoose! Really, there was nobody to stop Julian from having a mongoose in every room. He was so sick, one did tend to indulge him."

Oh Lord. Medlock as a sickly child cuddling wounded animals was just the limit.

"And our grandfather gave Julian whatever he wanted, mainly to annoy Papa." A cloud passed over her features.

Courtenay curled his fingers around the geode, temporarily stopping the play of light across the room, and studied his friend's face. They had known one another since Christmas and now it was just past Easter. This was the first time she had spoken of her father. He had noticed the omission, which, in his experience, was generally not a good sign. And now that she had mentioned her father, she hardly seemed to know what to say, as if she had never before spoken aloud of him. "Not a good sort?" he asked casually.

She opened her mouth and closed it again before finally saying, "What a gloomy topic."

"Is it?" he asked mildly.

"Papa was . . . I suppose you'd call him a bon vivant."

That didn't sound so bad, certainly not bad enough to warrant the way Eleanor was twisting the fabric of her skirt. "I thought he was some kind of shipping magnate." Courtenay was under the impression that those fellows did nothing but count their coins and arrange for them to multiply much in the way of Eleanor's cats.

"Oh, no. My grandfather kept the business out of my father's hands, and instead brought Julian up to manage all of it. And that's what he did, from the time he could add a column of numbers. Julian is excessively good at that kind of thing," she said with a hint of pride.

Eleanor stared pointedly at the letter she had been trying to write, and Courtenay took the hint and returned to his chair, still gripping the now warm rock. He didn't like any of the things he had learned about Medlock today: rescuing animals was bad enough, but being some kind of mathematical prodigy was worse. Courtenay could feel himself starting to like Medlock—or at least a theoretical version of Medlock—entirely despite himself. And then there were the circumstances under which he had been conscripted into the family business while his father had been idling about; that was far enough from common practice that Courtenay had no doubt there was an unpleasant story behind it.

He settled back in his chair, again watching the flecks of light from the geode sparkle across the room. It was impossible to think of anything else. Everything was glints of color, a universe of dazzling light that he held in the palm of his hand. Nothing else could possibly matter. It reminded him of the days when people had flitted in and out of his life like so many glittering flecks, everything dissolving into a confusion of dancing light, beautiful and joyful and fun. He had thought it would always be like that. That was what hope felt like, he realized. How long had it been since he felt that way?

He clapped his hand over the top of the crystal, causing the sparkles to die.

He didn't leave until the sun had set, long after Eleanor had forgotten his presence. He lit a lamp so Eleanor could continue to work, quietly shut the door behind him, and walked back to his own lonely lodgings.

With only half his attention on his horse, Julian put the animal through her paces. It was early enough that the park was still largely deserted, but for once he wasn't here to see or be seen. He had been restless since the opera, his fingers itching for something to do, and riding his horse was the best he could come up with. He didn't even enjoy riding, and had only learned because he thought it was something a gentleman ought to do, but at the moment, he didn't think there was a damned thing he did enjoy.

What Julian really wanted was to make himself useful at the dockyards. Perhaps he could inspect the shipment of silks he knew had recently arrived. Maybe he'd review the books, watch the numbers add up in the satisfying way money did when treated properly. But he had no place there now. The men he had hired to do the actual work of managing the enterprise wouldn't be able to get their job done with him prowling about, asking questions and recalculating sums. He'd only be a hindrance.

It had taken him years to accept that he couldn't properly run a business when he might be taken ill at any time. There were men whose livelihoods depended on Medlock Shipping remaining a going concern, and he couldn't properly ensure that when he was delirious and feverish. The realization that his bouts of illness were going to continue forever, bringing his life to a grinding halt with no warning, had finally dawned on him this past year. There would always be relapses and recurrences; he might not die, but he wouldn't get better. Regardless of how well he felt when he was healthy, there would always be another attack waiting for him around the corner.

Eleanor's tinctures only did so much. Bloodletting and special teas did nothing at all. He would spend the rest of his life trying to cram his living into the space between illnesses, his life a sentence with the ugliest punctuation.

All the more reason to polish the veneer that stood between his inner self—sick, sweaty, helpless, scared—and the rest of the world. All the more reason to keep everyone at arm's length. Nobody needed access to his humiliating reality.

He spurred the horse faster, feeling the still-cold spring air bite against his flesh. The horse had been as restless as he was, and now flew down the path as Julian bent low over her neck.

Ordinarily, when he was at loose ends, he went to Eleanor. She usually allowed herself to be persuaded to make morning calls or do some shopping or just have tea together. But when he had called on her yesterday, Tilbury gravely informed him that Courtenay had already arrived, and Julian had left with a request that Tilbury not inform his mistress of his visit. Julian was afraid that Eleanor, who had known him since he was a motherless infant, would immediately sense that something had happened between him and Courtenay. How could she not, when Julian felt that his own attraction to the man was practically a tangible, visible thing? And after he had been so rude to her about what he thought was her own liaison with the man, he couldn't very well let her know that he had actually done what he had accused her of.

He had a vague sense that he ought to be honest with her, that secrets would only compound this new chill between them. But lurking at the edges of his memory was what Courtenay had suggested to him about Eleanor's situation, and—worse—his own responsibility for it. He didn't want to think about Eleanor being lonely or sad or anything less than what he had meant to happen, which was for her to be rich and respected and safe.

But perhaps Julian had been a trifle ham-fisted in his meddling when he pushed Eleanor and Standish together. Even though it was quite clear that Standish needed to marry, his wastrel father having left him with nothing but debt, perhaps he ought to have let the two of them come to that conclusion on their own. At eighteen his meddling lacked the finesse he had since acquired. He knew Eleanor thought he ought to interfere less with other people's lives, but the fact was that most people needed help managing the simplest things, and Julian had both the talent and the time to be of assistance. It was a service, really.

He rode until the horse started to flag, and by then the sun was high in the sky. On his way back to the stables, he tipped his hat to a small group of ladies and gentlemen on foot. There was the barest pause before they greeted him in return, and he saw two bonneted heads tip towards one another, lips moving silently.

It had been years since he had been the subject of whispers. He didn't know whether the ladies had been whispering about his appearance at the opera with Courtenay or Eleanor's supposed affair with the man. Either way, it was Courtenay.

The only way to remedy it was to make Courtenay a success; then, there would be nothing to whisper about.

That wouldn't solve Eleanor's problems. But it would keep Julian busy. It might do something to abate the cold purposelessness that had driven Julian out to the park early in the morning. And it just might help Courtenay. Julian tried to ignore the fact that this alone felt like a good reason to exert himself.

CHAPTER SEVEN

Julian's machinations at the opera house had garnered Courtenay a dinner invitation from Mrs. Fitzwilliam. This wasn't precisely the top tier of London society, but it was a damned good start and Julian was quite satisfied with himself. As he allowed his valet to comb his hair and straighten his cravat, he was cautiously optimistic that if Courtenay could simply refrain from bawdy language or licentious behavior, they'd have the situation quite in hand.

"If you'll pardon me for saying so," said Briggs as he gave Julian's coat a final brushing, "you look pale. Might you be coming down with—"

"I'm quite all right," Julian snapped. And then, because Briggs had endured him and his illnesses for several years now, he added, "But thank you for taking care of me." And he probably didn't sound in the least bit grateful because he hated being taken care of almost as much as he hated being sick. But tonight, at least, he was fine. He'd had half a lifetime to learn the symptoms that signaled an oncoming attack, and he didn't have any of them now. He went to Mrs. Fitzwilliam's house in relatively high spirits.

By the time the fish plates were removed from the dinner table, Julian knew he had grossly misjudged Courtenay's abilities. The man was charm in human form.

Julian made the most perfunctory conversation with the lady sitting to his left, all the while keeping the bulk of his attention on Courtenay. He wouldn't have been surprised to hear that the other twelve dinner guests had their attention on Courtenay as well. They were leaning toward him like plants toward the sun. Julian, who had spent the entirety of his adulthood studying the ways of the *ton*, still couldn't quite put his finger on what Courtenay was doing to exert this magnetic pull on their attention. It wasn't just his notoriety—that would have been plain enough to see in people's narrowed gazes or inquisitive stares. Nor was it his good looks, for while preposterously handsome, he was hardly the only attractive gentleman to grace a London hostess's dinner table this season.

It had something to do with how, when he turned his sea-green eyes on you and paid attention to what you were saying, you felt like you were at the center of the universe. He seemed to genuinely like each person he spoke with. It was the same thing he had done to Lady Montbray's companion at the opera, only to the entire table. And it wasn't only the ladies—the gentlemen seemed equally under the influence of his charm.

Julian couldn't look at Courtenay without the memory of strong hands on him in the darkness of the opera, of forbidden pleasure and—

His mind stuttered over *pleasure*, and instead of seeing the china and crystal on Mrs. Fitzwilliam's dining table, all he could think of were balloons straining at their tethers and loose-limbed provocateurs.

Watching him, Julian had the sense that he could catch glimpses of the man Courtenay might have become if he hadn't been dogged by scandal and shame. He was intelligent and articulate, and when he wasn't deliberately trying to be provoking, he had effortless good manners.

The realization hit him like a blow: Courtenay could have been a man Julian might have admired.

After the ladies withdrew, the conversation turned to the blasted Poor Laws. Julian suppressed a scowl. As far as he could tell, some members of Parliament had realized that with two consecutive bad harvests and the vast number of unemployed soldiers returning from the recently ended wars, the two-hundred-year-old Poor Laws were increasingly useless. But instead of fixing them in a sensible way, they wanted to eliminate them entirely. Julian would have liked to ask the gentlemen at the table precisely what they had expected to happen to the poor after passing a series of laws designed to inflate the price of bread, and another series of laws designed to increase the rights of landowners and, necessarily, make it harder for country people to make ends meet. Junior clerks at his shipping firm could have puzzled that one out without too much trouble. But this was just the sort of topic he could never speak a word of in public lest people be too forcibly reminded of his origins and how he came by his knowledge of money and trade.

Julian caught Courtenay's eye and shook his head ever so slightly as a reminder for Courtenay to hold his tongue. Earlier this evening, he had told Courtenay all the things he was not to discuss. "Do not mention debt, radicalism, duels—"

"Why the devil would I want to talk about duels?" Courtenay had protested.

"Why the devil would you want to *have* a duel, but that's just what you've done. And on numerous occasions, no less."

"Fair point," Courtenay had conceded.

"Talk about the weather, the theater, and horses. Compliment a lady's attire, but not her appearance, and not overmuch. Praise the food and wine, but not in such a way as to make you sound as if you consider civilized refreshment a novelty. That's it."

But now Courtenay's mouth was twitching as if he had thoughts that were ready to spill out.

Don't you dare, Julian mouthed silently, fixing Courtenay with his sternest glare. Courtenay's only response was a dangerous smile, which Julian somehow felt on his person like a shivery caress.

"Shall we join the ladies?" Julian tried, attempting to forestall the calamity he foresaw. But the gentleman had only started their port and weren't apt to abandon it so soon.

"Can't just feed and house the blighters, otherwise why would they ever want to work?" said Fitzwilliam.

Julian reached blindly for his glass of port and drained it so he wouldn't be able to point out the incongruity of gentlemen, who by their very definition did not work, accusing the poor of laziness. They seemed to be under the distinct impression that the only reason people would work was if they absolutely had to.

"Wouldn't want to encourage them," Courtenay murmured in evident agreement. But something about the malevolent sparkle in his eyes told Julian that this was only the beginning. "Best to leave that to charities," Courtenay said slowly.

Wrong! Julian wanted to shout. Utterly wrong! Unless you wanted to raise a generation of men without a trade or the skills to acquire one, that is. In which case, sally forth with that scheme.

There was a general murmur of approval. When a footman filled his glass, Julian drained it again.

"I mean to say, who the devil are these upstarts who want to pass a bill forcing all the poor into workhouses, anyway?" Courtenay swirled the port in his glass. "I daresay they mean to line their pockets."

Julian gritted his teeth. The current, antiquated Poor Laws were administered by each individual parish; some gave food and money to the poor in their own homes, others required all the poor to relocate to workhouses. These institutions were generally considered an enormous favor to the poor, even though they were little better than prisons. Some men had the crackbrained belief that even workhouses were unnecessary, and that absent charitable relief, the poor would simply stop reproducing or somehow find work.

He wouldn't have thought that Courtenay, who surely didn't number chastity or diligence among his virtues, would harbor such a notion. Then again, Courtenay, despite being

Christendom's greatest scoundrel, had a pedigree stretching back to the Conquest. Julian knew that aristocrats and gentry looked on the rest of humanity as a different species, one that could be managed in the way of livestock.

There were the predictable sounds of assent from the half-drunk men around the table. Julian drained his own glass yet again, thinking at least he would keep his mouth too busy to tell them all how demented they were.

Courtenay then caught his eye, and Julian saw in it a glint of pure devilry that had nothing to do with workhouses. "The wife selling, though. That can't be right. Not sporting."

"But that's hardly common," said one very young gentleman. "I think it happened only that one time, in what was it, 'fourteen?" He was referring to an incident in which the workhouse governors had insisted a man sell his wife and children rather than have them supported by charity.

"No, Edwards, been going on for centuries. But no legal basis for the practice at all," said a gray-haired gentleman.

"If the fellow can't provide for a wife, best give her to someone who can," said a third, and based on the dark gleam in Courtenay's eye, this fellow had better keep his back to the wall.

"That's the part that bothers me," Courtenay said mildly. "The lass must have had some say about who she married the first time around. Letting her be sold to whoever pays the price doesn't seem English. Seems a bit like rape, to be quite honest. Not to mention bigamy and prostitution."

Having thereby discussed rape, bigamy, prostitution, and *politics*, Courtenay gracefully rose to his feet and smoothed his trousers. "I think I'll be joining the ladies in the drawing room." He flashed the stunned gentlemen a dazzling smile and strode out of the room.

Julian didn't know whether to be relieved to discover that they were of one mind about the bloody Poor Laws or incensed that Courtenay had in a few very deliberate sentences jeopardized his prospects, and Julian's good name right along with it.

"What is wrong with you?" Medlock hissed once they were outside on the pavement.

"What's wrong with *me?*" Courtenay began walking in the direction of his lodgings, hoping Medlock wouldn't follow. He hadn't expected Medlock to rise and follow him from the dinner table, nor to make civil excuses to the hostess explaining their early departure. But Medlock had done so all the same, smoothing over Courtenay's behavior in a way Courtenay didn't appreciate: he *wanted* to offend those men. "It's a sin and a crime that those lackwits are in charge of this nation."

"Strictly speaking, they aren't," Medlock said, keeping pace beside him. "You and Lord Lippincott were the only ones present with seats in the House of Lords. There were no members of Parliament."

"That's not what I mean." Courtenay shook his head, dismissing this unwanted reminder of his birthright. "They're the ruling class. These people who think poverty can be punished out of a person. And I saw your face, Medlock. You don't agree with them any more than I do. How could you sit idly by and let them talk such gammon? People will starve."

"Because it's tasteless to discuss politics at the dinner table," Medlock said primly.

"Rubbish. You tolerate it because you don't want anyone to dislike you. You're determined to be as bland as an unbuttered slice of *pain de mie*. Just like that wallpaper."

"*Pain de*—And what wallpaper are you talking about? Are you in your cups?"

He sighed. "No, Medlock. I'm not." But Medlock was. Courtenay could smell it on his breath. And if the man were sober he'd likely realize where they were heading and scamper off somewhere safe. "I'm angry. I hate this blasted country."

"You can't seriously mean to tell me that the poor are treated better in France or Italy or Constantinople or wherever else you've been?"

They most certainly were not. The situation of the poor in Athens was the stuff of nightmares. But that wasn't the point.

This was England. This was his bloody home.

This was a place where, as Medlock had reminded him, he had a seat in Parliament and could theoretically do something about injustice. He groaned.

"What now?" Medlock looked peeved, one hand on his hip, his lips in a tight line.

"We agree about the Poor Laws," Courtenay said.

"Hurrah," Medlock said unenthusiastically. "That's something we can talk about after neither of us is ever invited anywhere ever again."

"Surely that's a bit dramatic."

"You discussed rape, bigamy, and prostitution at Mrs. Fitz-william's dinner table." He strung his words together coherently enough for a man who had downed three glasses of port in half an hour. Probably long years of practice being inoffensive. "The entire point of refined society is to not discuss sordid things. We pretend the uglier aspects of life do not exist."

"I thought that after the ladies withdrew, it was permissible to discuss more interesting topics." He hadn't really. He also hadn't cared. If being accepted by society meant putting up with the type of ruinous palaver he had heard tonight, he simply wasn't capable of it. He'd figure out a different way to reunite with his nephew.

"At the absolute utmost, men talk about their mistresses, Courtenay. Or gambling. Not crimes against nature."

Courtenay shrugged. "In a few weeks they'll forget you ever . . . sponsored me, or whatever this is. You'll go back to being modestly appreciated by everyone, bland as bland can be."

"Modestly appreciated. What a pleasant thing to say. This is a far cry from the charm you exerted at the dinner table this evening and, one presumes, which you also exerted to fuck your way across Europe and back again. Modestly appreciated. Thank you kindly." Was Medlock *pouting*? If he knew how he looked with his hand on his hip and his lips pursed like that, he'd stop. Courtenay was suddenly very aware of how close they were.

"But I'm not trying to get you into my bed." Lord, he wanted Medlock to stop following him.

"I gathered as much." Medlock suddenly stopped walking and looked at his surroundings. "Where are we?"

"I'm going to my lodgings," Courtenay ground out. He was fast losing patience with Medlock, and didn't want the man to know where he lived.

"On foot?"

"I was planning to fly but I only do that without witnesses, so kindly leave me be."

"We're on the edge of St. Giles. I'll see if we can get a hackney before we're beset by footpads. You can't possibly live near here. You're lost. Where the devil are your lodgings?"

"On the edge of St. Giles, in fact."

"Good God. And you're going home on foot in the middle of the night? You'll be killed."

"Perhaps," Courtenay said easily. He did not, as a rule, fret overmuch about his own personal safety. He had to have a cat's nine lives to have gotten out of the scrapes he had found himself in. "I can't see what good worrying about it will do."

"Worrying might have led you to hire rooms in a slightly less unsavory quarter," Medlock said crisply.

"Would it have summoned up the blunt I'd need to pay for such well-located lodgings?"

"You've been out of the country for too long—"

"Not nearly long enough," Courtenay muttered.

"—and you have no idea what things cost. A couple of furnished rooms tolerably close to Mayfair wouldn't be so very dear. I'll arrange it tomorrow."

"I can barely afford the rooms I have now."

Courtenay chanced a look over at Medlock in time to see his mouth briefly hang open.

"You're a peer of the realm, Courtenay. Surely you have an income from the land you own. You can't be utterly penniless."

"My affairs are complicated." He hoped that would put an end to it. "And none of your business."

"They most certainly are. My name is now tangled up with yours, so if you're about to be thrown into debtors' prison, we'll both be tarred with the same brush."

"One of the privileges of a title is that I can't be arrested for debt. At least not in England." It had happened once in Florence and the experience had not been very amusing.

"You're in debt, then?"

"It's possible."

"Possible."

"You'd talk a good deal less if you stopped repeating every damned thing I say. When I acquire a debt, I pay it off, but I'm not certain whether I have any debt, because my affairs are in some disorder."

"Some dis—" He stopped himself, and Courtenay had to suppress a smile. "Do you have a man of business, or . . . No, of course you do not. I assume you have records of some sort?"

"I do. In my lodgings." He threw them all into a trunk. Bills, inscrutable reports from land agents, letters from relations requesting funds. He tossed them in and shut the lid.

"I'm going home with you, then, and I'll get everything straightened out. You can move somewhere less undesirable and stay at a hotel in the meantime."

Courtenay sincerely doubted that. He was fairly sure he had no ready money, few assets, and little chance of those circumstances changing. "No." They were now on a street that had no pretensions to gentility. The signs were the same the world over: animals and children roaming freely despite the late hour, something cooking in a pot over an open flame, laundry strung between two houses, and the general sense of orderly facades having dissolved into something more chaotic. This wasn't outright a rookery, but the people who lived here were always thinking about the next meal, the next rent payment.

"Believe me, whatever it is, I'll have seen worse. You should have seen the state of my father's affairs. Shambles." He wasn't quite slurring his speech but Courtenay could hear the drink in his words.

"You're very drunk, or you wouldn't be telling me this."

"I'm slightly tipsy, and I can tell you whatever I want, because you don't matter."

Courtenay had been insulted behind his back and to his face since being sent down from Oxford. He had been disowned by his family and cut dead by his friends. But the way his fists clenched of their own volition at Medlock's jab proved that he still wasn't immune to having his pride hurt. "I see."

"No, that came out all wrong," Medlock said quickly, waving his hand as if clearing soot from a window. "Let me see. What I mean to say is that I don't need to impress you, because you don't care about any of that."

Surely he shouldn't have been so gratified to hear this. "Quite true."

"Anyway, let me at your books. I've been dying to see a real lord's books for ages now." He sounded like he meant it. This was the happiest Courtenay had ever seen the man. If Courtenay had a collection of dirty lithographs in his lodgings, Medlock could hardly have been more eager to get his hands on them.

"Fine," he said, and laughed when Medlock clapped his hands together like a child who had been promised a special treat. "But you'll be disappointed."

CHAPTER EIGHT

Julian was horrified.

"Where are your things?" he asked. Courtenay's lodgings consisted of two rooms, each approximately the size of a hen coop, both furnished in what could charitably be called a Spartan style. In the first room was a plain deal table, a single hard-backed chair, and a tatty-looking sofa. Books were stacked against the walls with a careful neatness that Julian felt was nearly tragic. The fire Courtenay lit illuminated a room that was clean and orderly but dismal. If one closed one's eyes and summoned up the image of cheap furnished rooms, this was precisely the picture that would come to mind.

Through an open door he could see an equally depressing bedroom. Julian felt a wash of self-consciousness at the sight of the bed, and forced his gaze away from the open doorway.

"I've been traveling." Courtenay leant against a wall, his hands jammed in his pockets.

"But you had a house in Italy, did you not? Where you

lived with your sister and nephew?" Surely the man had more than this to show for the past decade of his life.

"Yes. I had a house there, but after Isabella died and Simon was sent to England, I had everything sold."

There was a note of sorrow in Courtenay's voice. Eleanor had said Courtenay was fond of his nephew and missed him terribly; persuading the child's father that Courtenay was not an outright menace was in fact the entire point of the charade. But this was the first time Julian had seen the man's sadness for himself. He imagined Courtenay suddenly alone, his sister dead and his nephew gone. Worse, he imagined a child having lost his mother and then being taken away from the only other relation he had known.

"I had a bad few nights at the card tables," Courtenay added. "I needed the money."

But Julian didn't think that was why Courtenay had sold his things. He remembered the time he had arrived at Eleanor's house to discover that she had put away nearly all the trinkets and mementos from her childhood; he remembered a jade figurine and beside it a tiger Standish had whittled for her when they had all been children. He wondered what she had done with them.

He quickly shook his head, as if to dislodge the unwelcome thought. "I see," he said, and he knew it was an inadequate response, but it would never do to dredge up feelings. His gaze drifted again to the bedroom door, the unmade bed, the rumpled sheets.

"In Istanbul, I had a set of silk bedsheets made up in a

green to match my eyes," Courtenay said, as if he needed to apologize for the depressing state of his current bed linens.

"Impossible," Julian said promptly.

"Extravagant, ill advised, and slightly vulgar. But not impossible," Courtenay said.

"I meant the color." In *The Brigand Prince*, poor, witless Agatha had described Don Lorenzo's eyes as being the color of emeralds. But Agatha was given to triteness rather than specificity. Courtenay's eyes were the color of the darkest jade—the exact color of Eleanor's missing figurine—with flecks of the green of a warm, foreign sea. Emerald, indeed. "There's no dye that could match your eyes."

Courtenay stared at him, and Julian realized he perhaps ought not to have admitted such an interest in Courtenay's eyes. "Come now," Julian said briskly. "People likely say all manners of nonsense about your person. Don't act shocked. Why don't you bring me whatever records you have?"

From the bedroom, Courtenay dragged a large trunk that he placed at Julian's feet. When the lid opened, it revealed a heap of miscellaneous papers.

"I just throw everything in there," Courtenay explained. "Done so for ages now."

Julian managed not to rub his palms together in glee. For years, he had wanted to see for himself where aristocrats made their money. He had seen Standish's accounts when negotiating Eleanor's marriage settlements, but that had been six years ago and Julian had still been wet behind the ears; besides which, Standish hardly had a sou to his name—

which was why he needed to marry in the first place. And even though Courtenay's scattered finances and negligent record-keeping could hardly be representative of his class, it gave Julian a sense of what he had longed to know.

He had always suspected that the gentry couldn't possibly afford to live exclusively on the income from their land in England, even though that's what they liked to pretend, and the paltry income from Courtenay's land proved it. Even accounting for the likelihood that Courtenay's acreage was grossly mismanaged, even if the man had the worst farmland in the kingdom, there was no way even triple this income could allow for a townhouse, balls, dowries, and all the other expenses aristocrats considered necessary. In order to finance their lavish way of life, Courtenay's peers had to rely on their investments in canals, factories, and enterprises not unlike Medlock Shipping. And a lot of them had income that came from holdings in the West Indies, a sordid business that made Medlock Shipping look like a May Day festival.

Well, Courtenay certainly did not have a damned farthing invested in anything, as far as Julian could tell. He had no valet, kept no horses, lived no better than a clerk, and yet he owned thousands of acres of land. Most of the land was either mortgaged to the hilt or entailed, and Courtenay wasn't seeing much income from any of it. Julian gritted his teeth and made notes to himself about what precisely needed to be done.

Throughout Julian's investigations, Courtenay lounged on the sofa. His eyes were shut but he couldn't be sleeping, because whenever Julian asked him a question, he answered promptly, and when the candle burnt down, he noticed and lit another one.

"Why are you living here when you have a house on Albemarle Street?" Julian asked, shocked to find a letter indicating that Courtenay owned the property.

Courtenay, sprawled out in a way that made Julian think terrible, terrible things, lazily opened one eye. "I let that house years ago."

"Indeed, but I have a letter here saying that your tenants left at the start of the year. You need to sell the house immediately."

"It's entailed."

Julian groaned. It was sufficiently stupid to entail land, but to entail a townhouse—a property that required an outlay of expense rather than earning an income—spoke of immense foolishness on the part of Courtenay's forebears. Perhaps bad management was in his blood. He had long suspected that he and Eleanor's sense for business had been inherited from their grandfather in much the same way they had inherited his hair color. It had evidently skipped a generation.

"What are you thinking? You look like you tasted something sour." Courtenay was looking at him with both eyes open now. His hands were hooked behind his head in a way that did interesting thing to his biceps and torso.

Julian tore his gaze away from the man's body and focused on his face, but that was no improvement. He was too damned handsome, with his half-closed eyes and the edges of his mouth quirked ever so slightly up, his expression hovering in between sleepy languor and something obscene. Or maybe that was Julian's imagination. He dragged his attention back to the letter he was holding.

"I can't decide whether you'd be better served by the income from new tenants, or by the cachet of living in a proper house. Even if you only hire a skeleton staff . . ."

"How would I pay them?" Courtenay drawled sleepily, stretching his arms over his head.

Julian was pleasantly surprised that Courtenay believed in paying his servants. "That's what I'm working on now."

He also seemed to believe in paying tradesmen and settling his debts, judging by the canceled notes he found in the trunk. "Courtenay," he began, trying to figure out how to phrase this as delicately as possible, "do you have any debts that perhaps I might not know about from the contents of this trunk?"

A shadow passed over Courtenay's face. "I pay my debts."

"I don't mean to give offense," Julian said hastily. "Most people don't." Hell, when Julian had moved Medlock Shipping's principal offices to London in advance of selling off his India interests, he had needed to borrow money, which he hadn't repaid until the last possible minute because that was how these things worked. Julian's understanding of profligate gentlemen suggested that they were even less inclined to promptly repay debts.

"I pay my debts. It's one correct thing that I can do, so I do it." Then he shut his eyes, and Julian was given to understand that the conversation was over.

Later, long after a clock in the distance had chimed two, Julian reached over and tapped Courtenay's shoulder to rouse him. "What's this property near Stanmore?" It was very close to London, and if the house were halfway decent it could command a decent price. "Is it entailed?"

"No. But I can't sell it."

Julian narrowed his eyes. There were several letters in a feminine hand requesting funds for what seemed to be the running of this household in Stanmore. Had Courtenay pensioned off a former mistress? Was he supporting an illegitimate child? Surely he hadn't been in England long enough to have acquired a new mistress, not when he spent all his time in London and seemed to haunt Eleanor's house like a particularly alluring ghost.

"Carrington Hall is where my mother lives."

Julian gasped. "You have a mother?" He collected himself. "I mean, a living mother?"

"Alive and well and only a few miles away."

"Who is she?" He searched his memory for any recollection of a Lady Courtenay, and came up with nothing.

"Mrs. Blakely."

Julian paused. "Your mother remarried after your father's death yet lives in a house you inherited from your father? And you support her? What does your stepfather think of this?"

"I couldn't say, as I've never met him."

Julian checked the signature on the letters that tersely demanded funds. "Who is this Miss Chapman who writes on your mother's behalf?"

"I believe she's the vicar's daughter."

Julian pursed his lips in disapproval. "Your mother is very infirm, then? She cannot hold a pen nor even dictate a letter?"

"As far as I know, she's quite well. She disowned me a good ten years ago, so I'm not certain."

Julian barked out an astonished laugh. "Disown? You pay for her upkeep. She lives on your sufferance. She's not in a position to disown you."

"I don't suppose she's bogged down by the technicalities."

"Well, I am. It's admirable to support your mother, presuming she has no money of her own, and please don't correct me if I'm wrong, because I'm not sure I can stand to hear it. But you might keep her in a considerably more modest style. You pay for over a dozen servants. And based on the grocer's bills, which Miss Chapman helpfully encloses, she seems to entertain a fair bit."

"I believe Blakely's children live there as well." Somehow Courtenay delivered this information as if it were in the least bit normal. "I daresay they eat their heads off."

"And so do their horses. If I'm reading this correctly, she has three grooms and at least six horses."

Courtenay was silent for a moment. "I had to sell my own horse in January. Couldn't keep him anymore."

Julian would not hear another word and held up his hand to stop Courtenay from elaborating. "Where's your writing paper, Courtenay? I'm putting a stop to this nonsense immediately."

"You will not. It's my affair."

"This here"—he nudged the now-empty trunk with the toe of his boot—"is testament to how unfit you are to manage your own affairs." Julian took a deep breath. "Your mother evidently thinks she's above your touch. Perhaps she is. But in that case, she and her husband and stepchildren don't need to take your money." Julian had never heard of such a preposterous arrangement. "I think not. I'll write a very cordial letter informing Miss Chapman that you find yourself in straightened circumstances and will happily relocate your mother and her hangers-on to a cottage someplace more suitable."

"It needs to be near Somerset," Courtenay said blandly. "That's where my sister lives."

"I didn't even know—Oh, I suppose she disowned you too." "Correct."

Julian narrowed his eyes. "I suppose you support her in a style of great elegance as well?"

Courtenay laughed with no rancor whatsoever, which was more than Julian was capable of. "No, thank God. She's married and has a couple of children."

"How many other relations are you supporting?"

Courtenay paused, as if performing a mental calculation. Julian inwardly grimaced.

"No other relations, but there are a few former servants. An old nurse, a groom. I can't quite remember who. They get annuities."

"Of course they do," Julian said acerbically. "Who needs the Poor Laws when instead we can have viscounts living in squalor in order to pay annuities to aged servants and estranged parents. That's quite a system." Perhaps it was the lateness of the hour, perhaps it was the ill-judged quantity of port he had consumed earlier, but he was developing odd protective urges where Courtenay was concerned.

"It's not squalor," Courtenay said, sounding peeved. He

had now rolled to face Julian, his head propped in one hand. "These lodgings suit me as well as any."

"Then why do you spend all your time with my sister?" Julian didn't mean for it to sound like an accusation, but perhaps it was. "Aren't you meant to be gaming and whoring and doing all the things reprobates do?" But even as the words left his mouth, he realized what he ought to have noticed weeks ago: whatever Courtenay had done in the past, he wasn't dissipating himself in that manner currently.

Courtenay held his gaze for a moment before speaking. "Your sister is my friend. And, besides, I suppose I don't like to be alone." He said this almost sheepishly, as if he were confessing a great secret.

"Nor do I," Julian admitted.

Julian was suddenly aware that at some point in the last few minutes, he had twisted in his chair so he was fully facing Courtenay, in fact leaning towards him. Courtenay was evidently aware as well, because when Julian's gaze caught on Courtenay's, Courtenay raised a single dark eyebrow.

It had to be some kind of witchcraft, that was the only explanation, because during the hours of sifting through Courtenay's papers, Julian had let the idea creep into his mind that perhaps it wouldn't be so terrible to pick up where they had left off at the opera. He wasn't opposed to discreet affairs, in fact considered them necessary to the orderly functioning of his life. An interlude in the privacy of Courtenay's lodgings was nothing if not discreet, entirely safe, nothing to worry about.

He was dimly aware of a voice deep within some very

sensible but utterly tired part of his mind that was shout ing at him not to be such a blasted fool. There was nothing safe about Courtenay, not when Julian's desire for him was so drastically out of proportion to what he was used to.

But in the dark and the quiet and in such close quarters, it didn't seem to matter.

"**W**ell, this is a regular orgy of emotions we're having," Medlock said briskly. The fellow really had no idea about emotions or orgies if he thought this qualified as either. "On to your affairs. Why did your mother disown you?"

Courtenay regarded Medlock quizzically. This topic had nothing to do with Courtenay's financial affairs, and in fact was a direct route to the dreaded emotional orgy. "Why wouldn't she have disowned me?" he said easily. "I've been a thorn in her side since I was in leading strings. Imagine such a one as me as your only son."

"Oh, your mother sounds charming." There was something about the angry twist of Medlock's mouth that went straight to a part of Courtenay's heart that he hadn't known was still there. It had been years since anyone had thought to defend him, even longer since he had believed he merited any kind of defense. And having a man like Medlock—stuffy, prim Medlock—take one's part made it worth even more.

"I expect she's very pretty," Medlock continued, wrinkling his nose. "Otherwise nobody would tolerate such airs. You probably got your looks from her, I daresay. Why are you laughing like that? I don't gamble, but if I did I'd wager twenty crowns that I have the right of it."

He did, of course. "I got sent down from Oxford for carrying on an affair with the chancellor's wife."

"Did you? Good Lord. How ambitious. And she disinherited you over that?"

"Not yet. My father died and she blamed my carousing and expensive habits for overtaxing his heart." Medlock sucked in an angry breath through his teeth and Courtenay had the demented sense that this was how people felt when duels were fought for their honor. "Then I came to London and started to run through my inheritance. Drinking, gaming, whoring. The usual." All the things Medlock had accused him of only a few minutes earlier. "My younger sister made her debut during that time, and I had the bad judgment to introduce her to some of my more dissolute friends." There were some things he wouldn't tell Medlock, because they weren't his secrets to share—properly speaking, they were Simon's—and they didn't matter much anyway. "She found herself ruined—"

"Wait. You're missing some crucial steps. One doesn't go from an introduction to ruination without a good many adventures in between. Had she no chaperone?"

"Our older sister—the one in Somerset—was supposed to—"

"But she made a terrible job of it, evidently."

"I suppose she did." He hadn't ever really thought of it in that light.

"And that's why your younger sister, Isabella, married

Lord Radnor so precipitously. I see." He only saw part of it, but it was enough. "Then Simon was born, and within the year your sister had run off with some blackguard. One of your acquaintances?"

"Yes." The same married man who had gotten her with child, in fact. "I didn't trust him, so I followed her to Italy to make certain she was safe. She eventually tired of the fellow, and he of her, but of course she would have been a pariah in England, so we stayed in Italy. My mother thought I ought to have brought Isabella back to England, tail between her legs, and forced a reconciliation with Radnor."

"What an idiot."

That was a bit too much. "You really can't talk that way about my mother, Medlock."

"No, I meant you. You're an idiot to have put up with such ill treatment. The entire world knows you're a menace with your lusty ways and your dissolute habits. Did your mother imagine that disowning you—I hope you can hear the inverted commas around that—would help in the least bit?"

"You yourself took issue with my friendship with your sister," Courtenay pointed out.

"Because I didn't want her to be considered a loose woman for associating with you. I should hardly think your mother had that to fear. If she hadn't cast you off, you could have come back to England without this cloud of ignominy surrounding you." He made a noise of sheer frustration. "Instead she has the vicar's daughter write to you and you send her hundreds of pounds a year in addition to letting her live in what I have no doubt is a very fine house."

Courtenay was still struck by the novelty of hearing someone defend his character, but he didn't quite believe Medlock to be correct. "It's the least I can do after costing her the life of her first husband and youngest child."

Medlock sucked in a breath of air. "Oh, so you're a murderer as well as an idiot, then. What was your weapon?"

"I know you're trying to make me feel better—"

"I am not," Medlock protested.

"—but this is no laughing matter. Isabella caught a fever that she never would have contracted in England. She was highly strung, and I ought never to have introduced her to any of my set in the first place. Of course I ought never to have countenanced her leaving her husband or taking up with other men. Her death is on my conscience." It always would be. "I miss her every day."

There was a long moment of silence, during which the close confines of the room seemed to get closer still. Courtenay could hear the man's breathing, smell his shaving soap. It would take the only the smallest effort to haul Medlock onto the sofa beside him.

When Medlock finally spoke, his voice was softer and lower than it had been. "I say, Courtenay. You've put me in the damnable position of having to argue that your behavior was defensible. And while I believe that ninety nine percent of the time you behave abominably and you've given me six white hairs tonight alone, in this single instance you acted well. Your sister had ruined herself, and it was probably best that she live abroad rather than stay here and be considered a harlot. I would certainly have taken Eleanor to the Continent in that situation." He scowled. "There, now my principles are in confusion and I hate it." He turned back to the papers on the desk before him, even though the candle was guttering and there was no way he could see well enough to read. "Now go to sleep and I'll wake you when I'm through."

Medlock's approval shouldn't matter, not to Courtenay, who didn't need anyone's approval and never had. But what made Courtenay's breath catch was that Medlock was admitting he'd do something improper, something the world would hold against him, if it meant caring for someone he loved. Courtenay found that his opinion of Medlock, which had been thawing over the course of the evening, suddenly got dangerously warm indeed. "I'm not going to sleep, Medlock."

"Fine. Stay awake and watch me work. That's peculiar but so are you and I shan't object."

"You know, before tonight I never would have thought sums were . . . erotic, but it seems I'm not too old to learn new things."

The only light was from the moon and a dying candle, but Courtenay could see the blush spread across Medlock's cheekbones.

"I'm sure I don't know what you mean." But he shifted in his seat, no doubt to accommodate his swelling prick. Courtenay watched in deep interest as he licked his lips and canted his body ever so slightly closer. There was no mistaking what this meant.

Keeping his eyes steady on Medlock's face, he reached out and wrapped a hand around the leg of Medlock's chair. He had done something similar at the opera, and he knew Medlock remembered that perfectly well. So when he saw nothing in the man's face but raw anticipation, he tugged the chair close.

CHAPTER NINE

"**Y**ou'll need a budget. Careful retrenchment," Julian said, clinging to the sides of his chair and also to the last shreds of his self-control. Perhaps this wasn't happening. Perhaps that wasn't Courtenay's hand on his thigh.

Courtenay was propped up on one elbow, the other hand inching slowly up Julian's leg. "You're terribly hard, aren't you?"

"Of course I am, damn you," Julian ground out. "What do you expect? I suppose everybody gets like this around you."

A soft chuckle. "Not really. How hard?" Courtenay's voice was an insinuating purr but his hand wasn't anywhere near Julian's cock and everything about this situation was unsatisfactory.

Julian made a sound of protest. "Hard enough to be damned distracting, thank you very much. Feel free to see for yourself, unless you prefer to torture me. It's all the same, don't mind me." It wasn't, though. He would have given three hundred guineas for Courtenay's hand to move six inches upwards or for this not to be happening at all. Either one, really.

"Likewise," Courtenay said, and of course Julian had to glance downwards, where indeed he could see a very promising bulge in Courtenay's trousers. "I got hard watching you be clever with my money."

Oh Jesus. Praise of his accounting skills really shouldn't make his cock actually pulse. This could not be a normal subject for bedroom talk. "What money?" Julian said, somehow managing not to reach inside his own trousers. "You haven't any."

Then Courtenay, bless his depraved nature, finally slid his hand up the final couple of inches and rested it on top of Julian's aching prick.

Courtenay made a low sound of approval. "The question is," he said, looking Julian right in the eye, "what you're going to do with it."

Julian drew in a deep breath. Was he really going to go through with this? The fact that he was even considering it meant that it was a terrible idea, meant that Courtenay's wicked charm had compromised his judgment. Courtenay meant scandal and wildness, improvidence and recklessness, all the things Julian went out of his way to avoid. Going to bed with him would be opening the door to chaos of a degree he didn't want to consider.

As a counterargument, there was the knowing caress of Courtenay's palm over his throbbing member.

Julian took a deep breath. "Get it sucked, I hope."

Courtenay growled, actually *growled*, and grabbed Julian by the hand, pulling him straight off the chair and onto the sofa. Or, rather, onto Courtenay's hard chest.

For a moment they stayed like that. Julian braced on his arms over Courtenay, Courtenay's hands smoothing down Julian's back. And then Courtenay grinned wolfishly and really what was Julian to do if not kiss that decadent smile right off his face? He bent down and pressed his mouth against Courtenay's, expecting to be met with the fierce collision of lips against lips that they had shared at the opera. Instead, Courtenay barely skimmed his mouth over Julian's, and Julian found himself responding with the barest insinuation of tongue. It was hardly a kiss at all, and Julian thought he might die from lust anyway.

Courtenay tasted of sugary tea, disconcertingly wholesome, and he kissed like he had all the time in the world. He had seemed sufficiently clean-shaven at dinner but now the stubble on his jaw rasped against Julian's cheek in a way that surely ought not to have been pleasurable. Every lick and nibble pushed Julian farther into a future in which he was a person who went to bed with Lord Courtenay.

Julian, slightly annoyed at being cast in the role of aggressor, pushed up so he had one foot on the floor and the other leg astride Courtenay. He began unfastening his trousers. Freeing his erection, he groaned with relief and heard Courtenay's rumble of interest. He took his cock in hand, gripping it as surely as he would in the darkness and privacy of his own bedchamber. "The question is, what are *you* going to do with it?" he said, echoing Courtenay's earlier taunt. Because if one couldn't be as bold as one pleased with Courtenay, Julian didn't know when one could.

"Up here," Courtenay said, and it was unmistakably a command. "Now."

Julian braced a hand on the arm of the sofa and with his other hand guided his erection just out of reach of Courtenay's parted lips. He needed to see Courtenay reach for it. He needed to know that this man wanted this, wanted him.

Courtenay's hands came to rest on Julian's hips and the same moment his tongue flicked over the head of Julian's erection. Julian hissed in pleasure. Courtenay pulled him closer, so Julian was now half-kneeling, half-standing over Courtenay's face when the man finally sucked him down.

"Oh God," Julian cried out. The warmth and wetness of Courtenay's mouth was heaven. He felt the man's tongue doing terrible magical things to the underside of his shaft, felt a hum that must have indicated Courtenay's own satisfaction. "Yes," he pleaded.

Courtenay pulled on Julian's hips and Julian groaned with pleasure and surprise at what that might mean. Tentatively, he eased himself farther into Courtenay's mouth. He saw Courtenay's lips wrapped around him, saw his eyes half closed in obvious pleasure. "Do you want me to?" Julian murmured.

Courtenay moaned around him, and Julian, unable to hold back anymore, began tentatively thrusting into Courtenay's mouth. It felt decadent, to be standing over this man, fucking his mouth, taking his pleasure in such a wanton way. He had never done such a thing. Oh, he had had his cock sucked, but his role in the business had always been passive, which only seemed proper and polite.

At the moment, the idea that there was a proper or polite way to have his cock sucked seemed the height of inanity. This was what he wanted. This was what he dreamt of, even if he hardly knew it himself. And, God almighty, Courtenay seemed to agree. Julian suddenly remembered what Courtenay had hinted at the opera. He liked being manhandled. Well, this certainly qualified.

Julian caressed Courtenay's head, combed his fingers through the man's hair, traced the outline of his ear, all the while feeling his pleasure build. When Courtenay tugged Julian's trousers below his hips and then slid a few of his fingers into Julian's mouth, Julian knew what to expect and sucked greedily at Courtenay's fingers. When he felt those slick fingers slide down the cleft of his arse and touch his entrance, he moaned and pressed back into them.

"Please, yes, please," he begged, and didn't care that he sounded unhinged, didn't mind the ragged desperation of his voice. Then he felt the welcome intrusion of fingers, twisting, probing. "I'm going to . . ." He meant it as a warning, but would have bet half his fortune that Courtenay didn't give a damn about warnings. When he came, the pleasure feeling almost ripped out of him, it was deep in Courtenay's throat, and Courtenay moaned and swallowed.

Panting and delirious with spent pleasure, Julian stayed there, not moving, as his cock softened in Courtenay's mouth. Courtenay licked and sucked and Julian only pulled back when the sensitivity of his organ outweighed the tender, filthy thrill of seeing his cock ministered to in such a way, by such a man.

Finally, he stood, tucking his prick away and fastening his trousers. He looked down at Courtenay, still sprawled on the sofa, his mouth red and his hair spread out beneath him, the picture of decadence. When Julian knelt beside the sofa and opened Courtenay's trousers, finally putting his mouth to Courtenay's own rigid cock, he did so with the intention of performing every fancy cocksucking trick he had ever learned, and maybe some he had only dreamt of, as a way to pay the man back for the pleasure Julian had just received.

But instead, when Courtenay's hand settled on Julian's head, idly stroking, all his grand plans went out the window. His brain turned entirely to mush, all thoughts replaced by the scent of Courtenay, the hot presence inside his mouth and throat, the garbled sounds of pleasure Courtenay was making.

Courtenay tried to tell himself that this was all perfectly normal, that gratified lust and simple exhaustion had muddled up his feelings and created the illusion that Julian Medlock, kneeling on the floor with his head resting on Courtenay's thigh, was a sight of uncommon loveliness.

Medlock was not asleep—Courtenay could see the moonlight reflecting off his colorless eyes. But he wasn't making any effort to move, either. He seemed stunned. Regretful and ashamed, in all probability.

"It's very late," Courtenay began.

"I ought to be going," Medlock interrupted, rising to his feet and fumbling with his trousers.

"Nonsense. It's past four in the morning, and as you pointed out, this is just the sort of neighborhood where bands of footpads roam unchecked."

"It isn't really. I only said that to be difficult." He cast a glance around the room, as if he were searching for something, but he was fully dressed. They hadn't even taken their coats or boots off, which seemed at odds with how utterly naked Courtenay felt. "You do need to find better lodgings, though."

A few hours ago, Medlock had offered to deal with that himself, but now he looked like he wished he had never come here in the first place, let alone offered to involve himself further in Courtenay's affairs. "Spend what remains of the night here," Courtenay said. He had confessed how little he liked being alone, and Medlock had admitted to the same. That's all it was, a convenient arrangement for both of them, and any silly notion Courtenay had about wishing it were otherwise was just his cock talking, surely.

Medlock shifted from foot to foot and ran his hands through his hair, which the moonlight had bleached to gray. Courtenay stood and took off his coat and waistcoat. When, after another minute, Medlock still had made no move toward the door, Courtenay took his hand and tried to lead the way towards the bedroom.

"No," Medlock said, pulling his hand swiftly away. "In the morning I'll send a servant to collect your records and I'll get everything in order. Or—no—I'll have my man of business attend to it." The longer he spoke, the closer his voice got to his usual peevishness, further and further away from the man who had given in to lust and tenderness. "That coat," he said, gesturing to the garment Courtenay still held. "It's Weston, isn't it?" He was referring to the tailor half the gentlemen of the *ton* patronized.

"Of course," Courtenay said. "I had to replace most of my wardrobe after coming to England." All his clothing had seemed foreign and strange, the attire of a different man.

"You can't afford any of it," Medlock said, now fully returned to his irritable self. "Your boots too. Everything of the latest fashion and highest quality."

It was a reproach. Courtenay had received worse, and surely should not have felt ashamed. "I'm very vain. And profligate. You knew that already."

Medlock sighed. "Good night, Courtenay." He grabbed his hat off the hook by the door and was gone before Courtenay could fully appreciate how disappointed he was.

Chapter Ten

When Julian got back to his lodgings—proper lodgings, not a hole in the wall on the outer fringes of civilization, he was pleased to remind himself—he didn't even bother trying to sleep. He had no interest in being alone in his bed with nothing but fevered memories of the previous few hours. The sun was nearly up, or at least it would be soon enough, and, for the first time in months, he had work to do.

Eleanor had mentioned that Radnor was having a hard time finding a house to let somewhere in the vicinity of Harrow, so as to be near Simon when he started school. Courtenay's house would do quite well. It didn't matter that it was currently inhabited; indeed, he took a vicious satisfaction in writing to Mrs. Blakely, informing her of Lord Courtenay's intentions to let Carrington Hall.

Next he wrote to Radnor's secretary. This was a Mr. Turner—or so he claimed—who had at some point been a sort of confidence artist. Julian had debated telling Radnor that his secretary was probably up to no good, but decided that polite, proper Mr. Medlock wouldn't discuss such a thing. So instead he wrote Turner a very cordial letter informing him of a house that might meet his employer's requirements.

This plan had the added benefit of putting Radnor in Courtenay's debt. Julian would see to it that Courtenay's house was offered to Radnor at well below the cost of similar houses in the neighborhood. Even better, he'd persuade Courtenay to allow Radnor to explode the conservatory or build canals in the rose garden or whatever other lunacy his scientific pursuits might require. They'd never find another owner willing to allow that.

He was perhaps overstepping by offering the property to Radnor without mentioning this fact to Courtenay, but if anything was clear, it was that Courtenay couldn't manage his own affairs. He paid his debts on time, which was so unusual a practice among gentlemen as to be nearly eccentric, and gave money to whoever asked him. Really, he wasn't fit to go outside on his own, let alone manage a complicated estate.

With the income from the rent of the Stanmore property, Courtenay would be able to properly staff and live in his London townhouse. And if Courtenay's own funds fell slightly short, Julian would quietly deposit some of his own money into Courtenay's account to make up the difference, and nobody needed to be the wiser. At the prospect of creating a budget and finessing the numbers until they were behaving themselves, he nearly rubbed his hands together in glee. Lord, he had been bored. His brain had been turning to rot these past months. This was the problem with living in the space between illnesses, always waiting for the other shoe to drop. He couldn't do anything more meaningful than arrange for Eleanor's furniture to be reupholstered.

And, well, he had done a bit more than that last fall while recovering from his last illness, although he tried not to think about it, as one always tried to avoid dwelling on one's lapses into vulgarity.

But the sad fact of the matter was that he had written a novel, for God's sake. A half-demented sensational novel. Julian had regretted it almost as soon as he had delivered *The Brigand Prince* to the printers. No doubt it had been slightly shabby of him to have used Courtenay as a model for his villain, but he had written the manuscript before even meeting Courtenay. Only later had he gone back to map Courtenay's looks and mannerisms onto the villain. At first he had though it rather Courtenay's own fault for behaving precisely as one expected an evil mastermind to do. All that lurking and brooding and sultry staring.

The truth was more complicated, though. Julian had poured everything into that book that he couldn't have in the real limits of his life. At a time when he was confined to his bed, he had written pages and pages of adventure. He, a man who hid his desires and obfuscated his background, created a hero and heroine who had no need for artifice or dissembling, so pure of heart and motive were they. He had given his sweet, dull-witted Agatha a clear purpose in life and an ally with whom to achieve it. At the end, they lived happily ever after.

He had filled the pages of that book with everything

he could never have, would never let himself admit he wanted. Courtenay—beautiful, dangerous, and indifferent to censure—had to go into the book as a matter of course.

Well, nobody would ever know he had written *The Brigand Prince*, least of all Courtenay. Perhaps if he used the proceeds from the book to right Courtenay's ship, that would be restitution enough. He could use the money to hire some staff for the Albemarle-Street townhouse. That way at least Julian wasn't actually profiting off Courtenay's shaming.

The trouble was that now he had allowed himself a taste of one impossible thing, he worried that he might keep wanting more. He'd want honesty. He'd want to be known for who he really was. He'd want to let people see past the carefully polished exterior to the man within.

It would be *dreadful*.

He was going to think only about Courtenay's money, or lack thereof, and not about the man himself. He would keep his mind busy, filled with things that were not memories of Courtenay's hands and mouth and the words he had spoken. He would not itemize and catalogue the ways in which their encounter had differed from the sort of discreet and cordial interlude he used to prefer—no, which he still preferred, because last night had changed absolutely nothing. If he went long enough without thinking about it, the memories would fade, or at least be covered up by more layers of protective varnish, and it would be like it never happened in the first place. He'd go back to his calm, friendly encounters and he wouldn't feel that his life was any poorer for it.

The morning post brought a stack of bills and a single letter. Courtenay didn't even bother opening the bills. He simply tossed them into the trunk with the rest of the lot for Medlock to deal with and tore open the letter. A quick glance at the signature told him it was from Radnor's secretary. Radnor hadn't even bothered to pick up the pen himself, which meant the letter could contain no good news. Indeed, it was terse and uncompromising, worded to cut him to the quick. Courtenay was kindly requested to direct all future correspondence through his lordship's solicitors, Messrs. Winston and Haughton, Lincoln's Inn. It was as efficient a dismissal as Medlock's had been in the early hours of the morning.

He balled up the letter and threw it in the trunk with everything else he didn't want to think about. The trunk was getting damned full.

He grabbed his hat and walked to Eleanor's house. She was home, thank God, because he didn't feel equal to spending the day on his own. The house was quiet, empty, the sound of his footsteps echoing off the cool marble of the vestibule. It was a grand house, richly furnished with the best of everything. A good many people would envy Eleanor, and for good reason. But, walking through the barren corridors, he thought he had been happier in that Florentine debtors' prison than Eleanor was in her fine house.

He found her in her back parlor, and it struck him that he hadn't seen her outside this room in more than a week. She wasn't going to lectures or salons, she wasn't attending the theater or any of the events that were beginning to be held even this early in the season. Watching her bent over the letter she was writing, he had the sense that her melancholy was spreading through her like a cancer.

He shut the door and, when Eleanor didn't look up from her work, he opened it and shut it again, this time loudly.

"Oh, good day, Courtenay. Did you come for luncheon?"

"Shouldn't you be going out to luncheons with your lady friends?"

"I could ask you much the same thing."

"I ought to go to luncheons? Not likely."

"You ought to be with lady friends. Or, any friends at all, really. As for me, you call on me every day. So does Julian. That's enough."

She made *enough* sound like a terrible fate. "Oh, Eleanor," he said. "I really am worried about you."

"I have my health and a good deal of money," she said crisply, "and with any luck I'll have a patent on a telegraphical device before midsummer, so there's nothing to worry about." Her voice faltered on the last few words. And then she burst into tears. He took her hand and drew her up into an embrace.

"I'm trying to figure out a way through the next few decades of my life," she said, wiping her eyes on his waistcoat, "but I haven't done it yet."

"You will," he said into her hair.

"I know, but it's nothing like how I thought it would be, and it's taking my mind some time to recalibrate, I think."

Courtenay had never had any vision of his future. He had

always played the hand he was dealt without too much concern over the next round. But he understood what it meant to look around at your lot in life and be sorely disappointed.

"Got a letter from Radnor's secretary," he said, thinking some outrage might distract her. "Basically told me to sod off in the most polite language."

She made a noise of frustration. "I don't know what to do with Radnor. I've made your case—Simon's case—but he isn't moved."

"I'm going to need to let it go. Radnor's very fond of Simon and they don't need me."

She pulled back long enough to look at his face. "Oh, Courtenay. Poor dear. You're another one with a couple of decades to fill and no idea how to do it."

Wrong. He knew what to do. He'd go back to Italy. No, Greece, because it was further. He'd fuck his way straight across the Continent, as Medlock had so charmingly put it, and then he'd keep going. That would keep him comfortably distracted until he died of the pox or succumbed to a fever.

When he heard the click of the door opening, he stepped away from Eleanor and dropped his hands to his sides. Looking over Eleanor's shoulder, he saw a man who was strangely familiar, but he couldn't place him. "Eleanor," he said quietly. "You have a visitor."

Eleanor turned and went so pale Courtenay thought she might faint. "Ned," she whispered. But then she tilted her chin up in her most regal manner and said, "Sir Edward, what a lovely surprise."

Courtenay's first thought was that he hadn't known that Eleanor's husband was Indian. Or, rather, by the looks of him, he had at least one Indian grandparent. He was dark, quite handsome, and only a few years older than Eleanor. Courtenay had always imagined an aged, bookish Englishman of the type who went off to travel the world and then simply never came back.

With a start, he realized how he knew Sir Edward Standish. Their paths had crossed more than once—several years ago in Constantinople, and later in Cairo when Isabella had taken a fancy to showing Simon the pyramids. Standish had been working as a translator and hadn't been using his title. He had never made the connection to Eleanor until now.

Courtenay saw the answering gleam of recognition on Standish's face, and also remembered that Courtenay had been carrying on an indiscreet affair with a married woman during that time in Constantinople. Standish was clearly not best pleased to find his wife in the arms of a man such as Courtenay. Really, if he cared so much about who she kept company with, he shouldn't have abandoned her in the first place. Yet, his jaw was clenched, his hands balled in fists at his sides.

"My lady," Standish ground out. "Do me the favor of an introduction, if you please." Courtenay wanted to clock him on the head if that was how he greeted his wife after six years' absence.

"Lord Courtenay, this is my husband, Sir Edward Standish."

"That's what I thought," Standish said, eying him up and down.

"A pleasure," Courtenay drawled. If he was going to be cast in the role of wife-stealing rake, he'd play it.

Standish folded his arms across his chest and stood silently. Plainly he wanted Courtenay to leave, but there wasn't a chance Courtenay was leaving Eleanor alone with a man who had a look of such fury on his face, not unless Eleanor explicitly told him to.

He sat on the sofa—right in the middle, so one of the Standishes would have to sit beside him if they sat at all— and smiled broadly. "I hope you had a pleasant journey," he said. "A couple years long, was it?"

There were advantages to being considered beneath reproach: if everybody already thought one rude and scandalous, it was almost satisfying to live up to their expectations. And Standish deserved a lot worse than a bit of drawing-room rudeness.

Eleanor rang the bell to summon a servant, then hesitated between sitting at her desk chair or sitting on the sofa beside Courtenay. She ended by pulling out the desk chair and pushing it to Standish, then perching on the edge of the desk. That at first seemed like a diplomatic solution, but when the tea arrived, she couldn't very well stay there, so she had to sit beside Courtenay.

"How long are you in London, Sir Edward?" she asked as she poured tea.

"That depends," he said curtly and without elaboration.

Courtenay supposed he needed money and had come to get some from his wife. He liked the fellow less by the minute. Or perhaps he came to demand an heir. Even worse.

"You'll find London much changed," Courtenay ventured, because it was the pleasantry he had heard the most since his return to England. It never failed to annoy him, and he was glad to pass the bad feelings on to Standish.

"I haven't set foot in England since I was a child," he said, looking at Eleanor. "I never planned to return." He stared at his tea, as if his cup contained something unfathomably wrong, like paraffin or hair tonic instead of perfectly normal tea. "We were married in India," he added abstractedly. His gaze seemed to fix on Eleanor's paperweight.

"You can leave, Courtenay," Eleanor murmured. "It's all right."

"Are you certain?" he whispered, aware that Standish had turned to watch them with a hawk's piercing gaze.

"He won't hurt me, if that's what you're asking. As for everything else, it could hardly get worse."

He kissed her hand and took his leave, sparing Standish only the most insouciant of bows on his way out the door.

As soon as he got to the street his smile dropped. Medlock needed to be informed right away of his brother-in-law's return, so he could be present to help his sister should the need arise.

After they had parted on such awkward terms, he had rather hoped to avoid Medlock, but now he had no choice.

"It doesn't make any sense." Julian collapsed, peeved and out of breath, onto a bench at the fencing studio. "You have one good leg. I ought to have beaten you handily."

Rivington—Lady Montbray's brother—sank onto the bench beside him. "I have a longer reach and better training," he said simply.

Julian grumbled and pushed a sweaty lock of hair off his forehead. He didn't begrudge Rivington the win, but he was deeply annoyed that his strategy of fencing until his head was on straight hadn't worked. It always had in the past. He had believed that his ability to overcome any stray licentious impulse was owing to his rigorous training and perhaps an innate strength of character. But that was before he met Courtenay.

In Courtenay's arms, Julian had let something off the leash he hadn't realized was restrained in the first place. He had gotten something he hadn't known he wanted.

He realized Rivington had been talking. "I'm sorry, what was that, Rivington?"

Rivington raised his eyebrows. "I was only saying that my other advantage was that your mind is elsewhere."

Julian muttered something about not having slept well, but this only reminded him of Courtenay, and that would never do. He rose to his feet. "After I get changed, I'm going to Manton's to fire some pistols." If physically exhausting himself hadn't worked to exorcise thoughts of Courtenay from his brain, perhaps forcing himself to concentrate on a target would.

"Another time," Rivington said, checking the clock on the wall. "I have to be going home." He paused and gave Julian a crooked grin. "Cook's making my favorite supper."

Julian regarded his companion with astonishment. Dining

at four in the afternoon in London was positively déclassé. Perhaps this was what happened when a man was cast out by decent society. Julian shivered. He'd dearly like to avoid finding out if this were typical.

He bid good-bye to Rivington and sat back on the bench, resting his head against the wall and letting his eyes droop closed. God, he was tired. And still his brain was assaulted by thoughts of Courtenay.

As if summoned up by his own imaginings, he heard his name spoken in Courtenay's drawl.

"Medlock, is that you in that getup?"

He opened his eyes and saw Courtenay peering down at him. He clenched his jaw. "This is perfectly normal fencing attire."

"If you say so. Your valet told me I'd find you here."

"Briggs? How the devil did you find my lodgings?"

"I asked your sister's butler."

Julian goggled. "Tilbury told you where to find me?" Tilbury hated Courtenay.

"Under the circumstances, he was happy to oblige."

Julian stood so he wouldn't have to keep tilting his head back to look at Courtenay. "What circumstances?"

Courtenay gestured to a sort of alcove where they wouldn't be overheard. "Your brother-in-law has returned. He evidently hadn't informed anyone of his intentions, so Tilbury may have an apoplexy over household arrangements."

"I should damned well think he might." Julian was feeling dangerously close to apoplexy himself. "How is Eleanor?" He couldn't imagine how she would feel, literally couldn't puzzle out whether she'd be happy or sad or some combination of the two, because he had worked so hard never to talk to her about this one topic. He had to go to her.

"Shocked." Courtenay had dark circles under his eyes and his brow was wrinkled in concern that was at odds with his usual careless manner. "She's safe with him?"

"With Standish?" Julian was taken aback. "Yes, of course she is. We practically grew up with Standish. His father was with the East India Company."

"What I mean is that . . . When he walked in he took us unawares. He might have gotten the wrong idea about what was happening."

Julian drew in a sharp breath. "Oh, might he have?"

"I had gotten some bad news and she was comforting me."

"Was she now? This comfort occurred horizontally, I take it? Christ, Courtenay, can't you keep your hands off my sister?"

"It wasn't like that." His voice was now a sinister whisper. "If you think I went from you to your sister you're bloody depraved. But I'm not going to stand here in a fucking corner and defend myself. You can think what you want as long as you see to it that your sister is well. I have an urgent appointment to keep with a couple of whores."

Courtenay doffed his cap ironically and left without sparing Julian another word. Shaken, Julian lingered alone in the alcove. He had heard the pain in Courtenay's voice, and felt an unexpected wash of shame at having put it there.

CHAPTER ELEVEN

Julian found Eleanor's house in the kind of deliberate silence that only comes when people have no idea what they ought to say or what they ought to do, so they try their hardest to not do or say anything. The footman who opened the door informed him that his sister was in her bedchamber. "The master," the footman informed him with wide eyes, "or am I to say his lordship?—is in the green bedchamber."

"Where is Tilbury?"

The butler was setting and resetting the dining table. "Oh, Mr. Medlock," he intoned. "What is to be done?"

Julian resented the old man's air of grief. To bemoan Standish's arrival seemed to assume so much about Eleanor that it was very nearly a violation of Eleanor's privacy. Had the entire household speculated about their mistress's situation? The entire *ton*, perhaps? Were Julian and Eleanor the only people who hadn't discussed the topic? Julian was ashamed for not having spoken to Eleanor months or years ago, to ask her if she was all right. He only hadn't because he feared what the answer would be, and that it was his fault, and that there was nothing to be done for it now.

"Put an extra plate out for me, if you please. How long is Sir Edward staying?"

"Nobody knows." Tilbury had the air of a man who was barely holding back a wail. "I didn't realize he was a foreigner. Somebody might have told me so I could have prepared the staff."

Julian bristled. "He isn't a foreigner. His father's family has been in England since the Conquest." His mother's family was also perfectly respectable, but Julian didn't think Tilbury was interested in that aspect of Standish's parentage. "If any of the servants take issue with their master's lineage, they're quite free to seek other positions."

"Indeed, sir," Tilbury murmured, sounding unconvinced.

"Lord Courtenay will be staying here for the next fortnight, so if you'll please ready one of the spare rooms I'd most appreciate it." Julian had come up with this plan on his way from the fencing studio. If Courtenay stayed with Eleanor and Standish, it would look like Standish was unconcerned about any rumors regarding his wife's relations with Courtenay. He probably ought to have asked Eleanor's leave before informing Tilbury, but the staff here had gotten used to taking orders from Julian. He probably ought to have asked Courtenay as well, but he'd sort that out later.

Tilbury looked as if he'd dearly like to scream, but he confined himself to a dour, "If that's what the mistress wishes."

He fiddled with a place setting. "If I may make a suggestion, sir, does Lady Standish have a female relation she could perhaps invite for a few weeks?"

Julian had had the same thought. "I'm afraid not, Tilbury." It had always been only him and Eleanor, with nobody to turn to but each other.

Eleanor appeared in the doorway. "Quite a pleasant surprise we had this afternoon, Julian!" she cried. Really, she was not any good at false merriment. Any hope Julian had that Eleanor had enjoyed a happy reconciliation with her spouse went straight out the window when he saw his sister's rictus of a smile.

"In your parlor, Eleanor." Not in front of the servants, was what he meant. Once the door was shut safely behind them, he asked, "How long does he plan to stay?"

"I can't imagine how you expect me to know." An irritated furrow appeared on her forehead. "He hasn't said more than ten words to me since arriving. First I thought he wanted to hit Courtenay, but of course he's too well bred for that, even if he did mind how I amused myself." The furrow disappeared and was replaced with a look of resignation. "I suppose I shouldn't be surprised."

"Are you all right, Nora?" he asked hesitantly, six years too late.

Her lips trembled a bit. "Not really, no."

He took a step towards her and then stopped. He knew he ought to do something, but what? Pat her hand? Embrace her? He had spent so long trying to avoid his own less presentable emotions that he didn't know what to do with another person's. "Is there anything I can do?" he asked feebly.

Eleanor looked as if she wanted to say something, but instead she gave her head a small shake.

There had to be, and he'd figure it out, but first he'd attend to a problem he could actually solve. "Courtenay needs to stay here."

"Here?" Eleanor looked bewildered. "Why on earth?"

"It'll put any rumors to rest that Standish came back because of your misbehavior."

"Do you think that's why he came back?" She looked slightly less bleak, which made no sense.

"I suppose it depends on how fast gossip travels. Where was he most recently?"

"His valet told my maid they had been in Vienna."

Vienna? He had always thought Standish farther away than that. "I dare say it's possible. What was Courtenay doing here this afternoon? He said you were comforting him."

"He got a nasty letter from Radnor's secretary and was cut up about it."

"Did he, now? Well, I think I have a plan to settle that business."

"I'm so glad." She gave him a bleak smile. "Will you stay for dinner?"

He did, and a wretchedly awkward meal it was. Julian couldn't speak freely to Eleanor with Standish sitting there stone-faced. And, oddly, Julian had the sense that Standish and Eleanor couldn't speak freely with him there either. They were studiously avoiding the issue of whether they used first names or titles, which seemed unnecessarily exhausting for two people who had climbed trees together as children and who were presently man and wife.

"Lord Courtenay is to make a visit with us," Eleanor said to her husband. "You don't mind, do you?"

"Of course not. Why ever would I?" said Standish in frigid tones.

"Oh. Good," Eleanor replied tepidly, and from that point on didn't even try to make conversation with either Julian and Standish, and instead fed morsels of fish to the cats who congregated around her feet.

Julian left as soon as decently possible.

He hired a hackney to take him to his lodgings, but when the carriage pulled up to his door, he hesitated. He didn't want to go upstairs and endure the ministrations of his valet, the unwinding of his tie and the hanging of his coat silent reminders of the status and position he only acquired through Eleanor's excellent marriage and subsequent unhappiness.

He had been deluded to think it was a bargain. Even at eighteen, he ought to have known that Eleanor gained nothing by leaving India. She didn't care about London society and he had been a rank fool to have believed her. She had done it for him; she had left her home and somehow lost her husband along the way, in order to convince Julian to move to a climate more conducive to his health. He never would have left for his own good and she must have known it. So she convinced him it was a bargain, a fair trade: she would go to London a newly minted baroness, and he would go with her to assist her rise to the top.

They had left the worsening cycles of illness that Julian had endured in India; he had never liked to dwell on how that required Eleanor to leave her bridegroom. But he had always assumed Standish would come along eventually. If he allowed himself to think about this for another minute he was fairly sure he'd puzzle out how that was his fault too.

He rapped on the roof. "I've changed my mind. Take me to Flitcroft Street." He didn't want to be alone, stewing in his guilt.

"You sure about that?"

It was the only thing he was sure of.

There was a dreadful pounding at the door. Courtenay ignored it and went back to staring at the liquid in his glass.

"Open the door, Courtenay." It was Medlock, and the people in the downstairs flat were not going to be impressed with this banging. "I know you're in there. I could see the light from the street."

Courtenay staggered up from his chair and opened the door. Medlock was all neat and tidy again, wearing his usual boring clothes and the beginnings of a frown. Courtenay had quite enjoyed the sight of the younger man rumpled and sweaty at the fencing parlor. "What do you want?"

"I came to tell you that you're staying with my sister for the next fortnight," Medlock said.

"That's a terrible idea." Courtenay hadn't missed the look of fury on Standish's face when he saw his wife with another man.

"It's a brilliant idea. You and Standish are to be the best of friends." Medlock peered over Courtenay's shoulder into the room beyond. "I knew you hadn't any ladies here!"

He shouldn't find it so adorable that Medlock referred to the sort of women who might be found in a bachelor's lodgings as *ladies*. "My plans changed."

"No, I don't think they did." Medlock shouldered past him into the room. "These are not the lodgings of somebody who does much in the way of whoring. It's like a monastic cell." He turned in a slow circle but stopped short. "Is that a bullet hole in the wall?" He stepped back and surveyed the wall. "Were you aiming for that stain?" He indicated a patch of damp.

Courtenay cleared his throat. "I was aiming for a pigeon across the way."

"You were—" Medlock looked at the open window, then at the bullet hole, half a yard away. "Either your pistol is faulty or you're a terrible shot."

"It's definitely the latter."

"Or perhaps you were drunk." Medlock looked around the room, his gaze catching on the bottle of brandy and the glass. He held the bottle up to the light, then approached Courtenay and performed an exaggerated sniff.

"You've noticed my irresistible scent, I see."

"Shut up," Medlock said. "You aren't drunk at all. There's hardly a glass's worth of brandy missing from the bottle, and your glass seems untouched. And I don't smell any spirits on you, so I know you didn't stop at a gin palace."

"I was working up to it."

Medlock gave him an appraising glance. "It's like that, is it?" And then he took the bottle and the glass and poured the contents of both out the window.

"What the hell are you doing?" He could ill afford another bottle.

"If you wanted to drink it, you would have done so hours ago. I think you wanted *not* to drink it, so I helped."

He was right, but that only made it more annoying. "It wasn't yours to pour out."

"I'll buy it off you." Medlock resumed his inspection of the room. "It was dark last night or I think I would have noticed the absence of vice." Courtenay suppressed a smile, trying not to imagine what Medlock would have considered evidence of vice if not the presence of his prick in Courtenay's mouth. "I think you've been trying to be on your best behavior since arriving in England."

"I'm too old to carry on the way I used to."

"That would hardly stop you if you really meant to continue debauching yourself. My father drank and caroused until he died."

Eleanor had hinted that the late Mr. Medlock had not been an exemplar of virtue. "What else did your father do?"

"Oh, the usual. Gaming, women, drink."

"I feel certain he and I would have gotten along swimmingly."

"I thought so too, at first," Medlock said without elaboration. "Monastic," he repeated, glancing around the room.

"Not entirely," Courtenay reminded him with a pointed glance at the sofa.

"Oh, that's different," Medlock said with a wave of his hand.

"True, I'd bet monks did a fair bit of what we did last night," Courtenay suggested. "It was probably the only way to keep warm."

Medlock's mouth twitched with the effort to hold back a smile. "What I meant is that we were discreet. Perfectly acceptable."

"Oh, yes, I'd wager most of the *ton* would find nothing indiscreet or unacceptable about what we did."

"Don't be daft. Of course I know they wouldn't. But I'd likely go mad if I were celibate." He said this as if it quite settled the question. "You're going to have to pay for that wall before quitting the lease."

Medlock had to know Courtenay didn't have cash on hand for that sort of expense. He sighed. "This visit's been lovely but I'm for bed."

Medlock held up a hand as if to halt Courtenay. "Eleanor told me you got a letter from Radnor's secretary. I have a plan to get Radnor to let you see Simon. Do you think you'd mind if Radnor sets fire to Carrington Hall?"

"I suppose it would depend on whether the house was inhabited."

Medlock furrowed his brow. "Unfortunately, I would have resettled your mother in Bath by then," he said apologetically.

Courtenay managed to keep a straight face. It had been so long since anyone had taken Courtenay's part, had thought him worthy of defense, that Medlock's venom towards the parent who had cast Courtenay off warmed a part of his heart he had long thought decayed. "Then I see no objection."

"I'll let you know when the papers are ready for you to sign."

Courtenay had no idea what papers Medlock was referring to and didn't much care. "I didn't want to pay for company. Not after last night, Medlock."

"I'm not sure I follow." He turned his back to Courtenay and suddenly became focused on tracing the bullet hole in the plaster.

"I think you follow perfectly fine." The man's mind went at twice the speed of any normal brain. He could certainly keep up with Courtenay.

"If you're intending to compliment me," Medlock said, still facing the wall, "I suppose I'm gratified to learn that my services compare favorably with those of a prostitute."

"Services be damned." Courtenay closed the gap between them so he was speaking nearly into Medlock's ear. "It had nothing to do with services. It was you." With one hand he drew the shabby curtain closed and with the other he brushed a strand of hair behind Medlock's ear.

Medlock shivered at the touch. "You probably say this sort of thing to all the people you consort with. It's why they jump back into bed with you time and again, I suppose."

He was half right. More than half. Courtenay knew what to say to endear himself to the people he wanted to consort with, as Medlock appallingly put it. But that wasn't what he was doing now—Medlock had no use for pretty words. "Is it working?"

Medlock rested his forehead against the wall. "Always. I think I get half hard whenever you start talking. It's a character flaw on my part, I'm quite certain."

"Good." Courtenay bent to kiss the tender spot beneath Medlock's ear. "You need more character flaws."

Medlock exhaled, almost a sigh, as he sank back against Courtenay's chest.

"I want you naked this time," Courtenay murmured into Medlock's neck as he slid his hands down the man's chest. "I want to see and kiss every inch of you. Later, after you've fucked me"—he felt Medlock's body jolt to awareness at those words—"I want you to spend the night, and when we wake up I want to do it all over again. You cheated me out of that last night, Medlock, and I won't have it happen again."

Medlock turned then, looking slightly dazed. "After I've fucked you," he echoed. "That's what you want."

"Want hardly covers it, Medlock. It's all I've thought of all damned day."

He licked his lips. "Me fucking you."

"Do you need a diagram?"

He slowly shook his head. "I think I can manage." A filthy grin began to spread over his face as he unknotted his cravat and lay it carefully on the back of the chair.

That was the last item of clothing either of them disposed of with any care whatsoever. Courtenay took a perverse satisfaction in Medlock's quickly evaporating concern for the state of his garments, or indeed anything that wasn't his hardening cock. He pushed Medlock into the wall, kissing him hard and savoring the man's moan. He tugged off Medlock's clothes and then his own, creating a pile of coats and waistcoats and then shirts and trousers and boots.

When they reached the bedroom, Medlock hesitated only the briefest of moments before pushing Courtenay onto the bed, then crawling over his body and pinning his arms over his head. Courtenay groaned in pleasure. He knew Medlock recalled their conversation in the dark of the opera and was giving him exactly what he wanted. When he was with a man, he wanted to be reminded of all the things that made men what they were, or maybe just what made that particular man what he was. Medlock was a half-suppressed smile and an imperious flash in his gray eyes; he was a firm grip on Courtenay's wrists and the ripple of ropy muscles.

"What do you want me to call you when I'm fucking you?" Medlock asked.

Courtenay's shivered at the words and the dark look in Medlock's eyes. "You can call me whatever you damned well please," he said, and he meant it.

"What's your given name? I'm not calling you Courtenay while I'm fucking you. That's absurd."

Courtenay had no idea why it was absurd, but if an answer helped Medlock get about his business and start fucking him, he'd give him one. "Jeremiah."

Medlock made an exasperated noise and let go of Courtenay's hands. "What can your mother have been thinking?"

Courtenay laughed, harder than he would have thought possible with a desperately aching erection and a deliciously naked man kneeling over him. "I really don't know."

"I mean, with a name like that you were either going to

become a Methodist preacher or you were going to rebel and become an infamous scapegrace. I rather think you went about things the right way."

Courtenay tried to roll away and bury his face in a pillow to smother his laughter, but Medlock wouldn't let him. He took hold of Courtenay's chin. "You must have another name."

"I have a laundry list of names. You'd hardly even credit it." Medlock's fingers were firm and sure on Courtenay's jaw. "I believe I was christened Jeremiah Lloyd Alexander Cecil Devere Illingham."

Medlock sat back on his heels, idly stroking his erection while looking down at Courtenay. He was lean, with more sinew and muscle than Courtenay expected in a gentleman. His chest was covered in pale hair that trailed down his belly. "What do people usually call you in bed?"

Something about the question—was it the *usually*, as if this transaction were as routine and unremarkable as having his grate swept or his hair trimmed?—set his teeth on edge. He felt his cock lose interest. "Just call me Courtenay."

Medlock tipped his head and looked down at him with an expression Courtenay couldn't read. "No. You've already told me to call you whatever I damned well please."

That tone—confident, a bit bossy—spoke directly to Courtenay's prick. God, that had been the best part of last night, watching Medlock let go, feeling and tasting and hearing him realize a desire he might not have known about.

Courtenay wanted that again tonight. Not a routine fuck, not a workmanlike grope and tumble. He wanted Medlock to give up some of that reserve he held so dear.

But if a commonplace roll in the hay were all that Medlock was offering, he'd take it. Looking at Medlock kneeling over him, wiry muscles tense, incongruously soft mouth slightly parted, a slightly wild look in his gray eyes, Courtenay knew he'd take whatever Medlock had to give.

Chapter Twelve

Courtenay sat up, shifting so that Julian was now in his lap, straddling him.

"What do you want?" Courtenay asked, his voice soft but heavy with an intent that Julian didn't understand.

"I think we've decided that I'm fucking you," Julian bit off, confused by their change in positions and at a loss as to what to do with his hands. After a moment of awkwardness, he settled his hands on Courtenay's upper arms, which turned out to be a terrible choice because he could then feel the flex and ripple of muscles when Courtenay touched him, somehow making the experience twice as overwhelming. And, damn it, Julian was hardly able to keep his want within reasonable boundaries as it was; each additional sensation threatened to send him to a place he hardly recognized.

"No, I asked what you *want*." Courtenay ran his fingers down Julian's back, and the shiver Julian felt in response seemed so exaggerated as to be a parody of a normal shiver.

As usual, his body was in an uproar of sensation where Courtenay was concerned.

"If you think I wouldn't enjoy fucking you, you're a deeply confused man." Julian indicated his own erection. Which was right there, plain as day, next to Courtenay's own, and it seemed to Julian a waste of two perfectly good erections to be sitting here talking about want instead of putting them to good use.

"That's not what I asked," Courtenay murmured into Julian's neck, gently biting the skin where shoulder met neck.

Julian felt that bite everywhere in his body. It sent trickles of awareness down his spine and tingles of confused pleasure even in his legs. "Yes," he managed, "I was just thinking how enjoyable it would be to negotiate this experience in bizarre detail like some kind of peace treaty, instead of getting down to the business of fucking."

In response, Courtenay threaded his fingers through the hair at the nape of Julian's neck, tilting Julian's head back so he could kiss the underside of his jaw. "Mmm," Courtenay sighed into the soft flesh there. "You didn't shave."

"I meant to," Julian protested, feeling suddenly defensive, "but *somebody* accosted me at the fencing studio with an emergency and I didn't have time to go home and shave before dinner. Besides, I hardly need to. My hair is fair and I don't grow much of a beard, and—oh!"

Courtenay was sucking on the tender skin beneath his jaw, then running his tongue along the place he had just sucked. "It feels good," he said. He rubbed his cheek against

Julian's jaw and Julian could feel Courtenay's own scratchy new beard.

It did feel good. Coarse and earthy and nonetheless very good. The polite, clean coupling he sought was becoming a distant memory.

Courtenay took hold of Julian's hips and tugged him closer, so Julian's cock was finally touching Courtenay's belly. At that slight promise of friction, he pushed forward helplessly and heard Courtenay's answering sigh. Then Courtenay raked his fingernails gently up Julian's back. It came as a strange relief, as if Courtenay were scratching an itch Julian hadn't realized he had, and sent more of those shivers along random, scattered areas of Julian's body.

"I like feeling you like this," Courtenay said, pulling back so he could see Julian's face.

"Cranky and overly aroused? Happy to oblige."

Courtenay smiled, and Julian knew as an absolute fact that nobody ought to look so handsome who was being this annoying. Julian was trying very hard not to think of how excessively attractive Courtenay was, because if he acknowledged even to himself how badly he wanted this man, how the perfect contours of his body and face made Julian almost dizzy with need, then Julian might dissolve into a sad frenzy of desperate lust.

"You like when I touch you," Courtenay said.

"That's rather the point. I think you're the one who needs the diagram. I really would have thought you'd have grasped the essentials by this point in your career, Courtenay."

In answer, Courtenay trailed an infuriatingly light touch

down the outside of Julian's thighs, making Julian's cock jump. "Like that."

Julian was about to say something snide, when Courtenay's mouth closed over his own. After all those too-light, infuriatingly diffuse touches, the kiss came as a terrible relief. Courtenay's lips and gently probing tongue felt like a drink of cool water after a day spent under the Madras sun. The slide of his big hands down Julian's hips to cup the globes of his arse felt like the answer to a confusing line of sums. His whole body sang with want and relief.

Courtenay squeezed and spread Julian's arse ever so slightly, almost absently. Julian found himself squirming, pushing back into Courtenay's hands. He had the sudden notion that it was he, not Courtenay, who was going to be fucked, and—worse—that he really wanted that to happen. But no, Courtenay had been quite clear on his intentions, and thank God, because Julian didn't think he could handle turning his body over to this man in that way.

"Come here," Courtenay said, pulling away from the kiss only long enough to speak. He lay down, taking Julian with him, still kissing and touching and stroking. Julian felt like a fire that had been built up with too much fuel, dangerously hot and bright, something that could easily become a disaster.

"Look at me," Courtenay murmured, and only then did Julian realize that his eyes had been squeezed shut. And they must have been closed for a while, because when he opened them, even the faint light from the candle Courtenay had lit dazzled his eyes. Even more dazzling was Courtenay himself, sprawled beneath him, his black hair spread out on the pillow and his eyes dark with want. Julian, against his better judgment, let his gaze travel down Courtenay's body, savoring the taut lines of his muscular chest, relishing the sight of Courtenay's cock resting dark and thick against his belly.

"Christ," he said, shaking his head. "Why do you need to look like that? You could look half—no, a quarter—as good and still get the job done." He knew he was being irrational, but he didn't care. He was so occupied with keeping his lust within acceptable parameters that he was genuinely exasperated by Courtenay's extravagant beauty.

"Moderation is not one of my virtues," Courtenay said apologetically, as if taking responsibility for his excessive good looks. "I'm very sorry." Only the faint quirk of his lip betrayed that he wasn't serious.

Julian did the only thing he could in the circumstances, which was to shove Courtenay's legs apart with his knees and pin his hands above his head with one hand. "You ought to be. Look what you've done to me." He thrust against Courtenay's hip, letting him feel the hard press of his desire. "I'm panting, for God's sake. If I don't get inside you I feel like I might die."

"Do it," Courtenay said.

It didn't sound like an order. If it had, Julian might have found a way to disobey, just to reclaim the upper hand or prove that he wasn't in total thrall to his baser longings. But the way Courtenay said it, low and urgent, jaw clenched and eyes wild, made it sound like a plea. A prayer. Like Julian had the one thing Courtenay needed.

Courtenay couldn't help but grin stupidly when Medlock shoved his knees apart harder than strictly necessary. This was the Medlock Courtenay had wanted to see tonight, the man without the filter of restraint or correctness. Pure, raw desire.

He felt triumphant knowing that he had chipped away at that blasted reserve.

Medlock's eyes were reflected firelight, lit with the same quicksilver glints as Eleanor's paperweight. His gaze, hot and seeking, traveled over Courtenay's body. Courtenay knew what he looked like and rather took for granted that people generally found him attractive. But Medlock always looked at him with the hunger of a starving man seeing a table laid for someone else. There was always something almost resentful about the heat he sometimes caught in Medlock's eye, as if Medlock were angry with Courtenay for making him feel the way he did.

Not now, though.

Medlock's hands were now on Courtenay's thighs, sliding down, ignoring his prick, skimming over his bollocks, and finally resting on his entrance. Courtenay shivered at the touch.

And then he froze. It had, he belatedly remembered, been rather a long time since he had engaged in this particular act. There was no way he was going to ask Medlock to play the part of the careful lover—that would be quite at odds with the tableau he had envisaged.

As usual, Courtenay had failed to plan ahead in even the most rudimentary way. It was the same story, over and

over again. It was too late to do anything about it now—
Courtenay believed in seeing his bad ideas through to the
very end. Reaching to the table next to his bed, he fumbled
until he found what he needed. "Here," he said, handing the
bottle of oil to Medlock.

Perhaps something in his tone gave away his stupid fit of
nerves. Or perhaps it was the way his entire body tightened
when Medlock's touch became more intent. Whatever the
cause, Medlock gave him a quizzical look as he poured some
oil into his hand. But that expression vanished as soon as it
had appeared, and when he returned his fingers to Courtenay's body, his touch wasn't hesitant. Not in the least bit careful or guarded, thank God, because Courtenay didn't think
he could bear it. The whole point of this encounter was that
he wanted to see Medlock become unhinged, and that wasn't
going to happen if the fellow made a great show of solicitude.

But Medlock was only looking at him with unchecked
lust as his slippery fingers slid over Courtenay's entrance.
Courtenay grinned despite his reservations.

"See something you like, Medlock?"

"Yes, damn you," Medlock said without rancor, and then
pushed a single finger inside.

Courtenay shivered and heard Medlock swear.

"More," Courtenay demanded, despite knowing he wasn't
ready. Medlock complied, stretching him slowly and . . . carefully? No, it couldn't be that. The expression on his face was
barely reigned in wantonness. And then Medlock twisted his
fingers and brushed against that spot inside that made him
feel like he might dissolve into a puddle of sensation. Oh,

God, it really had been a while. He had forgotten what that felt like. "Fuck," he ground out when Medlock did it again.

Medlock kept at it, bloody inexorable, his silvery gaze fixed not on where he touched Courtenay, but on his face, with an intensity that made Courtenay want to either crawl under the covers or pounce on the man. He kept stroking until Courtenay thought he might sob with need.

And when, finally, Medlock slicked himself with oil and pushed inside, there was only the slightest burn of intrusion. Then there was only pleasure, spiraling blindly out of control.

God, yes. This was what he had wanted. Medlock's grip punishingly hard on his shoulder, Medlock's breath heavy and ragged and interspersed with garbled oaths. Courtenay reached for himself, only to find his hand slapped away. Medlock wrapped his own hand tight around Courtenay's cock, stroking to the rhythm of his own thrusts. Courtenay wanted it to go on longer, wanted to watch Medlock abandon himself like this for the rest of the night, but he felt his climax bearing down on him. He let himself go, let the pleasure build up where Medlock filled him and touched him. He brought his hands to Medlock's hips and held on as he was shattered by his climax.

Spent, Courtenay watched Medlock lose his rhythm and abandon himself to furious thrusting, finally shuddering and collapsing on top of Courtenay. And when he mumbled something into Courtenay's neck that sounded like, "Oh, fuck, fuck, fuck," Courtenay stroked his hands up and down his spine and murmured reassuringly, as if Courtenay weren't the one in need of reassurance.

Medlock eventually pulled away, leaving Courtenay damp and quickly cooling in the night air. But he returned, cleaned them both with a wet cloth, and then, just when Courtenay was getting used to the idea that Medlock was planning to leave so soon, he crawled back into bed. Courtenay folded Medlock into his arms. Or maybe it was the other way around.

"Bring me the pistol you used," Medlock said after a while, when they were lying side by side and Courtenay was beginning to wonder whether Medlock meant to stay the entire night, and whether that was something Courtenay wished for slightly or very much indeed.

"What? Why?" Courtenay supposed Medlock meant to take it away, to dispose of it as he had disposed of the brandy, in order to prevent Courtenay from doing anything stupid.

"Just give it over."

Courtenay dragged himself out of bed and got the pistol out of the bottom drawer of his clothes press. Holding it by the barrel, he extended his hand to Medlock. "It's loaded," he cautioned.

In the gloom, Courtenay watched Medlock turn the weapon over in his hands and then narrow his eyes, focusing on some point across the room, through the open doorway. He held it out as if aiming it, one eye shut. "You're positive it doesn't pull left?"

"Positive," Courtenay said, still unsure where this was going.

"Don't move," Medlock murmured, sitting up against the headboard.

Before Courtenay knew what had happened, he heard the pistol's report. "What the devil are you doing?" he choked out, too stunned to even get out of bed. "You're mad."

"Go check and see if I got it."

Courtenay could smell the acrid smoke and his ears were ringing from the blast. The downstairs neighbors were shouting, and rightly so. "What you've got is some kind of brain fever, Medlock. You can't fire a pistol in somebody's lodgings."

"Says the man who started this whole business by firing a pistol in his lodgings. Fine. I'll check myself." Still naked, still brandishing the weapon, Medlock crossed to the curtained window and touched the wall. "You were quite correct," he called. "It does not pull left."

Only then did Courtenay realize what had happened. An instant later he was beside Medlock, examining the wall, which still bore only the single bullet hole. He touched the divot in the plaster, and it was hot to the touch.

"Holy mother of God," Courtenay muttered. Medlock had hit the bullet hole Courtenay produced earlier. "I wasn't expecting you to be a sharpshooter." There was barely any light, and the fellow had been in bed. Hardly ideal conditions for accurate shooting.

"It's just a knack." Medlock blew the residual smoke away from the pistol. He looked damned smug, though.

"Like hell it is."

Then Medlock adopted an entirely different tone, the brisk and businesslike register that meant Courtenay was about to get ordered about. Courtenay couldn't say that he minded. "I'm afraid I've made an awful mess of your wall, though, Courtenay."

"You know perfectly well I'm the one who put the hole there in the first place."

Medlock waved this concern away. "I'll settle matters with your landlord tomorrow."

Courtenay shook his head in bewilderment. Medlock was a madman. Courtenay had just been fucked ragged by a madman. A sharpshooting lunatic. And he wanted it again, as soon as possible.

"Don't look at me like that," Medlock snapped. "It's much better that I'm thought to have had target practice in your lodgings than it is for anyone to think you were attempting murder or that you might have been drunkenly playing with your pistol."

"I see," Courtenay said slowly.

"Now let's go back to bed."

Julian hadn't meant to spend the night, but he must have fallen asleep, because when he opened his eyes the sun was streaming brightly through the gap in Courtenay's tatty curtains. The room was silent except for the sounds on the busy street below. Courtenay was nowhere to be seen.

He made use of the ewer and basin and dressed himself as tidily as he could. Thank God he hadn't had time to change before dinner last night, or he'd have to make his way home in what was blatantly the previous day's evening clothes.

Upon further reflection, that was the least of his problems. He glanced at the bed out of the corner of his eye, as if looking at it head on would be too harsh a reminder of what had transpired there. He had been utterly lost to all sense of perspective and proportion. He had vague, disjointed memories of Courtenay's hands on his body, stroking and touching and coaxing him on like the devil he was.

The oddest thing was that Julian had the sense that Courtenay had been nervous. Julian had taken care to be . . . not gentle, but cautious. And now he felt strangely embarrassed about that, as if the care he had taken of Courtenay had exposed something he didn't wish to think about. Another night like that and Julian might not be able to pretend that he wasn't getting a trifle attached to Courtenay. How lowering to develop a tender for Courtenay. How cliché. Julian had thought he was made of sterner stuff than that.

At least Courtenay had the sense to leave before Julian woke. God only knew what kind of awkward conversation they'd resort to under the circumstances.

As he made for the door, it swung open, revealing Courtenay carrying a parcel. "I brought some rolls," he said, dropping the parcel onto the table.

Rolls. Were they to breakfast together? That seemed unwise. "I ought to leave," Julian said, suddenly conscious of the scratchiness of his jaw and the rumpled state of his cravat. But the yeasty, sweet scent of fresh bread rose to his nostrils and made his mouth water. He had hardly eaten dinner last night, and now it was—he pulled out his watch—"It's half past noon!"

"You were tired."

"Tired!" He shook his head, horrified. "I haven't slept past nine since I was a child."

"High time, then," Courtenay said, sitting on the arm of the sofa and helping himself to a roll. "Eat."

Julian sat at the table and bit into a roll. It was soft and buttery and studded with currants, simultaneously rich and light. It was quite possibly the most delicious thing he had ever eaten in his life, certainly in the last few years. He finished the roll and licked his fingers, not realizing what he was doing until he caught Courtenay watching him intently. He hastily pulled his finger from his mouth and wiped it on his handkerchief.

"Thank you. I'll arrange for your things to be brought to Eleanor's house this afternoon. Now I ought to be—"

"I got an invitation to the Blacketts' Venetian breakfast."

That was quite a coup. Julian had feared that after the events of Mrs. Fitzwilliam's dinner, Courtenay would never receive another invitation from a respectable hostess. "That's good. I'm going, and so is Eleanor."

"And Standish?"

"Hell."

"Quite."

"Wear your gray trousers," he snipped. "And endeavor to tie your cravat less terribly. And for God's sake, cut your hair."

His rudeness somehow put them back on comfortable ground. "You like my gray trousers?" Courtenay raised his eyebrow. "You think I'm handsome in my gray trousers?"

Julian bit back a smile. "Shut up. You'd be handsome in a tattered burlap sack or in—" He had nearly said *or in nothing at all*, which was true but not the direction he needed this conversation to go. "Your looks aren't the problem. Strive for some conduct and we might pull this thing off."

He headed for the door but was stopped by Courtenay, who silently held out a pastry.

"Fine," Julian sighed, as if taking another pastry were a favor and a concession. "Fine."

As he walked home, he tipped his face up to catch the bright midday sun. The buttery scent of the bun wafted up to him. The scent, the sunshine, and the memories of last night mingled together, and it was only when Julian got back to his lodgings—the bun now cool and the sun having passed behind a cloud—that Julian realized he was smiling broadly. He couldn't have stopped himself if he tried.

Chapter Thirteen

Courtenay wore the gray trousers. It wasn't as if his wardrobe had him spoilt for choice, and besides he would have worn pretty much anything to earn the look of hot approval he caught in Medlock's eyes when they met on the Blacketts' terrace during the party. That look quickly evaporated when Medlock's gaze narrowed on Courtenay's cravat.

"It could be worse," Medlock said, frowning slightly.

For some reason—likely his own perverse nature—Medlock's criticism delighted Courtenay almost as much as his stingy scraps of praise. The knowledge that Medlock wanted him despite everything was a sop to Courtenay's vanity.

Also, Courtenay suspected that if Medlock were honest and free with his criticism, then it might mean that his approval was equally sincere. Courtenay told himself that he wasn't interested in acceptance, nor in praise, not from anyone and especially not from Medlock. He had spent years telling himself that after being complicit in his sister's misfortune, he didn't deserve anything good for himself. But

Medlock's approval made Courtenay want more for himself.
It made Courtenay expect more from himself as well, and
wasn't that a bizarre novelty? This morning he had woken up,
read a segment in the newspaper about the mismanagement
of a workhouse, and seriously wondered if he ought to take
up his seat in the House of Lords and try to do something
about it. It was the height of lunacy, of course, but he found
his thoughts returning to it throughout the day.

"What's the matter with you?" Medlock asked, eyes narrowed. "You look very handsomely tragic. Stop that, before
the ladies swoon." His words were sharp but Courtenay
heard the concern in his voice.

Courtenay forced a smile and returned his gaze to the
lawn. The guests were valiantly pretending that it was fine
weather to be strolling about outside, rather than the unseasonably chilly and damp April day that it sadly was. They
ought to be huddled around a fire. It was too damned cold for
this mummery. But if one didn't look too closely, one wouldn't
see the shawls wrapped a bit too tightly around ladies' shoulders or the men's hands jammed too deep in their pockets.

"Come here," Medlock said, gesturing to a set of doors that
led off the terrace to an unoccupied parlor. Courtenay felt his
heart thump in anticipation, even though it was impossible that
Medlock of all people would risk exposure by carrying on with
a man in a room anyone might walk into. Still, when Medlock
raised his hands to Courtenay's shoulders, he felt a flush spread
across his body, as if he were a schoolboy instead of a jaded
debauchee of over thirty. It had been a week since that night at
Courtenay's lodgings, and he was hungry for more.

But instead of pulling Courtenay into an embrace, Medlock simply unknotted his cravat and deftly retied it. There was nothing in the least erotic in Medlock's efficient folding and knotting the length of starchy white linen, but Courtenay couldn't help remembering how clever—and bossy and gentle and maddening—those hands had been. He didn't know if he was only imagining a proprietary quality to Medlock's touch, but he felt marked.

"That's better," Medlock said, holding Courtenay at arm's length and squinting at his handiwork.

Courtenay cleared his throat. "Quite a trick to tie another man's cravat."

Medlock's gaze stayed on Courtenay's lapels, as if examining them for lint. "I used to tie my father's when his hands shook from drinking and we didn't have the money for a valet."

Before Courtenay could picture Medlock as a child administering to a parent, or as a person who had experienced deprivation and shame, Medlock led him back out onto the terrace, which by now had filled with party guests.

It turned out that Standish had indeed come, and looked about as miserable as a man could be at a blasted garden party. Eleanor was at his side, wearing one of her staid Medlock-approved ensembles. She had on the sort of smile that might as well be a grimace.

"What a pair of idiots," Courtenay said under his breath.

"Who?"

He gestured with his chin. "Your sister and Standish."

"What did they do?" Medlock looked confused. He *would* be confused, because he was just as much an idiot as they were, if Courtenay had the right of it. And after nearly a week under the same roof as the Standishes, he was fairly sure he knew which way the wind blew.

"She's fond of him. He thinks she isn't," Courtenay said patiently. "He's fond of her. She thinks he isn't. It would be the world's easiest problem to solve if either of them had any sense."

Medlock was still looking at him as if he were insane. "Of course they're fond of one another. They were children together." He hesitated, as if not sure the next bit of information really mattered. "They got married, for heaven's sake."

"They did indeed. And then they stayed away from one another for six years. I know you're a stranger to the ways of the heart, but that's not a typical mark of fondness, Medlock."

"Surely now that they're together, they'll manage to work things out." There was an unexpected tightness to Medlock's voice. "If that's what they want."

Courtenay turned his head. Medlock looked uncertain, maybe even confused. He was usually so smugly arrogant, it was something of a shock to see him less than entirely confident. He was worried about his sister, which was natural. But there was something more there. A touch of guilt, perhaps. Courtenay understood that very well indeed. But why did Medlock feel responsible for Eleanor's marriage?

"Why wouldn't that be what they wanted?" Courtenay asked.

Medlock looked pained. "I had only hoped that this was what she chose. This life." He gestured around him, encompassing the party and its guests. "Without Standish. And if it turns out that she wanted something different, then . . ." He sighed.

Was he saying that he would think less of Eleanor for wanting love? Courtenay felt a pang of disappointment at Medlock's ignorance. He nearly pitied the man for not being able to understand why his sister—or Standish for that matter—might want something more than a marriage on paper, might want to go to bed with and wake up next to a person they loved.

But he also felt vaguely embarrassed, because to be disappointed in Medlock's lack of interest in love meant that Courtenay must have harbored some slight hope of sharing such a thing with Medlock in the first place.

And he hadn't, not really; he had never let himself hope for a future that included anyone wanting to wake up next to him day after day, straightening his cravat and sharing his breakfast buns, a series of days unfurling infinitely and impossibly. But to know that it wasn't even a possibility—to know that Medlock hadn't even imagined falling in love with him or with anyone—made him grieve something he never would have had anyway.

"Watch," he said, suddenly wanting to prove his point to Medlock, without even knowing precisely what his point was. He sauntered over to Standish and Eleanor, affecting an ease he didn't feel, and engaged them both in dull conversation, strictly confining himself to the Medlock-sanctioned topic of weather. After five minutes, he bowed and returned to Medlock. "Did you see?" he asked.

Medlock rolled his eyes. "What I saw were two well-bred people conversing with . . . you."

"Exactly. Standish was terribly polite to me. He thinks I'm taking his wife to bed, but he was thoroughly affable."

"Would you prefer that he call you out?"

"No, but your sister might."

"That's ridiculous," Medlock scoffed. "Eleanor's a sensible woman."

"There's nobody more sensible," Courtenay agreed. "Which is why she can't see that her husband is barely containing his jealousy and disappointment. I wonder if I ought to go back over and slap him with my glove or something, give him a chance to make a proper display of his affections."

Medlock sighed. "Please don't provoke my brother-in-law to a duel. You're really a terrible shot."

Courtenay snorted with laughter. "The duels I've had the honor of participating in don't involve much aim," he explained. "Both of us delope, shake hands, and call it a day."

"That's shockingly pointless."

"I think shooting one another would be even more pointless, but reasonable minds may differ on that matter."

"Hmmm," Medlock said. "True. Then why the devil do you bother in the first place? I don't much see why you'd want to fire a weapon at someone unless you want them dead."

"It's a way out of a situation," Courtenay explained. "Let's say you've wronged a man, say you've called him a liar or gone to bed with his wife. The fellow can't just let that go, so you pretend you're going to kill one another. Everyone wins."

"What happens if the other man decides not to pretend?"

Courtenay shrugged. "It happens."

"Wouldn't it be a better idea not to take other men's wives to bed in the first place? Avoid the necessity of a duel entirely?"

Oh, poor Medlock. Sometimes Courtenay had no idea whether they even inhabited the same world. "Let's say a lady has a husband who is cruel or absent, or perhaps who doesn't care for female company. Should she resign herself to a life of celibacy?"

"And those are the women you've been with? You confined yourself to unhappily married ladies?"

"No," he said simply. "But I ought to have." Another thing to feel guilty about. As he looked out across the lawn at the brightly dressed guests milling about, he was conscious of Medlock scrutinizing him.

"Ever given any thought to getting married yourself, Courtenay?"

He kept looking over the lawn. "Not the marrying sort, Medlock."

"But you do like, ah . . ."

Courtenay didn't have to look to know Medlock was blushing. "Yes, I do. But I'd be a terrible husband. Any woman I liked enough to spend the rest of my life with, I'd be too fond of to punish with my presence." He had made the same general comment dozens of times over the years, and he had always more or less believed it. But this time when he said the rote words they didn't ring true.

Medlock, however, didn't argue that a life with Courtenay would constitute a punishment. "You have a title and some land, badly managed though it is. You probably ought to have an heir. We could find a woman with her own money—"

"Stop," Courtenay ground out. "I don't want the sort of marriage your sister has. Christ, look at them. I don't want to be purchased for my goddamn title. You think that's never occurred to me as a way out of my troubles?"

"That's a mercenary way of—"

"Stop," Courtenay repeated. He felt tears pricking his eyes, whether from anger or sorrow he couldn't tell. "Sometimes I don't understand what the hell is wrong with your brain. It's a fucking mess in there, isn't it? It's all columns of numbers marching in a row. I can't . . . I'm not like that, Medlock. That's not what I want."

"Then what do you want?" Medlock asked, exasperation in his voice.

Courtenay didn't know what he wanted. But he knew it wasn't a wife who looked down on him, nor was it the prospect of building a life and a family when he had robbed his sister of that chance.

Stupidly, he had the fleeting thought that what he truly wanted had something to do with deft hands on his cravat, a soft frowning mouth, and quicksilver eyes.

Julian cornered Eleanor in an alcove near the lady's cloakroom. It was not a dignified way to accost his sister, but at least this way they were alone.

"Courtenay told me you and Ned are having some kind of misunderstanding," he said, pitching his voice low, "and that you probably want to make things work between you. So you ought to get over whatever's bothering you and hash it out."

Eleanor's mouth went tight, her eyes blank. "I somehow doubt Courtenay said precisely that."

He had meant his remark to be light and helpful, a way of addressing the chasm that was growing between them, but now he felt defensive. "Those might not have been his exact words."

"You think it's so simple, that people's feelings can be arranged as easily as a column of sums."

"What the devil does everyone have against sums today?"

"But it isn't simple, Julian. You can't make yourself fall in love, let alone make somebody else. You can't even prevent it from happening."

Julian was getting peeved. "But—"

And then Eleanor slapped him. Hard, and right in the face. She had never laid a hand on him, not even when he had been a bratty child.

"What the—"

She was already gone, turning back toward the party.

This was the devil of a garden party. First Courtenay was in a state, now Eleanor. He didn't think he could stand another moment of it, at least not with any semblance of equanimity. He stepped out of the alcove with the intention of finding the hostess and taking his immediate leave. Instead he nearly ran into Courtenay.

"Good lord, Courtenay, why are you by the ladies' cloakroom? Do you follow my sister about like a spaniel?"

Surely he was imagining the fleeting look of hurt on

Courtenay's face. Whatever it was, it disappeared and was replaced by his usual lazy indifference. "I was looking for you," he said. He glanced pointedly at Julian's cheek. "I see Eleanor got to you first, though."

Julian automatically raised his hand to his cheek. "I think everyone has gone mad today."

"I don't think you want to get caught with me in an alcove. Let's go."

"I need to find Mrs. Blackett and take my leave."

"Not with your face like that, you don't. Come along. Very casually, to the street, as if we're having a conversation and simply forgot to do the pretty with the hostess."

Julian realized Courtenay had the right of it, damn him.

"After you left the terrace, Standish was flirting madly with a young widow," Courtenay said when they were on the pavement. "I daresay he was doing it to make your sister miserable, and he was quite successful."

Julian sighed. "Poor Eleanor." They walked another minute in silence. "I still don't understand why they can't just talk and agree to make it work," Julian burst out.

"I know you don't, Medlock. I don't suppose you've ever been in love?"

"Of course not."

He heard Courtenay sigh. "There's no of course about it. Anyway, love involves making your heart sort of . . . available. Unprotected. And you can't properly love a person who at any moment might step on your heart and toss it into the gutter. Or, I suppose you can, but it's a bad practice."

To Julian's ears, Courtenay sounded like he knew exactly

how bad a practice this might be. "You know this from experience?"

"I'm the sort of poor sod who can only learn things the hard way."

They reached Julian's lodgings, and Courtenay walked with him up the stairs. While they waited for Julian's valet to arrive, Courtenay took Julian's chin in his hand. "It was a bad day, but tomorrow will be better. Let your sister and Standish figure this out on their own. This is not your problem to solve."

It was, though, but he couldn't admit that to Courtenay. It was bad enough to admit it to himself. "Thank you for walking me home," Julian said, hating that Courtenay knew more than he did about anything.

Courtenay leaned in and brushed his lips over Julian's.

"I can't," Julian protested, but still found his hands resting on Courtenay's arms. "Briggs will be here any moment now."

"I only wanted to kiss you," Courtenay said, and he did it again.

Kisses that didn't lead up to some kind of release were totally foreign to Julian. He had never quite understood why a person would want to get themselves all worked up without an end in sight. But now he knew: this embrace was the point, the tasting and exploration, the knowing touch of hands.

Later, when the sun had set and he was alone in his bed, he couldn't help but think that things had all been much simpler before Courtenay had entered his life.

Chapter Fourteen

The next morning Julian sent a note to Courtenay at Eleanor's house informing him that he was visiting Carrington Hall, Courtenay's property near Stanmore, in order to inspect it for the new tenants. He asked whether Courtenay wished to accompany him but was positive Courtenay would decline. Julian wasn't very much looking forward to the errand himself.

He was finishing his toast and tea when Briggs solemnly informed him that Lord Courtenay had arrived.

"Here?" Julian asked stupidly.

"Indeed, sir. Shall I show him in?"

"Of course, of course."

Courtenay sauntered in, looking indecently handsome. At some point in the last week he had done as Julian had asked and cut his hair. But instead of cropping it, which was what Julian had intended, he had trimmed the ends so now his almost-shoulder length hair looked like a deliberate aesthetic choice rather than the result of laziness. It was, if possible, even less acceptable than before, a glaring reminder that Courtenay was not like other men. Julian desperately wanted to touch it. As if sensing Julian's gaze, Courtenay pushed a lock of hair off his forehead.

Julian interested himself in assembling his toast crumbs in an orderly pile.

"You were going to evict my mother without even informing me beforehand?" Courtenay said without rancor.

"I mentioned it to you," Julian protested.

"I dimly recall some such thing. But I had no idea it was to be today."

"Do you object?" Julian was prepared to fight this matter to the death.

"No, good God, not by any means. But I'll be damned if I'm going to sit out the match of the decade. If you're going to take on my mother, I'll have a front row seat, please and thank you." He tossed a parcel onto Julian's breakfast table. "I brought buns."

Julian could smell the cinnamon and butter even through the paper. "You may as well sit." He gestured reluctantly at an empty chair. He wanted to leave, not linger over pastries, but he didn't want to get sticky sugary crumbs all over the plush upholstery of his carriage. And leaving anything behind that smelled so good was quite out of the question. Gingerly, he opened the parcel and gave one of the buns to Courtenay and dropped one onto his own plate, then wiped the sticky glaze onto the napkin in his lap. Leave it to Courtenay to choose the messiest pastry in the land. But it smelled divine, and his dry toast seemed a very distant and irrelevant memory.

He picked the bun up carefully, and then—"Oh my God," he said, his mouth still full. "These are even better than the last ones." There was cinnamon and butter and a vast quantity of sugar, but also lemon rind and the barest hint of a spice that reminded him vaguely of his childhood in Madras.

"It's the one thing I missed when I was abroad. Bath buns, Chelsea buns, the whole lot. Can't get them in France or Constantinople or anywhere else."

Julian took another bite, conscious that the glaze was now all over his fingers and mouth. But, well, no use worrying about that now.

He shoved the rest of the bun in his mouth.

And then he took another.

"Hungry?" Courtenay asked. He was taking catlike bites of his own bun.

"Oh shut up." Julian stared at his now empty plate. The toast crumbs were not only scattered but compounded with cinnamon-bun crumbs and globs of glaze.

He ran his finger through the mess and licked it. He would never do such a thing around anyone else, not even his manservant, but what could Courtenay possibly care? What was finger licking compared to participating in orgies and eating opium and doing whatever else Courtenay had gotten up to in his past? Julian scooped up another fingerful of pastry and licked his finger again.

Courtenay made a choked-sounding noise and shifted

in his chair. Julian paused with his finger still in his mouth, realizing what he looked like.

"Does your valet knock before entering?" Courtenay asked, his voice low and promisingly raspy.

Julian knew what Courtenay was really asking, knew he ought to say something quelling, but the man looked so appallingly delicious. So instead, he licked another finger, looked Courtenay directly in the eye, and said, "Always."

Courtenay let out his breath and slid his chair closer to Julian's. Then he took hold of Julian's wrists, and, bending his head, he systematically licked each of Julian's fingers. Julian somehow managed not to whimper when he felt Courtenay's tongue circling each fingertip, or when Courtenay drew a finger deep into his mouth, sucking much harder than was necessary to remove a bit of sugar. But when Courtenay leaned in and licked the corner of Julian's mouth, the warmth and roughness of his tongue made him gasp aloud.

"Sweet," Courtenay murmured, before flicking his tongue along the seam of Julian's lips.

Infuriating man. Julian wrapped his fingers around the arms of his chair, hoping that would keep his hands from doing anything embarrassing, like petting Courtenay's hair or something. "Kiss me properly," he said with a little sniff. "Otherwise, let's get in the curricle and get on with the day."

Courtenay let out a huff of silent laughter and pressed another exasperating little kiss on the edge of Julian's mouth. "I can't imagine how you think propriety enters into this. There's very little that's proper about this situation." Another stupid, teasing kiss. "Even your table manners are atrocious."

That really was the outside of enough. "There's a right way to do things. And chaste little kisses that don't go anywhere aren't the right way." He was gripping the arms of his chair so tightly his fingers were beginning to hurt. "I should have thought that you, of all people, would have grasped the concept."

"But I'm enjoying this," he murmured into the skin below Julian's ear.

"Because your head isn't on right." It was taking all Julian's composure to keep his voice neutral and his clothing on. "I always suspected it." Julian could feel Courtenay's smile against his flesh.

Then Courtenay finally cupped Julian's jaw in his hand and tilted his head back for a real kiss. He licked into Julian's mouth, and he tasted sweet, like messy pastry and a confusion of spices. Julian moaned—he hadn't meant to—but the sweep of Courtenay's tongue against his own was so good, so exactly what he craved, such a relief after that prolonged torment.

Julian let go of the chair and threaded his fingers in Courtenay's hair, tugging him closer, kissing him deeper. He tasted so good and his mouth was so warm and right. Each kiss stoked the lust that had been building in his belly since Courtenay walked into this room. No. Wrong. The lust had been building since he had first laid eyes on Courtenay, only temporarily relieved in Courtenay's arms.

Courtenay pulled away. "We ought to go."

Julian gaped. "The bedroom is *right there*."

"It'll still be there later." He rose to his feet, straightened his lapels, and headed for the door.

"I think that what you really like is discomposing my state of mind. Turning me into a babbling fool."

Courtenay became very busy adjusting his cravat.

"Oh my God, I'm right. That is what you like. You like seeing me desperate for you." It was mortifying, this knowledge that his sad own lack of control was what Courtenay sought.

"You're so pretty when you're desperate."

Julian gasped. "Nobody has ever called me pretty. Or desperate."

"You've been keeping terrible company, my dear."

Courtenay felt his light mood evaporate with every furlong as they got closer to Carrington Hall. Looking out the window of Medlock's predictably first-rate carriage, he saw a road that he remembered all too well. It wasn't so very long ago that he had happily traveled along this route to visit his mother and Isabella. Even then, his mother had blamed him for his father's death, but she still received him, albeit grudgingly and with a good deal of drama. Isabella had been a different story. He remembered her half hanging out the schoolroom window, awaiting his return.

Medlock must have noticed Courtenay's quiet, because he was babbling nervously in a plain attempt to fill the silence.

"If you don't want to toss your mother out part and parcel, do you perhaps have a dower house you can put her in somewhere on the property and let Radnor have the main house?"

"I daresay Radnor and that secretary of his want more privacy than that. They're used to rattling about in that old pile down in Cornwall. They most certainly won't want my mother and her family poking in the windows, which is exactly what she'd do if she knew she had the famous Mad Earl on the premises." Only after the words had left his mouth did he realize he shouldn't have exposed Radnor, even though he knew Medlock shared the same secret. "Let's forget that I said anything."

Medlock made a frustrated noise. "Give me some credit, Courtenay. But Radnor and the secretary," he said musingly. "I wouldn't have thought Radnor needed privacy of that sort. But the secretary. Yes, I can see that. I met him before, you know."

Courtenay looked over at Medlock with some interest. "Did you? I tried to find out who he was, since Simon seemed terribly fond of the fellow and I wanted to make sure he was all right. But he seems to have materialized out of thin air."

"He was using a different name when I knew him. He duped an acquaintance of mine. Poor fellow had to go to South Africa."

It took Courtenay a second to realize what Medlock was saying. "Are you telling me my nephew is being raised by a confidence artist?"

"He seems aboveboard now." Medlock said this with the naive certainty of a man who still believed that a person could change his ways.

"Why didn't you tell me?" Courtenay might have used that information to barter in exchange for time with Simon.

"Because I can't see how it's my business what Radnor's

pretty secretary did to keep his bread buttered. We've all done things we're not proud of," Medlock snapped. Courtenay wasn't sure whether to ask what Medlock meant. Then, in his earlier offhand tone Medlock asked, "But he and Radnor, you say?"

"Can't be sure. I never saw them together. But I used to know Radnor rather well. Radnor, was, shall we say, inclined as we are. And nobody would go to that dilapidated rabbit warren of his in Cornwall without damned good reason, so I'm deducing that there's more to their dealings than that of a typical employer and secretary."

They drove on for a moment, their silence only interrupted by hoof beats and carriage wheels. "Well, then," Medlock said blandly, "nothing for it but to toss your dear mama out. And," he added with relish, "the rest of them. Disown, indeed." This last he muttered under his breath.

Courtenay bit back a smile. He would never get tired of trying to figure out Medlock's strange code of ethics. Lingering kisses were improper, almost shocking; the fact that these kisses occurred between two men was entirely unremarkable. Confidence artists were nothing to be too terribly concerned about; Courtenay's mother, on the other hand, was a villain of the rankest nature for having cast off the child who sent her money. Courtenay himself was a worthless scapegrace, or at least that was the decided impression Medlock had given him at first. But now . . .

He chanced a sideways glance at Medlock. Now, he wasn't so sure. He had sensed less rampant disapproval from Medlock since that night at the opera. Perhaps he had grown on Medlock. Perhaps Medlock believed that Courtenay, like Radnor's reformed criminal lover, was capable of change, was capable of good intentions despite the mischief that seemed to trail in his wake no matter how hard he tried.

The idea that Medlock might approve of him, respect him even, gave him a warm sort of feeling. God, he had thought his need for acceptance had petered out years ago. And maybe it had—he still didn't give much of a damn what people in general thought of him. But the idea that Medlock—fussy, high-hat Medlock, with his rules about cats and his penchant for soporific wallpaper—might see something worthy in Courtenay gave him a peculiar feeling.

Whatever it was, he knew he was very glad to have Medlock with him on this trip, on this road, to the house where he had been raised. To see the woman who had cast him out.

The closer they got to Stanmore, the more familiar the landscape seemed. There were the predictable markings of time—a tree that had been felled, a gate repaired, an inn's sign repainted in new, bright colors. But overall the terrain was familiar. It was his. This was where he was from, and no exile could change that. No matter how much he wished it.

"Have the coachman turn onto that lane," he said, indicating a divergence from the main road.

"But the map—"

"Trust me."

Medlock surprised him by rapping on the roof of the carriage and doing as he was told. Courtenay felt the carriage turn.

"This will take us back behind the house, so we'll approach by way of the stables, rather than the main gates."

Another silence, interrupted only by hoof beats on soil that somehow even sounded familiar. His soil. He owned this land, this dirt, these trees. Another shirked responsibility, but he was dismally certain he'd bollocksed up Carrington as much as he had bollocksed up everything else he'd ever tried to do.

"I hate going back to places," Medlock said, as if reading Courtenay's thoughts. "I'd swallow lye before going back to Madras."

Courtenay sighed, relieved to be understood, if only partially. Behind a copse of trees, he could see the game warden's cottage, now half tumbled down. "Bad memories in India?" He knew this to be true, but hadn't quite considered that Medlock might be running away from something, that his flight to England might have had as much to do with starting fresh as it did with social climbing.

"Some bad, some good, but I'd rather not think of any of it. I prefer moving forwards."

"Yes," Courtenay agreed. He hadn't considered that perhaps that feeling of not wanting to revisit the past was a common thing; he had assumed it had to do with not wanting to dwell on scenes that had memories of his failings sprinkled liberally over the top like coarse pepper on a cheap cut of meat. Before he could think twice, he reached over and squeezed Medlock's hand. He felt Medlock go still beneath that layer of fine kidskin. But Medlock's fingers wrapped around his own, briefly but unmistakably, before he pulled his hand away.

CHAPTER FIFTEEN

As they approached the stable block, Courtenay realized that his heart was racing.

"Needs a new roof," Medlock muttered, indicating the stables. "Four servants sitting idly about. Terrible use of that money you so kindly send." Medlock's voice was tight with irritation. Courtenay smiled, distracted momentarily by Medlock's annoyance.

After Medlock's coachman had turned the horses over to the stable boys, Courtenay led the way along the path that led to the main door.

Courtenay had no preconceived vision of what this visit would be like—what he would say, what his mother might look like after the past ten years, whether he would meet his mother's husband and stepchildren. It was all a blank. So, he was entirely grateful when Medlock took the matter in hand, producing his calling card and his best manners when a footman—too young to recognize Courtenay as the exiled master of the house—answered the door.

After a wait that Courtenay found disorienting and Medlock, judging by the sad shake of his head, found grossly improper, they were ushered into a sitting room that Courtenay remembered as his mother's morning room. And there, half reclined on a sofa, sat his mother. Her hair was the same black it had been ten years ago, unspoiled by gray. Her back was to the window, but Courtenay saw no signs of increased age on her pale face. Her gown was the soft green that she always favored because it brought out the unusual color of her eyes. Their eyes.

He was filled with the old, futile desire to please her, to do something right for once.

"Mrs. Blakely, how kind of you to receive us," Medlock said in much the same tone he would likely use to inform a person that they had a something embarrassing in their teeth.

His mother murmured something about the visit being a pleasant surprise, in a tone that left no doubt about the visit being deeply and profoundly unpleasant. Then her eyes cut over to where Courtenay stood, slightly behind Medlock, and he saw recognition dawn slowly on her face. Just as quickly, her expression resumed its indifference.

"Jeremiah, my dear, I had no idea you were back in England."

Courtenay opened his mouth but Medlock spoke first. "Dear Mrs. Blakely, of course you did not. Perhaps the vicar's daughter knew, but I dare say she wouldn't trouble you with such unwanted information." As he spoke, he angled his body slightly, as if to shield Courtenay from the conversation. Before the lady could reply, Medlock briskly changed the topic. "I came to see if you required assistance in removing from the house before . . . what day was it I specified?"

As if he didn't know perfectly well. Courtenay's mouth twitched in the beginning of a smile he hadn't thought possible in this room, in this company.

"It was Midsummer, I believe," Medlock continued, without waiting for an answer. "And now it is halfway through April. When you supply me with the address to which you intend to remove, I can provide whatever assistance you may require."

Courtenay watched as his mother calculated how best to manage her unwanted visitors and how to thwart their purpose. "Who precisely are you, Mr. Medlock?" she asked, not bothering to rise from her sofa or to offer the gentlemen seats. If anything, she sank even deeper into the cushions as if to signify her contempt for her visitors.

Medlock glanced at Courtenay over his shoulder. "I see you learned from the best," he said, loud enough to be heard across the room. Much lower, for Courtenay's ears alone, he murmured, "And I was right about your looks." Courtenay stifled an unexpected laugh.

"You wouldn't have heard of me, except that I'm managing your son's business affairs. He requires that this house be emptied." He glanced around, as if noticing his surroundings for the first time. "Except, of course, for any property belonging to the estate." From his coat pocket, he produced a small book and a pencil.

Courtenay hadn't expected that Medlock would cast himself as the humble man of business, it being very close to the origins he had tried so hard to rise above.

"Lord Courtenay," Medlock continued, "will you do me the favor of indicating which items you recall as being the property of the estate rather than your mother's personal effects?"

That might have been the first time Medlock used his title, and it was all to remind his mother who she had cast off and that she was about to find herself without the lion's share of her possessions if that was what her son wanted.

Courtenay nodded, helplessly borne along the current of Medlock's wishes.

"Now, Mrs. Blakely," Medlock said, cordiality underlaid with a core of ruthlessness that Courtenay found made him want to simultaneously take a step backwards and take the man into his arms, "against my advice, your son has decided to settle an annuity on you and to assist you in procuring a suitable house."

Courtenay could see how this negotiation would go: every time his mother balked, Medlock would remind her of what she stood to lose by being difficult, and what she stood to gain—or retain—by cooperating. No wonder the man had been able to manage his family's company when he had been little more than a child. He was frankly terrifying.

"I read that book about you, Jeremiah," his mother said in a blatant effort to regain the upper hand. "It seems like you've had a good many adventures."

Medlock opened his eyes wide. "What book is this?" he asked innocently. "The only book I can possibly think of is that coarse novel people like to say is about Lord Courtenay but is likely nothing but the filthy imaginings of a pamphleteer. You can't mean that one, though."

Courtenay watched as his mother's green eyes narrowed ever so slightly. He knew that look. It was like watching a man reload a pistol.

"I was so relieved to hear that Simon was settled in England. All that gallivanting around Europe in such low company can't have been wholesome." She gave a sad shake of her head. "Have you seen him lately?" she asked, a sinister smile playing over her mouth. "I heard his father is . . . protective. I'm so glad that somebody is."

Courtenay felt cold, as if an icy hand had wrapped around his neck. Being kept away from Simon was bad enough, but the fact that virtually everybody else—even his mother—thought that he was a bad influence made him want to sink into the earth. Simon had learned at least four languages by what his mother was called gallivanting, and had been happy and loved. Courtenay had been a part of making that so.

"Oh, heavens, I'm so glad you brought that up, Mrs. Blakely. I thought it was going to be devilish awkward, because nobody really wants to mention the fact that Simon doesn't like to see you or his aunt. Sporting of you to get that out in the open. I say, my sister, Lady Standish, will be so glad to hear that her dear friend Lord Courtenay has been restored to the bosom of his family. I'll be sure to tell her to spread the good news far and wide."

Courtenay nearly choked at that. He realized that he was watching his mother get blackmailed, and that he was perfectly fine with it. Medlock sank gracefully, albeit uninvited, into one of the pretty fireside chairs. "Now, how about you ring for tea and we can hash out the details?" Medlock spoke with all the affability of a viper. And then he turned deferentially to Courtenay. "Is that acceptable, my lord?"

"Of course, Mr. Medlock," Courtenay agreed, and it felt right that the first words he uttered in this house—his house—after so long should be to this man.

"What the devil was going on in there?" Julian muttered as soon as they were back in the carriage, finally heading away from Carrington Hall. "You hardly spoke. I was expecting an onslaught of your usual charm but instead you were as meek as a kitten."

"I'm perhaps not at my best around my mother," Courtenay said with a weak smile.

"Well, no. I can't imagine you would be. One usually expects one's mother to at least feign affection. That woman's like Lady Macbeth." This earned a faint laugh from Courtenay. Julian shook his head. "I've never seen you like that." But as soon as Julian spoke he realized he was wrong. He had seen Courtenay meek and undemanding once before, and it had been in Courtenay's bed, when the man had been unwilling to ask Julian for the care he so plainly required. No—that he so plainly craved. Courtenay wanted affection and kindness and warmth, but didn't want to ask for them. Julian let a thought creep to the forefront of his mind, a thought that he'd been doing his best to ignore and deny: he wanted to give Courtenay all those things and more. He wouldn't, of course, because that would mean giving Courtenay access to all his hidden vulnerabilities, and he didn't think he could live with that.

Impulsively, he reached out and grabbed Courtenay's hand, squeezing it once before releasing it. "At any rate," Julian said hastily, "I understand why you don't like being called by your Christian name. The way she says it makes it sound like something a witch would whisper over her cauldron. *Jeremiah.* It gives me the shivers."

Courtenay was silent a moment. "As soon as I inherited, everyone called me Courtenay. Even Isabella. It was a relief."

"I should damned well think it would be. Is there an inn nearby?" Julian asked, striving for a normal tone. "I'm half starved."

Courtenay's infernal mother had made things as difficult as possible, insisting that her husband be present, and then pretending to forget what she had agreed to mere minutes previously. But Julian had finally gotten her to understand that she was to leave Carrington Hall in June, along with her husband and stepchildren, for a perfectly reasonable, although significantly less grand, house in Bath.

Now Julian's stomach was growling. For the sake of appearances, he had only had a single tea cake, not wanting to look ravenous during negotiations. He had taken a diffident nibble of the cake, then turned directly to Courtenay and congratulated him on the proficiency of the cook whose wages he paid. Courtenay had nearly spit out his tea and Julian had been quite satisfied with himself.

Really, Julian was all around satisfied with himself today. A few times during the afternoon, he had caught Courtenay looking at him with something like wonder, maybe even gratitude, as if he had never seen anyone half so clever. Courtenay's opinion on Julian's cleverness really shouldn't have mattered. Julian already knew he was clever. But knowing Courtenay thought so too—knowing that Courtenay thought anything good about him at all—made him almost giddy. Besides, he enjoyed the sense of coming to Courtenay's defense. It seemed that nobody else had for a good while.

He tried to remind himself that he was only helping Courtenay because Eleanor required it. But he couldn't quite keep up the pretense. He was helping Courtenay because he cared about the man, damn it. And maybe because he owed him after that blasted book had caused him such trouble.

"What was your father like, Courtenay?" Julian asked after they had settled into a table in the private parlor of the tavern Courtenay had indicated. "I take it he was bewitched by your mother's looks, but that can happen to the best of men. Was he terrible as well?"

Courtenay stared into his ale—thus far untouched, Julian noticed—for a moment before smiling slightly. "You might think so. I honestly don't know. He died around the time I was sent down from university, you know." He flicked a glance across the table, and Julian remembered that Courtenay had been made to feel responsible for his father's death. "He was disappointed in his children. And he wasn't shy about letting us know about it."

Julian pursed his lips. "Hmph," he sniffed. "That ended

in the usual fashion. One child dead, one married to that sapskull in Somerset—I looked her up in the peerage, and if she's married to who I think she is then I sincerely doubt it was a love match, so I have to assume she married the first eligible soul to offer so she could get out from under your father's thumb—and one—"

"A washed-up dissolute?"

"No," Julian retorted. He hated the way Courtenay was looking at him now, like a criminal in the dock waiting for a guilty verdict. "One is a self-pitying, self-censuring dilettante with no sense of his own worth." That sounded too warm, so he added, "And who is execrably bad at maths."

"I'll grant you that last bit," Courtenay said, cracking a smile. He swirled the ale in his mug.

"I'm surprised you didn't harangue your mother about the state of the village."

Courtenay looked up, his brow furrowed. "I don't follow."

"For a man who has such concerns about the plight of the poor—and I'm not disagreeing with you, so save your argument for people who need it—your own tenants could be doing better. Every cottage we passed needed a new roof, and there was at least one footbridge that had collapsed. And those are only the things one can see from the road."

"I hadn't noticed," Courtenay murmured, sounding troubled.

"It's a good thing you're to take the property in hand."

"I hadn't planned on it. But yes, I daresay I will." He spoke slowly, as if realizing the import of what he was saying only as he spoke. "I daresay I will," he repeated. Then he absently lifted the mug of ale to his mouth before quickly putting it back on the table.

"Order tea for God's sake. You'll be taken ill if you don't have anything to drink, and we both know you're not going to drink that ale." Courtenay froze, and Julian realized he had spoken too freely. Damn it. "Or do what you please," Julian added with belated nonchalance.

"No, you're right," Courtenay said. "I'm not going to drink it."

He had better stop buying the stuff, then, but Julian wasn't going to be the one to point that out. "It's damned hard, what you're doing. There was no getting between my father and the bottle. What you're doing . . . I admire it."

"Well," Courtenay said. "I see." He looked bashful, as if he had been issued a compliment rather than told a basic truth. "Your father . . ." His voice trailed off, as if he weren't sure he ought to ask. Strictly speaking, he shouldn't.

"Hasn't Eleanor told you?" Julian asked, pushing his own mug of ale to the center of the table beside Courtenay's. "Our father was a sot. Useless. Stupid. And he knew that because his father told him so. Left the business to me, even though I wasn't of age, bypassing my father. He died shortly after." Julian had no fond memories of his father but couldn't help but wonder if his father's vices were driven by his own father's scorn, and what he might have become with a bit less criticism and a bit more kindness.

"How old were you when your grandfather died and you took over? I've done the sums in my head but I can't make you out to have been anything more than a child."

"Sixteen."

"You *were* a child, then." Courtenay said, staring at him curiously.

Julian felt his breath hitch. "I was never a child!" He hadn't meant it to sound so vehement, so angry. But he hadn't had any kind of childhood, not when it was divided between the sickroom and the counting house.

Courtenay didn't look surprised, though. He nodded, as if to indicate that he had guessed as much, or that he commiserated without the need for further elaboration. His silence felt like a gift, and Julian didn't know how to respond. He felt like he ought to be grateful, and hated it. He had gone a good long time without accruing debt of any kind and didn't want to start today, and especially didn't like the notion he had that he might not mind so much being indebted to Courtenay.

The deliberate clink of dishes interrupted them, saving Julian from figuring out how to proceed. The inn servant placed hot platters before them with an amount of clatter and fuss that Julian would ordinarily have found excessive and ill-bred, but now he was glad to have a few moments to collect himself.

Julian pointedly ordered a pot of tea. When he turned back to Courtenay, he saw that the man had carved a joint and heaped slices of it onto both of their plates. He found that he was pleased by this bit of domesticity.

"Stupid habit," Courtenay apologized, holding the carving knife with an air of embarrassment. "But I used to do it for Simon and Isabella."

Again, the hint of a Courtenay he hardly knew, somebody who had sat at a table with a family he had lost. It should have been hard to reconcile this man with the man whose sprees of libertinism were common knowledge. Then again—he glanced at the untouched ale, thought of Courtenay's vicious mother—maybe not so hard after all to reconcile those two sides of the coin.

"Tell me about them," Julian said.

And Courtenay did. By the time their plates were empty and their teacups drained, Julian had heard tales of Courtenay's travels with his sister and nephew around Italy and through the Mediterranean and Adriatic. He also told Julian stories about trying to teach his nephew to swim, and the dog he had taken in during a cold winter, the times his sister and nephew had both fallen ill with fevers.

"My sister wanted to see everything. At the beginning, there was a year or two when she insisted on not waking up in the same bed more than seven times in a row. Simon thought it was all a grand adventure, but what he really wanted was to visit the stables at every inn we stayed at. He wound up learning every language the stable hands spoke."

"It all sounds very jolly." Julian felt unreasonably envious of Courtenay's nephew, allowed to explore and wander and never confined to sickrooms or forced to contend with ledgers.

"I ought to have known better," Courtenay said. "Isabella's health had always been delicate and the constant traveling took a toll."

Julian's heart stuttered. He hadn't realized Courtenay's

sister had been unwell, hadn't realized Courtenay believed he could have saved her by acting differently. "Based on what you've told me, there wasn't anything you could have done to persuade your sister to settle down in one place. Am I right?"

"Yes, but—"

"So, your guilt over the matter is predictably self-indulgent." He tried to imagine what he'd want someone to tell Eleanor if she had chosen to stay in Madras, if she hadn't managed to convince Julian to leave before another summer weakened him further. "You loved your sister and you did your best."

Something of his tension must have bled into his voice, because Courtenay reached across the table and briefly touched Julian's hand. Courtenay couldn't possibly understand why Julian found this topic personally disturbing, but he could tell that Julian was disturbed, and he cared. And that meant more to Julian than he could have anticipated.

When Courtenay picked up his tale again, he let it veer into anecdotes that were slightly off color—he'd reference a former mistress or being caught *in flagrante* in a delicate situation—and he'd hesitate before proceeding.

"You'd better not be thinking of leaving that out," Julian said in one such instance. "I'd feel cheated." And he would feel cheated, not only because those were the juicier parts of Courtenay's tale, but because they were at all part of Courtenay's tale. He wouldn't be the man he was, sitting across a scarred wood table from Julian if he hadn't been the sort of man to run off to Athens with Italian princesses (a lady who had since reunited with her husband) and have an affair of long standing with his sister's coachman (a man who now owned a tavern near Naples).

Julian had initially thought the roast a trifle dry, but by the time they rose from the table, he considered it was the best meal he had had in his entire life.

Chapter Sixteen

The sun had set by the time they returned to the stables where Medlock kept his horses near his London lodgings. It was an unseasonably warm evening for April, and it was the first time Courtenay felt agreeable about the weather since he had set foot on English soil.

"Care for some tea, Courtenay?" Medlock asked with the too-casual tone of somebody with an ulterior motive.

"Not really, Medlock," Courtenay responded, amused. Not well-practiced in seduction, was Medlock. And that only made Courtenay like him more, damn it, because any other man would leave the seduction up to Courtenay—but Medlock liked being in control. Courtenay rather liked Medlock being in control too.

"You'll come up anyway, I dare say," Medlock retorted.

Yes, God help him, he would. He followed Medlock up the stairs and settled into a low chair, watching as Medlock dispensed with his manservant. Medlock never looked better than when he was telling people what to do. He wasn't precisely handsome, nor even striking or any of the other adjectives people used to describe men with unconventional looks. No, Medlock was the opposite of striking. He was aggressively neutral. But the way he moved, the way he spoke, the things he said—Courtenay's heart thumped in his chest whenever he caught a look at the man. He was aware of a growing conviction that Medlock looked precisely the way he wanted a man to look like, whatever that even meant.

"Come here," he said after Medlock locked the door behind him. His trousers already felt too tight.

Medlock came and stood before him, his usual haughtiness tempered by a hint of awkwardness that made Courtenay want to laugh with happiness. Courtenay took hold of his hands and tugged him down into his lap. Medlock adjusted himself so he was straddling Courtenay's knees, and it wasn't clear whether Medlock was sitting on Courtenay's lap or pinning him down. Courtenay was fine with either option.

"Thank you," Courtenay said, looking up at Medlock. "For today."

Medlock's quicksilver eyes gleamed. "It was a rare pleasure to deal with your mother. It's not every day I get to be as rude as I like."

Courtenay smoothed his hands down Medlock's sides and felt the man shiver. "You're very good at being rude."

"I know." Medlock tucked a strand of hair behind his ear, almost preening.

"But I didn't only mean what you did at Carrington, though. Thank you for the whole day." He felt Medlock go slightly stiff under his hands. "I enjoyed being with you."

"You're going to make things awkward, Courtenay."

"Yes, I damned well am, and you're going to listen to me do it. I enjoyed spending time with you and I think you enjoyed spending time with me. If it doesn't terribly bother you, I'd like to continue to do so. Is that acceptable?"

Medlock was silent for a moment. Courtenay heard nothing but their own breathing and the distant ringing of church bells. His chest felt tight with a suspense that was surely disproportionate to the situation.

"Is this how you usually carry on affairs?" Medlock chided. "So businesslike?"

He was going to be difficult, then. He always was, and strangely, Courtenay wouldn't have it any other way. "There is no *usually* where you're concerned." Courtenay was well out of his depths. In the past he had generally preferred warm, affectionate sorts of people. Medlock was made of ice and thorns, venom and gunpowder. It ought to be hard to get anywhere near him, let alone fall into love with Medlock. But it hadn't been hard at all, had it? It had been as easy as breathing.

Courtenay had always thought love had to be the stuff of grand declarations. Hothouse flowers and gifts of great price, not to mention the kind of poetry Medlock would dismiss as being rife with self-indulgent sentiment. Courtenay nearly laughed at the thought of how appalled Medlock would be by any of that. Courtenay tried to think of some way to tell Medlock what he felt, what he wanted, what he yearned for, but without saying anything that would scare the man off.

Instead, he settled for taking Medlock's chin in his hand and stroking his thumb along Medlock's cheekbone. "Come to bed with me," Courtenay said. "Then let's wake up tomorrow and we'll have pastries. You'll fence or have tea with duchesses or do whatever it is you do. I'll go to your sister's house and count how many new cats she's taken in. Then we can go for a ride in the park and dine at Simpson's."

"You don't keep a horse," Medlock said, as if that were at all the crux of the matter. But Courtenay could hear the thickness in his voice and he knew Medlock wasn't unaffected. "You sold it to line your mother's pockets."

"I'll hire one," Courtenay said, suppressing a smile. "Then we'll come back here, you'll get rid of your servant, and I'll fuck you."

Medlock gave a sharp intake of breath. "Is that something you want?"

Courtenay pulled Medlock closer so he could feel for himself how much he wanted it. "Would that be acceptable?"

"It's . . . ah. Hmm." Medlock's eyes were glassy, his lips parted. Watching him try to look aloof was the most arousing thing Courtenay had ever seen. "I'm not opposed. Rather, I'm amenable. What I mean to say is please do that."

Courtenay could feel through the layers of wool and linen that separated them that Medlock was indeed far from opposed. "I'll fuck you, then," he murmured. "Tomorrow afternoon."

"Why are we talking about this instead of you actually fucking me?"

"Because I like feeling how hard you get when I'm talking about it." Also because he wanted to make sure Medlock would see him again, wanted to hold out the prospect of a good fucking like a sugar lick for a horse.

"I want it now." Medlock was only a shade this side of arrogance. Courtenay loved it.

"No." He cupped Medlock's arse in his palms and pulled him even closer.

"Why the hell not?"

"I'm leaving something on my plate for Miss Manners."

"You have got to be—"

"Don't worry." He pressed his fingers into the seam of Medlock's breeches, tracing the cleft of his arse, just enough to give the man ideas. "I'll bring you off before I leave."

"I should damned well think you will."

Courtenay pulled him close then, because there was nothing else to do with such a sharp tongue than to silence it with a kiss.

"Take off your coat," Courtenay murmured into Julian's neck. The rasp in his voice made Julian's head swim with lust. It was heady, this sense of having a man like Courtenay— handsome, experienced—want him so badly. He felt intoxicated on the strength of Courtenay's want alone.

"No," Julian said, just to be contrary, just to keep Courtenay on the knife's edge of desire a little longer. There was also that bothersome memory of Courtenay's meekness the last time, and now it was all tied up with his demeanor today at Carrington Hall.

Julian would not tolerate any more of that. He would have Courtenay, he'd have his body and his pleasure, but most of all he'd have Courtenay's words.

"I'm sure we can work around it," Courtenay said, his gaze dragging down over Julian's body and leaving a wake of heat behind it. "Unconventional, but hardly unheard of."

"No." Julian got to his feet. "If you want me to be in charge—"

"Yes," Courtenay said immediately.

"—then I want to tie you up."

"I . . ." Courtenay cleared his throat. "Medlock, I hadn't seen that coming."

And that was another thing. "I've had it with this Medlock business. I'll happily call you Courtenay if you like, but for God's sake call me Julian. Now, are you going to let me tie you up or not?" Julian tried to sound like a man whose mouth hadn't gone dry at the thought of Courtenay bound up beneath him. "I do recall that you said you liked being manhandled."

"You remember that." Courtenay passed a hand over his mouth.

How could he not? "I remember everything." Julian felt his cheeks heat as he spoke.

"I've never done that." Courtenay rose to stand before Julian. "I mean, I've done the tying up, but nobody's ever offered to return the favor."

"No time like the present," Julian said briskly. "The only condition is that you need to tell me what you want."

"At the moment, I want you to tie me up, damn it. Who knew?" he added under his breath.

"That's a good start. Now, into the bedroom."

Julian systematically divested Courtenay of all his clothes, kissing newly exposed skin—a hard shoulder, the dent beside his hip, the inside of an elbow. Julian could have spent all night pressing worshipful kisses to Courtenay's body, but he had the sense that would not be a new experience for Courtenay. He pushed Courtenay flat onto the bed. Julian kept his own clothes on. He had an inkling that Courtenay would find that arousing, and based on the state of the man's cock, which was rigid and arched up towards his belly, he had been right.

Courtenay obligingly presented his wrists, and Julian bent down to bite one before using Courtenay's own cravat to bind them to the bed frame over his head. He could hear Courtenay's breaths, fast and shallow, and knew that the man was panting for *him*.

Julian stood back to admire his handiwork. Or, really, to admire Courtenay, who was now testing Julian's knot in a way that did very interesting things to his biceps and chest.

"Comfortable?" Julian asked, shoving a pillow behind Courtenay's head.

"Yes, actually." He did look decadent, sprawled on Julian's soft featherbed, surrounded by fine linen, and yet tied up.

"Would you rather, ah, not be comfortable?"

"No, this suits."

Thank God. There was a limit to how much Julian could

manage in the name of manhandling. He knelt between Courtenay's legs and smoothed his hands up the man's thighs. He hadn't yet seen Courtenay properly naked. The first time they had kept their clothes on. The second time the only light had been from the moon. But tonight Julian's valet had lit a fire in the grate and there was enough light to see that Courtenay was every bit as splendid naked as he was fully clothed. For a man who seemed to spend most of his time lounging about and reading, he was surprisingly muscular. Perhaps his dalliances tended to be athletic in nature. Julian felt his cock pulse at the thought of the fucking he'd get tomorrow. He traced a finger along Courtenay's hard belly and down across his hip and thigh. "I damned well expect you to exert yourself when you're fucking me," he said. "Put all of this"—he gestured to Courtenay's physique—"to good use."

Courtenay's eyes went wide as he made a low rumbling noise at the back of his throat.

"But that's for tomorrow," Julian added, palming himself through his trousers and watching as Courtenay's erection jumped in response. "What do you want me to do?" With his other hand, Julian stroked the line where Courtenay's leg met his torso.

Courtenay's chest was rising and falling quicker now. "Whatever you please."

"No, that won't do," Julian chided. Tonight he wanted Courtenay to tell him exactly what he wanted, to admit to himself and to Julian everything that he desired and then let Julian give it to him. "Where do you want my hands?"

"On my cock," Courtenay said promptly.

Julian immediately complied, wrapping both his hands loosely around Courtenay's cock. Very lightly and perfectly still. He looked expectantly at Courtenay's face.

Courtenay groaned. "Feel free to move them."

Julian gave a halfhearted little wiggle of his fingers. He had to bite the inside of his cheek to keep from laughing at Courtenay's outburst of incoherent rage.

"Now, now. Keep your voice down or you'll disturb the entire building. Weren't you the one who lectured me about balloons and pleasure? Now tell me what you want."

"I really regret that metaphor," Courtenay groaned, helplessly thrusting upwards into Julian's hand. "Profoundly."

"How did you manage to debauch yourself so completely if you can't even tell me what you want?"

"I have to say, Med—Julian, that most people, when confronted with my naked, tied up, obviously aroused body would have a pretty good idea of what to do with it."

Julian narrowed his eyes. "I think you usually give people what they want. And, because you're basically a hedonist with a broad range of tastes, you enjoy yourself perfectly well despite never articulating what you actually crave. Is that how things usually work for you? You just sort of drift into these situations and then drift through them?"

Courtenay was silent for a moment, as if he had never considered the matter in that light. "Well, yes?"

"There will be no drifting tonight. Now, tell me about what you require for your pleasure."

"I require . . . Oh, kiss me, you maniacal bastard."

Julian crawled up his body and by the time his lips were

near Courtenay's he was smiling too broadly to manage anything like a proper kiss. Instead he pressed his silly, uncooperative mouth to Courtenay's and then buried his face in Courtenay's neck.

"I'm glad you're amused," Courtenay said, but he had been smiling too. "But I still want that kiss."

Julian lifted his head and kissed Courtenay fully, rewarding him for having said what he wanted. He bit Courtenay's lip, then licked it, then thoroughly tasted Courtenay's mouth, as if kissing was the point. That was what Courtenay had asked for, and so it was the point.

"Now what do you want?" he asked into Courtenay's ear.

"Take off your clothes," Courtenay said promptly, his voice low and raspy.

Julian complied, if a bit leisurely. He saw Courtenay's eyes, black with desire, focused on his erection. He'd been hard since they walked in the door and now it was taking all his effort not to touch himself, so he gave his cock one lazy stroke. "What now?"

"Touch me. Please. Anywhere. I just want your hands on me."

Julian lightly skimmed his fingers along Courtenay's bound arms, enjoying the hardness of his biceps, then down his chest. He felt Courtenay's body tense when he skimmed over his nipples, but he didn't linger there because he wasn't doing a damned thing that he wasn't asked for. He rested his palms on Courtenay's flat belly. "I wonder what I should do now."

"May as well put your mouth on my cock if it'll keep you

from talking." He must have read something of Julian's intent on his face because he quickly added, "And don't you even think about just kissing it or whatever torture you have in mind. Put it in your mouth, as much as you can, and suck it, as hard as you can. And use your tongue," he added, as if an afterthought.

Two seconds later Julian had the head of Courtenay's cock at the back of his throat and was following the man's instructions to the letter. He was determined to give the best cocksucking performance of his life, to lavish every attention he could on Courtenay. He'd never be able to put into words what he was starting to feel for Courtenay, and even if he could he wouldn't want to. But he could show him. He could use the tips of his fingers and the length of his tongue, and maybe Courtenay would know this was meant as an offering.

He only raised his head when he tasted the beginnings of saltiness on his tongue. Courtenay's jaw was set and he was straining deliciously against his bindings.

"Is there anything else you'd like?" he asked innocently. It was taking all his self-control to keep his hands off his own prick, but he wanted to make it clear that his foremost goal was Courtenay's own pleasure.

When Courtenay didn't answer, Julian swung one of his legs off the bed as if he were going to leave the room.

"No! Oh, damn you. Touch my arse."

"With my fingers or with my mouth?" Julian asked sweetly.

Courtenay groaned. "Fingers. This time. I can't take the other right now."

Julian spread Courtenay's legs further apart and pushed

his knees back, then returned his mouth to the damp, swollen head of his erection. He took only the tip in his mouth, sucking and kissing while slowly trailing his fingers lower. He paused for a moment at Courtenay's bollocks, which were already drawn up tight. He gave them a gentle tug and heard Courtenay's strangled groan. Then he brought his fingers lower and circled Courtenay's entrance.

"Tell me if you like what I'm doing," Julian said, raising his head. He needed to hear it.

"Yes. God. That feels good." Courtenay's voice was a thready rasp and it made Julian's prick throb. "Keep touching me like that."

And so, Julian did. He kept touching Courtenay as if it were the only thing he had to do in the world, because at the moment it was.

"Fuck me with your fingers."

Julian smiled. Courtenay was getting the hang of this. Good. Julian licked his fingers, aware of Courtenay's gaze intently on him. Then he slid the tip of one finger in, then the other, stretching and stroking, enjoying every quiver and sigh of Courtenay's response. He knew when he had brushed against the spot he was seeking when Courtenay arched off the bed.

"There," Courtenay groaned. "Keep touching me there."

Julian sat back on his heels so he could watch but he didn't stop moving his hand. "Look at you," he murmured. "Just look at you." Courtenay was trying not to writhe, but his fists were balled and his arms taut. Sweat beaded on his brow. He was desperate and wanting, and it was all for Julian.

"Come up here," Courtenay said. "Please. But keep your fingers—yes!"

Julian stretched himself out over Courtenay, taking his mouth in a desperate kiss as their erections rubbed together. It was an awkward position but it would get the job done.

"Don't stop," Courtenay pleaded. "Julian. I'm going to—"

And he did. He came, Julian's name on his lips, shuddering around Julian's fingers, his body tense beneath Julian's own, his arms straining and his mouth parted in pleasure.

That was all it took to bring Julian off, the sight of Courtenay's release along with the friction of his erection rubbing between them.

"That was—"

"Julian." Courtenay whispered the word into Julian's hair. "Julian," he repeated, and he sounded almost wondering. He lifted his head to look at Courtenay's face. Courtenay raised a single eyebrow, as if asking a question they both knew the answer to.

Julian buried his face in Courtenay's neck, a halfhearted attempt to prevent Courtenay from seeing the emotion Julian suspected was written all over him.

"Shhh," Courtenay whispered soothingly, even though Julian hadn't said anything. Probably Courtenay knew what a person looked like when he was a welter of half-resented emotions. Probably this sort of thing happened to Courtenay all the time. Julian almost laughed, because he realized he could tell Courtenay every bizarre notion flitting across his brain and Courtenay would likely have heard stranger things.

He could probably have told Courtenay everything—except about the book, of course. He went rigid at the thought.

"It's not that bad," Courtenay said, misunderstanding Julian's reaction. "Happens to people every day."

"Oh, Courtenay," Julian sighed. "You don't know."

Reluctantly, he pulled away from the warmth of Courtenay's body. He got a wet cloth and cleaned them both up before finally untying Courtenay's bindings. He rubbed and kissed each wrist as he released the knots, even though the time for tenderness was gone and if Julian were half as clever as he thought, he wouldn't let it happen again. But he couldn't resist, and when Courtenay pulled him down, he realized how much he had missed the feeling of those sure hands on his body. He sank on top of Courtenay, reluctant to leave his arms before he absolutely had to.

Chapter Seventeen

When Courtenay woke, it was still dark. He was surprised to find Julian still in his arms, their limbs intertwined, Julian's open eyes colorlessly reflecting the moonlight.

"Trouble sleeping?" Courtenay murmured.

"I told you I'm in the habit of waking early." And then, in a softer tone, "It's when I get most of my thinking done."

It was very early, so early it was more accurately late. No sounds rose from the street—no costermongers calling to one another on their way to the market, no servants pattering back and forth in the mew, no hoof beats or cart wheels in the street. Nothing.

But Julian seemed to be wide awake, and judging by the look in his eyes, he had been thinking for a while. He hadn't gotten up though, he hadn't pulled away from Courtenay's embrace. Whatever he was thinking about—interest rates, taking over the world, whatever it was that flitted through the minds of financial geniuses in the small hours of the morning—he could have done his thinking in his sitting room, fully clothed, far away from Courtenay.

Instead he was here, tucked against Courtenay's side. Courtenay pulled him close and Julian melted against him, his head nestled into Courtenay's neck.

Last night had perhaps been the strangest sexual encounter of Courtenay's life. If anyone had asked him yesterday afternoon whether there were things he didn't know about pleasure, he would have laughed in their faces. He had spent years pursuing pleasure as his only real goal and it might be the only field of knowledge he could be said to have made a study of. But tied up, helpless, with Julian ruthlessly forcing him to say aloud everything he wanted? That had undone him completely, even though nothing they had ultimately done together was so very exotic.

It had been the combination of Julian's mastery with his own grudging awareness that Julian had somehow found out a secret he had kept from himself: he had, more or less, drifted from pleasure to pleasure without any real thought as to what he really wanted. The world, as far as he could tell, was filled with people who would happily take him to bed; once they got there, Courtenay tended to defer to the other person's pleasure. He wasn't entirely devoid of strategy: obviously scrupulous attention to a partner's pleasure made it more likely that rumors of one's prowess would spread, making it easy to keep one's bed warm in the future.

But at some point he had lost sight of what he really wanted, lost the ability to name and demand and beg for things. And throughout it all, anchoring the entire experience, was the sight of Julian's barely checked passion, watching him so carefully not touch himself, so thoroughly devoted to simultaneously annoying and pleasuring Courtenay.

Something changed in Julian's breathing, and when Courtenay looked down, he saw that the man's eyes were once again shut. He was sleeping, and Courtenay felt like it was a benediction, or maybe proof that he wasn't the only one whose heart had taken a dangerous turn.

When Courtenay woke—after procuring and delivering the required buns for Julian—he went to Eleanor's house.

That infernally high-hat butler could hardly conceal his delight in informing Courtenay that the lady of the house was not at home to visitors.

Courtenay refrained from rolling his eyes. "I'm staying here, Tilbury. And I have been for the past week." Upon leaving the house yesterday morning, optimistic about his prospects with Julian, he had left a note for Eleanor informing her that he had business that would take him out of London until perhaps the next day.

"Let him in, Tilbury," said a deep voice that came from behind the butler. The door swung open, revealing Sir Edward Standish.

Courtenay bowed and wished Eleanor's husband good morning as the butler shuffled off.

"Care to have some brandy, Courtenay?" There was a flash of something unpleasant in Standish's eye.

It was eleven o'clock in the morning and Courtenay had

no intention of drinking brandy at any time, but Standish's words sounded like a challenge. Courtenay had never been wise enough to stand down a challenge. "Yes, I've been meaning to speak with you."

Standish led the way into a room Courtenay had never known Eleanor to use. It was a small book room of vaguely masculine character: the walls were papered in a dark green stripe and the furniture appeared to have been chosen more for comfort than for style. The bookcases were filled with elegantly bound volumes, each row arranged in the orderly fashion that books acquire only when they are not read. Eleanor's own study had shelves that looked like they had been arranged by a hurricane. This room, he realized, had been put together as a study for the master of the house, at a time when Eleanor hadn't realized her husband's absence would stretch so far into the future. Unlike the rest of the house, which in its strict adherence to rules of fashion was unmistakably the work of Julian, in this room he thought he saw Eleanor's hand. On the chimneypiece, instead of the symmetrical and pristine arrangement of clocks and figurines, a jade elephant stood next to a whittled tiger. Neither object was particularly interesting in its own right, so Courtenay supposed they had sentimental value to Eleanor and perhaps to Standish.

Courtenay thought he could almost smell the aroma of hopes gone stale.

His good mood having quite evaporated, Courtenay sat in the seat Standish indicated and took the glass he was offered. He wouldn't drink it, but he found it easier to say yes to spirits and then simply not drink them. Hardly anyone ever noticed or cared except Julian. He remembered what Julian had said about Courtenay's habit of saying yes, of spending his life drifting between yeses. Julian had been right. He usually was.

"I'm not having an affair with your wife," Courtenay said abruptly. He ought to have said as much a week ago, but if Eleanor preferred to let her husband believe she had a lover, that was her business and he didn't like to interfere. But looking at this room, thinking of Eleanor's past hopes and her best chance of future happiness, he couldn't keep silent.

Standish didn't seem surprised. His handsome face betrayed no reaction of any kind. "I hoped as much, given how you quite clearly are carrying on with her brother."

A wave of cold swept over Courtenay's body. He thought he could brazen out a blackmail attempt, but didn't relish the prospect, especially not if Julian's name were to be dragged into it. "I don't know what you're talking about."

"I had you followed yesterday. I'm not blackmailing you, so you don't need to look like that. I'm quite aware you aren't touching my wife. But I'd almost rather she have an affair than simply pretend to have one, which is what she's doing by letting me believe you're lovers. I can't understand what's going through her mind, but I gather she must want me to leave as soon as possible."

Was it possible that Eleanor—brilliant, ingenious Eleanor—had somehow married an utter fool? He spoke like an intelligent man and had obviously devoted a good deal of thought to coming to this outrageously wrong conclusion.

"Have you considered that she might have another reason? From her perspective, you married her and then traveled everywhere in the world where she wasn't."

"That's not what—"

"I know," Courtenay said patiently. "But put aside the circumstances that precede your marriage—please," he hastily added, seeing a look of fury dawn on Standish's face, "just put them aside. Medlock told me you were fond of one another. Did Eleanor negotiate her marriage settlements herself?"

"Of course not." Standish's brow creased. "Julian arranged everything, of course."

Courtenay tried to imagine eighteen-year-old Julian negotiating his sister's marriage settlements, and how protective he would have been. "Well, I daresay he felt justified in keeping Eleanor's settlement as safe as possible. He is"—how to put this delicately—"rather dedicated to defending the interests of people he is fond of. He put you on allowance, did he?"

Standish sat back in evident surprise. "Something to that effect. She—he—paid off my late father's debts, which were . . ." His voice trailed off, and Courtenay was given to understand that these debts along with the death of Standish's father were the circumstances that made his marriage an immediate necessity. "They tied up all Eleanor's funds for her own use and left me with a token amount."

"Which I doubt you've touched," Courtenay said with a sigh.

"I've refused to draw on the account." Standish had his chin in the air.

Courtenay was striving for patience. "Which Eleanor

has no doubt noticed and interpreted as a sign you regret the marriage."

Understanding finally dawned on Standish's face. "I see."

"She seems to have been under the impression you would eventually join her in England—no, don't point out that you have in fact joined her, because we both know six years is enough to make a lady doubt the strength of a man's affections."

Standish ran a frustrated hand through his dark hair. "I know you think I ought to have had faith in her constancy, or whatever rot you're thinking now, but the fact of the matter is that I think Eleanor and Julian tend to forget I'm Indian."

"Pardon?"

"I didn't—oh damn it—I didn't know whether she'd want an Indian husband with her in England."

Courtenay did not know what to say. "I hadn't thought of it in that light. Did she ever say anything to make you suspect—"

"No, nothing like that," Standish said, shaking his head. "But sometimes the stories we tell ourselves in the dead of night are hard to forget in the daylight."

Wasn't that the truth. "You can look around this room and come to your own conclusions."

Standish glanced around him, as if noticing his surroundings for the first time. When he reached the trinkets on the chimneypiece, his cheeks flushed. "I see. I'm afraid I don't know what to do. We've spent six years thinking the worst of one another and that can't be easily undone."

If there were words or deeds that could silence the night-time stories of doubt and pain, he certainly didn't know about them.

"That isn't why I asked you in here today, though," Standish said, fiddling with the edge of his cuff and not meeting Courtenay's eyes. "Oh, damn it, this is none of my business but there's something you need to know about Medlock."

For the second time that morning, Courtenay felt overcome with cold.

Julian was the first to arrive at the stables where he kept his saddle horses. He wanted to make sure the chestnut mare he meant to lend Courtenay was ready.

He had been almost jubilant all day. The vision Courtenay had sketched—sharing breakfasts and rides in the park and nights in bed—had left him positively optimistic about the future. He hadn't ever contemplated the possibility of going through his life with another person, but now that the idea had crept into his mind, he couldn't shake it loose. He wanted whatever Courtenay had to offer, and he wanted it with a force he hadn't thought himself capable of. All the grasping and climbing he had done in society had occupied his mind like a particularly challenging word puzzle might, and had allowed him to drop invitations and recognition at Eleanor's feet as a cat might bestow mice upon his owner. But he hadn't yearned for any of it. He hadn't thought he was meant for yearning—that was for warmer, gentler people.

It was tempting, this promise of days filled with shared kisses and tea cakes. He could see it so clearly it felt almost within reach. All he would have to do was to let Courtenay in past his polished façade, but that was never going to happen because he hardly even let himself consider what lay beneath that façade. He didn't want to think about illness or loneliness or frightened purposelessness, and the idea that somebody else was thinking those things about him was terrifying. His suspicion that Courtenay wouldn't think less of him only made it worse, because that made him like Courtenay even more. The last thing he needed was more affection for Courtenay. He was already almost drunk on it. The fact that he was even thinking of letting Courtenay inside his heart was cause for alarm.

"Medlock." Courtenay's voice came from behind.

Julian heard the ice in Courtenay's voice before it registered that he had reverted to using Julian's surname. Turning, he saw on Courtenay's face a glacial expression that matched his tone. Courtenay's jaw was set, his eyes as cold as Julian had ever seen, with none of the usual laughter in them.

"I had this chestnut saddled for you," Julian ventured, but stopped talking when he realized Courtenay wasn't wearing riding clothes. Instinctively, he led to the way to the stable door. They could have a measure of privacy in the lane.

Once outside, Julian could see exactly how grave Courtenay looked. He wanted to touch him, even to comfort him, but when he reached out, Courtenay stiffened. Julian pulled his hand back as if from open flame. Instead he wrapped his fingers tightly around the riding crop he still held and waited for Courtenay to speak.

"We're not riding today." Courtenay took a deep breath

and paused just long enough for Julian's mind to race through every bad piece of news Courtenay could deliver. Had his nephew fallen ill? Or Eleanor? "How much of it was an act?"

"Pardon?" Julian wasn't following. He couldn't make his brain work when Courtenay was looking at him like that. Had it only been last night that Julian thought Courtenay's eyes the green of a warm, foreign sea? Today they were ice.

Courtenay made a scoffing noise. "When you fucked me, Medlock, did it give you an extra thrill knowing you had ruined me beforehand? I never would have guessed that you hated me enough to write an entire book about it."

The blood drained from Julian's face. He wanted to grab for something to steady himself but he didn't. He opened his mouth to speak, but for once he had nothing at the ready. His years of calculating his every utterance to strike the precisely the right tone left him without anything to say in this situation. "What book?" he asked, hoping against hope that there had been a mistake and Courtenay didn't know the truth.

"Don't lie to me," Courtenay said, his teeth clenched. "Standish told me. Aren't you going to say anything?" he demanded. "Don't you think you owe me at least that? I'm trying to understand why you would do this and you aren't making it easy for me."

Julian recognized this as a chance to make things better but he couldn't for the life of him imagine what he was supposed to say. "I didn't lie," he protested feebly, and even as he spoke he knew he was making things worse.

He could see the disappointment and rising anger in

Courtenay's face. "You saw me reading it. Christ, Medlock, I read parts aloud to you. You had every opportunity to tell me early on, to get it out of the way. Why the devil didn't you?"

"I didn't tell you because it was a secret," Julian said. "I wrote it anonymously. I couldn't admit to having written such a thing."

Courtenay sucked in a breath of air. "I'm to understand that in addition to penning an entire volume dedicated to itemizing and immortalizing my flaws, you also didn't trust me to keep a secret. I see."

"No! I meant at first. The first days, I didn't trust you. Later on—"

"Later on you had reasons to keep me in good cheer. I see. Quite understandable. I would not have taken you into my bed if I had known you held me in such low regard."

"That's not what I meant." Julian shook his head in frustration. "I didn't write the book about you. I hadn't met you when I wrote the first draft of the manuscript. It was only later that I saw you at Radnor's house and I borrowed some of your quirks."

"Some of my quirks," Courtenay repeated. "Just enough to convince the world that I'm as much a villain as they always suspected."

"First of all, I didn't think anyone would read the stupid book. And even if they did, I assumed they wouldn't recognize you based on my description. But even if I had done what you think, that was before I knew you." It was different now, couldn't Courtenay see that? "It was before . . ." He gestured between them, because he couldn't find words to describe what he meant, and even if he could he wouldn't have had the courage to speak them aloud.

"That is my point. You were content to slander and libel a man who had done you no wrong. You think that I'm beneath reproach, but I never stooped to such a depth as you did when you published that book. I ought to have realized that this fucking obsession of yours with propriety was to cover up something truly vile."

The words hit Julian like a slap. The riding crop fell from his hands into the dust and he didn't stoop to pick it up. *Something truly vile.* That was how he thought of himself when he was ill—sweaty and dirty and the exact opposite of the face he tried to present to the world. And he knew that wasn't what Courtenay meant, but it didn't matter. Julian recognized it as the truth he tried to conceal from the world and even from himself. He straightened his back and tried to draw on the reserve of sangfroid and rectitude he always relied on.

"Why me? Why not choose somebody else to ruin?"

Somebody else? There wasn't anybody else. "It wasn't like that," he said, hardly believing he was about to admit this. "You were the most beautiful thing I had ever seen and I had to put you in the book. That's what the book was. It was everything I couldn't have."

Courtenay's eyes somehow got even colder, his jaw harder. "You were angry that I didn't want to fuck you and so you decided to destroy my name?"

That wasn't it at all. Julian had thought that maybe Courtenay would understand, but he didn't, and Julian wasn't going to waste his breath and humiliate himself by trying to explain it any further. He wasn't going to grovel, he wasn't going to demean himself when their friendship—or whatever it had been—was over now, and nothing Julian could say would change that. "You didn't have much of a name," Julian hissed.

For a moment Julian thought he was going to get thrashed. Courtenay's fists were clenched at his sides, his cheeks livid with fury. This was so far from the bored, languid man he had first met that Julian was suddenly struck with the idea that Courtenay's entire demeanor was as much a series of illusions as Julian's own. Then Courtenay shook his head and took a step backwards, holding his hands out as if dismissing his temper and Julian all at once.

The look on Courtenay's face was one of pure disgust. "Spare yourself the trouble of another falsehood, Medlock. I know you're not a particularly honest man, that whatever matters in your warped mind, it isn't earnestness or sincerity. I knew you were wrapped up in layers of propriety and pomposity but I thought there was something real within all that. More fool me. But I never could have guessed you were capable of this level of deceit. You were contemptuous of me from the beginning. I ought to have known. But now I do, and I can stop wasting my time. I only wish I had known earlier."

He turned on his heel and walked away, leaving Julian alone in the lane.

Chapter Eighteen

Julian didn't know how long he stood in the lane behind the stables. He couldn't even think of Courtenay without a fresh wash of shame. He knew he had done wrong by writing that book, and he was not used to being in the wrong, but beneath that obvious problem was the fact that he had hurt Courtenay, which was the one thing in the world he wished to prevent. He had the sense that another man—a better man, a more honest one—could have said something to make Courtenay understand how much he regretted harming him. Another man could have said something to reclaim that future of shared pastries and rides in the park. But Julian wasn't that man. It was just as well that Courtenay had walked away from him. The life he had deluded himself into thinking possible was a figment of his imagination.

He managed to get back to his lodgings and out of his riding clothes. Once he was properly attired he was at an utter loss as to what to do with himself. He couldn't go to

Eleanor's house—that was where he was most likely to run into Courtenay, which was obviously something he was going to spend the rest of his life avoiding. Besides, he now realized that Eleanor, the one person who knew Julian had authored the book, had told Standish. He didn't know if this was a betrayal or a normal thing for a wife to tell a husband, and the fact that he couldn't puzzle it out only went to show how sadly unfit he was for any kind of partnership.

He had taken extra care in dressing, seeking the fortification of a perfect cravat and excellently polished boots. Briggs, sensing that his employer was in need of extra defenses, combed and pomaded his hair to an unnatural degree of brilliance and brushed his already pristine coat. He set out from his lodgings with no real destination. In the end he found himself on the doorstep of Lady Montbray's house. When he handed his card to the surpassingly stoic butler who answered the door—really, he was developing grave misgivings about Eleanor's Tilbury and his presumptions—he doubted Lady Montbray would see him. It was a strange hour for callers, that awkward period when everyone in polite society seemed to be dressing for dinner.

But the butler showed him into the drawing room, where he found Lady Montbray sitting among the remnants of tea with her brother. When the butler opened the door, both Lady Montbray and Rivington sat up a bit straighter, an irritating reminder that they were at their ease around one another and he was an utter outsider.

That's what he always had been, always would be. It didn't matter that his desk was covered in invitations. It didn't matter that the finest gentry in the land treated him as an equal. He had arrived where he was by making a study of how people responded to everything he did, by calibrating his every decision—from the cut of his coat to the company he kept—to achieve a favorable reaction from society. And it had worked.

But there was a difference between acceptance and friendship, and Julian had never felt that gap as acutely as he did now. He tried not to think about the fact that Courtenay had been glad to see him. The last few times they had seen one another, Julian had seen Courtenay's face light with a lazy smile at the sight of him. It had been a mistake, Julian now realized, to let things get to that point. It had been safer to keep everyone at a comfortable distance. He hadn't let himself want real friendship until he had a taste of it with Courtenay. Now that it was gone, he didn't know how he would settle for less. His polished façade now seemed more an obstacle than a protection.

"Good heavens," Lady Montbray said, rising to her feet and ushering him toward a chair. "Were you accosted? Is Lady Standish well?"

Oh, damn. He must have distress writ across his face. He made an effort to compose himself, but judging by Lady Montbray and Rivington's increased expressions of concern, he didn't quite manage it. He touched his immaculate lapels, as if confirming that they were still there, his only armor.

"No, I just . . ." He nearly made up a story about an accident, some way to preserve the illusion of anodyne Mr. Medlock. But suddenly he wanted to shatter that illusion. It hadn't done him any good and now he didn't know why he had bothered in the first place. It had started as a sort of gift for Eleanor, but it had never meant anything to her and now he realized it had come at a cost to himself.

As things stood, he feared nobody cared much for him except as a bachelor to even out the numbers at a dinner table, a gentleman whose presence was guaranteed not to offend. He might as well toss that away too. He would tell them something true, something ugly about himself, and see what happened.

"I wrote *The Brigand Prince*," he blurted out. He was tearing up his reputation and scattering it in the breeze. What did any of it matter, anyway?

Rivington and Lady Montbray stared at him, then flicked a glance at one another, the sort of telling glance that he used to share with Eleanor before he ruined everything.

Inferring that he would no longer be wanted after divulging that information, Julian rose to his feet and prepared to leave. But before he could get out the necessary words, Lady Montbray put a hand on his arm.

"Wait. You wrote that? Anne and I spent a week reading it aloud to one another and trying to sneak the book away when the other wasn't looking. We adored it."

"So did I," Rivington chimed in.

"So did everyone. But—" Lady Montbray paused, and looked as if she were doing a sum in her head "—you must have written that book before meeting Courtenay, so it can't truly be about him. How disappointing."

"It is not about Courtenay," Julian said firmly. "I was idle last autumn and you know what they say about idle hands. I did add details about Courtenay later on and I regret it. Eleanor is most displeased with me."

"Oh, that is bad, then. Does Courtenay know?"

Julian hesitated. "Now he does."

"Will he spread it about?"

"I don't much care." And that was the truth. If he were known as the author of a book in questionable taste, the betrayer of a friend, that was the least of his problems. "It's his tale to tell, if that's what he wants."

Before he knew what had happened, he had been drawn into conversation about nothing in particular—the virtues of private tutors as opposed to public schools for educating Lady Montbray's young son, the talents of Rivington's new cook, the fact that Lady Montbray was nearly finished with her mourning.

It wasn't until Julian was half asleep, alone in his bed in his impeccable lodgings, that he realized what had been different about this afternoon at Lady Montbray's house. It was the closest thing to friendship he had experienced in the years since coming to England. And it had happened after he had deliberately aired some of his dirtiest laundry in front of the son and daughter of an earl, the very sort of people he had always sought to impress.

He felt slightly less alone, slightly less miserable, but his bed was still empty and his future as bleak as it had ever been. But perhaps he wouldn't be going into that future entirely alone.

Courtenay went to a brothel. It was a time-honored tradition, this ceremonial visiting of a whorehouse on the occasion of a broken heart. He had left the stables, gone directly to Norton's lodgings and roused him, and embarked on a round of drunken carousing.

Except for how he was neither drunk nor engaged in much carousing. This was the soberest he ever had been in a whorehouse, to say nothing of how his breeches were resolutely fastened and his prick bored. Instead, he was leaning against the wall of Madame Louise's parlor, watching Norton entertain a damsel who had artfully disposed herself on his lap. She was whispering in Norton's ear, no doubt telling him exactly what she intended to do with him upstairs. One of Norton's hands was on her ample hip, the other trailing across the bodice of her satin gown. Another place, another time, he might have followed them up and either watched or joined in—he knew from a holiday in Venice that Norton was game for that sort of thing.

Now he had no appetite for anyone but Medlock. It wasn't possible to go from his bed to paid company, no matter how compelling and beguiling. The pleasures of Madame Louise's establishment were as ashes in his mouth.

Courtenay idly felt for the piece of card stock he had in his coat pocket. The invitation had come in this morning's post and he had been eager to show it to Julian, proof of their joined success embodied in a piece of expensive stationery requesting the pleasure of his company at the Preston ball.

But to hell with that now—to hell with parties and society and most definitely to hell with Medlock. He would have ripped it up, but for how stupidly solid it felt in his pocket. It was just the right shade of ivory, with just the right linen-like texture and the perfect slanting script to remind him of everything he would never have, to remind him of the world that had cast him out. To remind him of Medlock.

It wasn't an Eden, this polite society symbolized by inconspicuous yet costly ivory card stock; more like an inner circle of Dante's hell. But it had cast him out all the same, all those years ago, and as such it was more important to him than perhaps it ought to have been. Or perhaps it was the fact that the only three people he cared about in England—Eleanor, Simon, and Julian Medlock—swam in this very sea that he was barred from.

He'd leave as soon as possible, even if it meant borrowing the money from Eleanor for a packet to Calais. No, not Calais. He'd let his exile take him farther than had been possible the last time, when he'd had a woman and a small child to consider. He'd go to the Argentine or to Siam. Far enough that nobody would have heard of him and he could fill his eyes and ears with new sights and sounds to replace the memories he didn't want. His mistake—well, one mistake on a list as long as his arm—had been coming back here in the first place. London—hell, all of England, as far as he knew—was filled with regret and disappointment. He was made for warmer weather anyway.

"Lord Courtenay?"

Courtenay looked in the direction of the voice to see a

slim man with dark hair looking up at him. He looked dimly familiar. "At your service," he said.

"I'm George Turner, Radnor's secretary. We met only briefly."

Well, well. "Right before you stole my bag and all the money in it, in fact."

Turner only shrugged vaguely, neither confirming nor denying the accusation. "I came to London to meet with you regarding the lease of your house."

Courtenay tried to cast his mind back over the past forty-eight hours. "But I only visited my estate yesterday."

"Mr. Medlock wrote last week. But I thought I'd speak to you directly."

Courtenay remembered what Julian had said about recognizing Turner as a confidence artist. "I'll bet you did," he said.

Turner examined his nails, as if Courtenay's insinuations failed to hold his interest. "I visited it this morning. It will suit."

"Oh will it?" Courtenay didn't know whether to be amused or affronted that a confidence artist and thief considered Courtenay's own property a suitable residence for his eccentric employer. "How gratifying."

"It's near enough to Harrow that we'll be able to visit Simon when he's at school, and there seem to be several out-buildings nobody would mind sacrificing to Lord Radnor's scientific achievements, so yes, it will suit. And the amount Mr. Medlock proposed is likewise satisfactory."

The rent Medlock proposed had been enough to keep Courtenay in reasonable funds for the duration of the lease. Courtenay had thought it preposterous, but Medlock had insisted it was low enough to buy Radnor's goodwill. Which just went to show that Courtenay would never understand money.

Courtenay's thoughts were interrupted by a trill of high-pitched laughter and he was forcibly reminded of his surroundings. "How did you hunt me down at a whorehouse?"

Turner looked at him as if he were an imbecile. "I asked around. You're not exactly inconspicuous. People do recognize you."

Another reason to get on the first ship leaving Southampton, then. Suddenly he was angry. "But why bother following me tonight? Why not wait until tomorrow? Your employer has already made up his mind that my moral turpitude renders me unfit company for a child. You hardly need more evidence." Radnor had already made up his mind about Courtenay, and now was twisting the knife in the wound. "Let me tell you, my good man, I'm quite out of patience with people acting as if my character is so egregious it puts me in a different class from the rest of the world. I'm no different from most any other man, except that I don't make a secret of my vices. I hardly gamble anymore, it's been months since I had anything to drink, and I'm not going to apologize for taking my pleasure in the beds of willing partners."

Courtenay didn't lose his patience often, and certainly not with a roomful of lookers-on, but he was furious. He had enough shame and guilt without the rest of the rest of the world compounding it. If he wanted to castigate himself, he'd bloody well do it, but he didn't need Medlock or Radnor or anybody else to make it even worse.

"Good night," he said, and headed for the door.

He was already on the street when he heard his name being called. He assumed it was a footman bringing him the hat he had left behind in his haste. But it was Turner.

"I don't have time for this, Turner. Leave me in peace. I'll sail for Calais on the next tide, and I'll be sure not to burden Radnor or my nephew with any correspondence." Damn his voice for cracking on *nephew*.

"If you'll listen to me for half a minute, please," Turner said, not bothering to conceal his irritation at having to run his quarry down. "My employer has been entertaining the idea that despite your personal failings it might do Simon some good to see you, considering how close you were during his time on the Continent. I was simply making sure that you weren't engaged in round-the-clock orgies. I believe Lord Radnor will be satisfied. I'll be in London for three days, and I brought Simon with me so he could visit Astley's again. I thought you might want to come with us."

Courtenay thought he might weep with relief. "Yes," he managed. "Yes."

Chapter Nineteen

"Why didn't you tell me you had been invited to the Preston ball?" Eleanor asked, looking up from the letter she was reading at the breakfast table.

Courtenay was in an agreeable mood, having spent the past two days taking Simon about London. It had felt like old times, but more than that it was the promise of a future that wasn't totally devoid of joy. "There's no point, thank God. Radnor saw reason, and now I can go back to behaving normally," he said.

"But I'm going," Eleanor argued. "It would be lovely to see you at one of these dos for once."

"*I* have to go," Standish said, appearing in the open door of the breakfast room. "I don't see why I ought to be the only one suffering."

At some point while Courtenay had been distracted by Simon's presence, Standish and Eleanor had reached a slight detente. Standish now leaned against the doorframe, his hands jammed in his pockets and a smile on his lips. His words were addressed to Courtenay but his eyes were on Eleanor.

Eleanor, who was blushing. *Very* interesting.

"Julian did go to all that trouble to get you invited." Eleanor said, blissfully oblivious to the fact that Courtenay and Julian hadn't spoken in days. "It seems a waste if you don't go."

Standish made a strangled noise and Courtenay shot him a reassuring look. Courtenay would hold his tongue. If Eleanor knew that Standish had told Courtenay about Julian's novel, she'd be upset with her husband for violating her confidence, and it might undo some of the progress they had made in reconciling. Courtenay, however, was unspeakably grateful to Standish for telling him the truth before Courtenay had fallen even more dangerously in love with Julian.

Besides, it would be damned hard to explain why Standish had felt it necessary to tell Courtenay Julian's secret without revealing their affair. Courtenay wasn't entirely sure if Eleanor knew that her brother's tastes ran to men, let alone whether he had been intimate with Courtenay. And as disappointed as Courtenay was with Julian, and with himself for having been stupid enough to fall for a man who held him in such low regard, he wasn't exposing the man's secrets.

"Perhaps I'll go," he said, wanting to be agreeable.

"Eleanor said it will be very crowded." Standish spoke with an offhand air, but Courtenay understood him to be reassuring Courtenay that he wouldn't need to see Julian if he didn't want to.

Well, he damned well didn't want to, so that was good. He also didn't want to look like he was shrinking away from all decent society. It was rather a coup for him to have gained this invitation to the Preston ball, and declining to attend would feel like a defeat, as if he were admitting he had no right to be among civilized people.

Courtenay pulled his watch from his pocket. "I need to leave if I'm to see Simon off." He pushed his chair back and rose from the table. "I told him I'd go to the hotel and admire the carriage horses."

As he left the breakfast room, he saw Standish sit in the chair he had vacated. Courtenay dearly hoped Standish and Eleanor managed to make this work and was almost annoyed that they had spent years resentfully apart when they could have been together. They could have had what Courtenay never would.

Medlock had made him start to second-guess his belief that he didn't deserve happiness, didn't deserve lasting companionship after his part in robbing his sister of her future. For how many years had he implicitly allowed his own opinion of himself to be tarnished by his mother's contempt? She had never given a damn about him, and he ought to return the compliment.

And now, walking along the sun-dappled springtime streets of Mayfair, on his way to see his sister's beloved child, he couldn't help but think that Isabella wouldn't have wanted him to deny himself happiness. Of course she wouldn't—people wanted their loved ones to be happy. The only person who wouldn't want Courtenay to be happy was his mother, and—

And he didn't care what his mother thought of him.

Or, rather, he did care but realized he shouldn't.

He thought that he could maybe try to see himself through the eyes of the people who thought the best of him—Isabella always had, Simon did now. So did Eleanor and maybe even Standish.

So had Julian, despite what he had written in that book; that had been before he had really known Courtenay. Courtenay knew that. He had gone over the timing a hundred times. He had remembered, unbidden, every kind word Julian had told him.

That didn't mean he could ever trust Julian again, but he could know that Julian had cared about him, as much as Julian was capable of caring about anyone. He told himself that had to count for something.

That night, settled in the spare room, he took *The Brigand Prince* out of his valise. He hadn't read it since learning that Julian had written it. But he hadn't burnt it either, or tossed it out the window.

As he turned the familiar pages, he found himself catching traces of Julian—a turn of phrase, a cutting remark. And he realized these words were always from the mouth of the villain Don Lorenzo. The rest of the characters were as good-hearted a lot of simpletons as ever graced the pages of a novel and Julian made them all say the most appallingly sentimental things to one another. Any notion Courtenay had about Julian not understanding the workings of the human heart were proven utterly false. He was a damned expert in the treacliest of sentiment.

Courtenay remembered Julian's insistence that Don Lorenzo wasn't based on Courtenay, that Julian had only borrowed Courtenay's looks and mannerisms. And now he saw that this was the truth. Julian, not Courtenay, was Don Lorenzo: conniving, ruthless, cold, friendless.

Courtenay rather wished he hadn't figured that out.

He flipped to a passage he remembered well. Agatha and Don Lorenzo were trapped in the crumbling tower of the monastery. Don Lorenzo had very flamboyantly thrown the key out the window.

"You'll never get away with this," Agatha cried, clawing at the velvet folds of Don Lorenzo's robes. Wind whipped through the open window, bringing with it pelting hail and blinding gusts of frigid air. Agatha's own humble cloak was in tatters, a poor defense against this gall.

"My child," Don Lorenzo drawled, his emerald green eyes glinting with cold malice, "I already have." He opened his palm to reveal the golden contours of the prince's locket. He held his hand out through the window, dangling the locket over the abyss.

"No!"

"Without this locket you'll never have proof that you and your appalling infant brother are the rightful heirs of the prince, and his fiefdom will revert to me." He ran the long white fingers of one hand through the ravens' wings of his hair. "The ancestral curse will finally be lifted from my bloodline after centuries of despair."

"What do you want from me?" Agatha begged, falling to her knees on the cold, hard flagstone of the tower floor. "I would do anything to restore my family's honor."

"Sweet, stupid Agatha. Don't you wish it were that simple? I know I do."

He was interrupted by the sound of a tremendous crashing. The stone floor creaked and trembled and it sounded as if the tower itself was in danger of collapsing into dust. The ancient oaken door burst inward, sending a spray of splinters into the room.

Agatha turned toward the hole in the wall where the door had once stood. It was empty. She had expected to see a party of rescuers armed with a great battering room, but instead there was only a gaping void of shadows.

"No!" Don Lorenzo cried, flinging an arm over his eyes in terror at a sight only he could behold. "Not that!"

"Nothing is there," Agatha protested, shaking her head in meek confusion. "It must have been the storm."

"Don't take me!" Don Lorenzo begged to the unseen entity. "It isn't time!"

"Who are you speaking to?" The mist in the tower seemed to be coalescing into a shape. Agatha knew it had to be a trick of her tired mind. She had spent weeks chasing this villain over hill and dale. She had travelled nearly the length of the country tracking him down and now her mind must be fevered. But if she stared too long at the mist it seemed to take the form of a hooded figure who loomed over them.

"I thought I'd have longer," Don Lorenzo cried, tears streaming down his face. He seemed to be diminishing in size and substance. With what seemed to be every reserve of strength in his body, he leaned out the window and released the locket. Agatha watched in frozen horror as she saw the golden object drop from his long fingers, plummeting into the abyss.

The wind in the tower stopped for an instant and a silence fell over the monastery, so eerily still Agatha could hear her

own heart beating. It was over. The locket was gone and her
hopes were dashed. Don Lorenzo sagged with relief against the
window casement, and for the first time Agatha could see what
the man would be without the prophecy compelling him to black
deeds and awful feats. His visage smoothed, relaxing into some-
thing devoid of rancor, empty of all traces of the villainy that had
spurred him on for perhaps his entire life. As Agatha watched,
a sigh escaped his mouth, a white puff in the darkness, and his
eyes fell shut.

Suddenly the wind picked up again, furious and violent, and
before Agatha could realize what was happening she saw Don
Lorenzo fall out the window as if pushed by an invisible hand.

"No!" she cried, even though vanquishing this man had been
the object of her life.

Courtenay closed the book. Julian hadn't even made Don
Lorenzo fall into the abyss by his own greed or treachery.
Courtenay didn't know what the curse signified, if anything.
He closed the book and put it on the nightstand, but it was a
long time before he fell asleep.

Julian's head was throbbing. It felt like there were shards of
glass where his brain ought to have been. When he moved, he
set off a chain reaction of pain throughout his body.

But it was the night of the Preston ball and it would take
more than a simple cold to keep him away. Because that's
what this was: a cold. Nothing more. Never mind that when
he crawled out of bed after his nap he felt that he could just as
easily curl up on the floor and sleep until the next day. Never

mind that when his valet tied his cravat, the smooth linen felt like coarse rope against his flesh.

"If you'll pardon me, sir," Briggs said after watching Julian wince through having his hair combed. "Will you let me take the liberty of calling for the doctor? Or perhaps Lady Standish? She always knows what to do in these, ah, situations," he said diplomatically.

"No," Julian croaked. "It's a summer cold." It wasn't summer and it was becoming increasingly clear that this wasn't a cold but Julian didn't care. He would not sit this ball out. He had worked blasted hard to get to the point where his invitation to such an event was a matter of course. "I daresay I'll feel better once I'm distracted." His voice sounded like it was coming from far away.

Later, he couldn't say how precisely he had gotten to the ball. Briggs must have poured him into his carriage and told the coachman where to bring him, because the next thing he knew he had drifted through the receiving line and gone down the stairs into the ballroom.

He lasted about two minutes in the ballroom. It was stifling hot and infernally loud. Were balls always like this? Impossible. He would have remembered. It was like something dreamt up by one of those medieval Dutch fellows who were forever painting their deranged imaginings of a hell populated by jolly demons torturing the damned. Courtenay would have found that vastly amusing, but he was not thinking of Courtenay, because that made his head hurt even worse, to say nothing of his heart. He made his way through the crowd and out into the garden.

Why did the soles of his feet ache so much? That was bloody new. Perhaps he'd tell Eleanor, so she could write the symptom in that little book in which she detailed his illnesses. He hated that book. The cool night air, at least, was blessed relief. Julian wanted to crawl onto a garden bench and fall asleep. The sound of the breeze rustling through the immaculately maintained shrubbery was somehow as loud as a monsoon.

Leaning on the balustrade that overlooked the garden, he let his eyes fall shut. He peeled off his gloves so he could feel the cool of the stone with his hot, painful hands. He didn't need to open his eyes to know what the Prestons' garden looked like. The first year he had attended this ball, he had been wide-eyed with astonishment that such a large garden existed behind a private home in a crowded metropolis. Even most wealthy people contented themselves with a modest patch of greenery, but the exceedingly wealthy—and the Prestons were very rich indeed—had obelisks and follies, bridges crossing picturesque streams, cleverly situated temples and grottos. Houses like this must require armies of gardeners—always out of sight, even though a garden like this must need hours of work daily to coax flowers to bloom coincidental with the ball. He wanted to tally the likely cost of such an enterprise but his mind wouldn't cooperate.

Even with his eyes squeezed shut, Julian could smell the plants—flowering shrubs and trees, blooms that belonged in Madras, not Mayfair. When he heard a burst of conversation, for a moment his aching brains thought he was hearing the Hindustani voices of his grandfather's servants, the laughing chatter of Eleanor and Ned as they slipped through the moonlit gardens, Julian watching from an opened window of the upstairs room where he balanced the account books, Julian listening from his sickbed while grandfather's valet made him drink that infernal tincture.

It was time for the tincture.

"Nora," he heard Standish say, and Eleanor laughed. They had always been laughing, thick as thieves from the moment they met. He thought he could hear them now, and even in his disoriented state he knew it was not a good sign to be hearing things. He lifted his head but there were Eleanor and Standish in the garden below him. Eleanor was wearing a gown he dimly recalled having bought her, far away in London—dark blue silk shot through with silver thread, and even from this distance he could see the adoring look on Standish's face as he regarded her.

"Thank God," Julian said aloud. Maybe he hadn't made a mess of their lives as badly as he had his own. Maybe Eleanor would have what she wanted, all the things she hadn't ever spoken aloud to Julian. Julian hadn't deserved those confidences, because he wouldn't have understood anyway, at least not before knowing Courtenay. Now he thought he could begin to grasp what Eleanor's sorrow had been like. "Thank God," he repeated, when he saw Standish pull Eleanor behind a shrub and kiss her. Then he shut his eyes again and rested his forehead against the blessedly cool stone of the balustrade.

He didn't know how long he stayed like that, but after a while he felt a hand between his shoulder blades and smelled tobacco.

"Is that you, Medlock?" It was Courtenay's voice, low and rumbly and out of place among the exotic blooms.

"Why are you in Madras?" Julian asked without lifting his head. He felt a hand, wonderfully cool on his brow.

"You're feverish. You ought to be in bed. Or in a vinegar bath. Why are you alone out here?" He sounded angry and worried.

Julian turned his head so his cheek rested against the too-warm wool of his sleeve. The burning tip of Courtenay's cigarillo seemed as distant as a star in the sky.

"Come here." Courtenay wrapped an arm around Julian and hauled him upright.

Julian tried to explain that his legs weren't working properly, but his mouth wasn't working properly either. He collapsed against Courtenay's hard chest.

"Christ, Julian."

"That's what you were supposed to call me," Julian said, his words garbled, "if I hadn't ruined everything. I ruin everything that isn't money." It had been better when he thought he was still in Madras, the future laid out before him in all its dazzling potential. Now he was in London and there was no future, nothing to plan for.

"I think you have the influenza." Courtenay's voice was stern. "Damn. Is there a doctor here? No, impossible that the Prestons would have invited a lowly professional man."

"He's the Chancellor of the Exchequer. But he also has a model village. You ought to talk to him." Julian couldn't remember why he thought Courtenay might want to know about model villages, but it had something to do with the Poor Laws and the bad roofs at Carrington.

"You're delirious."

Julian thought he very well might be. The world seemed to be spinning about his ears. Music wafted out on the breeze, and as he rested against Courtenay's chest, he felt like they were dancing together. "We're waltzing," he murmured. He had never danced with anyone he loved, and he supposed that wasn't what was happening now anyway. They weren't dancing so much as standing still while music played and Julian tried not to faint. Besides, Julian didn't want to think about love. Whatever it was, it would have been pleasant if he weren't growing increasingly certain that he might drop dead at any moment.

"I miss you," Julian said, as Courtenay scooped him up in a pair of strong arms and the world went dark.

CHAPTER TWENTY

Where the devil was Eleanor? Courtenay braced Julian against his chest and called out her name. She would know what to do, while Courtenay could only offer brute strength, and even that was barely sufficient to get Julian out into a hackney. He dismissed the idea of having one of the Prestons' footmen fetch Eleanor—it would take too long, and create a scene that he knew Julian would abhor. Besides, Julian's illness was getting increasingly worse. He needed a doctor. He told the hackney driver to bring them to Eleanor's house. It was only a few streets away, much closer than Julian's lodgings.

Julian was half conscious, opening his eyes only long enough for Courtenay to see how glassy they were. Beads of perspiration dotted his forehead despite the chill of the evening. Courtenay untied Julian's cravat and attempted to remove his coat, but it was too closely tailored for Courtenay to manage on his own, so he settled for unbuttoning both coat and waistcoat. He had never touched flesh so alarmingly warm, not even Isabella during her final illness.

"Mr. Medlock has taken ill," he told Eleanor's butler after half carrying, half coaxing Julian out of the carriage. Tilbury was regarding him with a degree of suspicion unusual even for him. "He needs a bed. Now!" he added when Tilbury didn't move immediately.

A footman—the same one who he recalled not wanting to help the opera girl into her cloak—materialized to help carry Medlock up the stairs and through the door. Every time they moved one of Julian's limbs, he moaned. "Never mind a bed," Courtenay barked. "I'm taking him to the back parlor." It was the room he had once told Julian was Eleanor's cat room. God, that felt like a hundred years ago.

"Call for the doctor," Courtenay called over his shoulder in his most commanding tones.

"Stop touching me," Julian moaned as Courtenay and the footman undressed him. "My skin is prickly."

"Too bad," Courtenay said. Now, in the well-lit parlor, he could see how badly Julian was. His cheeks were livid with fever, his pupils dilated so much that his gray eyes were entirely black. This was how Isabella had looked in the days before her death. Courtenay gritted his teeth.

"Vinegar," he said to the footman after they had eased Julian onto the sofa and covered him with a thin sheet. He wracked his brain but couldn't think of the name for the tea that was good for fevers. "And . . . goddamn it, I don't know any of these things in English." He cursed himself for not knowing.

"I'll ask the cook," the footman said on his way out the door. "She'll know."

The doctor came while Courtenay was bathing Julian's head with the vinegar the footman had brought. He nearly collapsed with relief to see the man, but his relief was short-lived when the medical man ordered that the windows Courtenay had opened be closed immediately.

"Nonsense," Courtenay argued. "Feel him. He's hot. He needs to cool off."

"The night air is unwholesome," the doctor insisted. "Besides, Mr. Medlock is shivering. He needs warmth."

He was shivering because he had sweat through the sheets. Even Courtenay understood that. He felt a rising sense of panic at what he felt was the doctor's potential incompetence. If this doctor couldn't save Julian, then that would be another death on Courtenay's conscience. He watched the doctor rummage in his bag, finally producing a lancet and a cup from his bag. "In order for the fever to break, he needs to have one of his veins breathed."

Courtenay wrinkled his brow in confusion. Did the doctor mean bloodletting? Because there was no way Courtenay was letting this doctor put a knife to Julian's arm.

"That won't be necessary," said a voice from the door. It was Eleanor, still wearing her ball gown, with Standish just behind. Courtenay nearly sagged with relief to see her. She would know what to do. She always did. "It was so kind of you to come to us so late, Dr. Abernathy, but I'll see to things from here. Tilbury will pay your fee on your way out."

"Thank God you're here," Courtenay said.

Eleanor approached the bed and put her hand to her brother's head. She frowned.

"Is this a recurrence . . ." Standish's voice trailed off.

"I can't be sure. We don't use Dr. Abernathy for these instances, so he wouldn't have known."

Courtenay had no idea what they were talking about. "What instances?"

Eleanor unwrapped her shawl and absently held it out. Standish promptly took it from her. "You did right to cool him down with vinegar. Bloodletting," she added. "In my own house. I think not." She spoke with a degree of venom that reminded Courtenay of Julian. A fresh wave of panic swept over him at the idea that he might never hear Julian complain about Courtenay's cravat or hair or anything else.

"The cook sent this tea up," Courtenay said, gesturing to a cup on the bedside table. "But I didn't want to give it to him without knowing if it was right."

Eleanor sniffed it. "Willow bark. It won't do any harm but what he needs is the Peruvian bark tincture. I have some in my study in case he has an attack while he's with me. You can spoon some into his mouth if he'll take it."

"An attack?" Courtenay still didn't understand. "I thought it was influenza."

"Eleanor," Standish said. "Why don't you get changed and have someone send up the tincture? And we may as well send for your brother's valet. We'll need help tending to him. How long did his last attack last?"

"I don't know. He's always very cagey about it. We'll ask Briggs when he gets here."

"Could somebody tell me what is going on here?" Courtenay's voice came out too high, panicked, all wrong.

"Get changed, Eleanor," Standish said firmly with a pointed look at his wife which apparently she knew how to interpret. She shut the door quietly behind her on her way out.

"He has malaria," Standish said calmly. "He fell ill when he was a child, and it comes back from time to time." Standish must have read something of Courtenay's shock on his face because he added, "He's healthy, though."

"Healthy?" Courtenay gestured at the sofa where Medlock was fitfully turning, his breathing labored. "Evidently not. Why was he at that blasted ball? He oughtn't to have been out of bed."

"Had to go." Julian's eyes were wide open but vacant. "Otherwise you'd think I stayed away to avoid you."

"You're fucking daft," Courtenay said, and only after he had spoke them did he realize that this insult and obscenity might be the last words he ever spoke to the man he loved. "I'm furious with you," he added, as if that were better.

"I ruin everything," Julian said. "I'm not good at people."

"Were you under the impression that letting me believe I killed you would improve things?" Courtenay knew he only felt guilty because he was tired, too tired to separate the strands of death and guilt and shame that became so easily knotted in his mind. He hadn't made Julian write that godforsaken book. He had been entirely within his rights to end their friendship because of it. But if that was what had made Julian venture out when he should have been in bed, and then he died, how could Courtenay not feel responsible?

"I'm not dying, you pillock," Julian croaked. "Haven't died of this yet."

"It looks like you're trying your damnedest to make an exception." The door was shut and Standish was trustworthy, so Courtenay squeezed Julian's hand.

Standish cleared his throat. "He's always been damned healthy, despite the malaria."

"He looks the picture of blooming health," Courtenay said dryly.

Julian laughed, and it sounded like a death rattle.

"In India he suffered from recurrences several times a year, each much worse than this. Eleanor wanted him to go to England on the chance that a different climate would make him less vulnerable, and she seems to have been right. It's a very good sign that he's so coherent."

There was a soft tapping at the door and Standish rose to answer it, returning a moment later with a goblet filled with dark liquid. This, Courtenay gathered, was the tincture.

"If you'll make sure he takes that, I'll have somebody set up a bed for the valet when he arrives." Standish slipped from the room, closing the door behind him.

Julian's eyes were closed again, but Courtenay wasn't letting him fall back asleep before taking his medicine. He slipped a hand behind Julian's sweat-damp head and lifted him to a half-sitting position. Julian winced.

"I'm sorry," Courtenay said, bringing the cup to Julian's lips. "Take this and I'll let you be."

Julian drank the tincture. It must have tasted terrible,

because his entire body was wracked with a shudder as he swallowed.

"I'm sorry," Courtenay repeated as Julian collapsed onto the pillow. "So sorry."

Julian drifted in and out of alertness. He couldn't manage to properly sleep, not when his head was filled with jagged rocks and his body was on fire. But whenever he opened his eyes, Courtenay was there. Sometimes Eleanor was in the room too, poking and prodding him as she always did during these episodes.

"I'm reminding myself that you mean well," Julian croaked. His mouth was dry and it was taking all his effort to speak. He couldn't quite be sure—his mind wasn't right—but he thought this was the first time he and Eleanor had seen one another since that awful garden party. "But please stop touching me."

She wrote something in that damned book. "You're not as sick as you were the last time. At least not the last time I heard about." She was annoyed, which was probably a sign that she didn't think Julian would die. At least not this time.

After she left, Julian painfully turned his head to see Courtenay. He was leaning against the wall near the empty grate.

"Your valet arrived," Courtenay said. "I can leave . . ."

Julian felt the gears of his mind turning despite the illness and the pain. Courtenay could have left hours ago. Either he was here because he wanted to be, which was good, or because he felt guilty, which was intolerable.

"None of this is your fault. I know you find it convenient to wallow in guilt and self-recrimination." He took a deep breath and tried to keep his voice normal, tried not to fall back into the non-sleep of delirium. "It's impossible for you to imagine that you aren't responsible for the misfortunes of anyone . . ." He grasped for a word that wouldn't imply more than Courtenay might feel. "Of anyone in emotional proximity to you. But my illness has nothing to do with you, and I didn't go to that blasted ball just to show you up. I wanted to go because my fevered brain wasn't working right."

Courtenay said something, but Julian couldn't follow. He closed his eyes, and when he opened them again, Courtenay was sitting by the bed, holding another glass of that god-awful tincture. Julian reached out but his hands were still too shaky. The shivers had started. He couldn't even force his body to sit up. Courtenay brought the glass to his mouth and Julian drank, only wincing slightly from the taste. This experience was nightmarishly familiar: the ache in his head, the fire on his skin, the bone-deep sense of wrongness in his body. Even the taste of the tincture was something that had been with him for almost his entire life. The only unfamiliar element was Courtenay.

"You can leave if you want," Julian said as Courtenay plumped the pillow under Julian's head.

"I don't know what I want," Courtenay said after a while.

Julian shut his eyes when the edges of his vision dissolved into emptiness.

When he woke he felt a warmth on his arm. He opened his eyes and saw a jet-black kitten curled in the bend of his elbow.

"I tried to get rid of them," Courtenay said. He was still sitting by the bed, still wearing evening clothes despite the faint light coming in through the open windows. "But every time I shut the door another kitten crawls out from under a cushion."

"That's how kittens work." Julian's mouth was dry. He was dreadfully thirsty and didn't complain when Courtenay held the cup of tincture to his lips. This time Julian was able to half sit up, and Courtenay put a hand to the back of his head to steady him. The touch was startlingly intimate, but not the embarrassing bodily intimacy he usually associated with the sickroom. He sipped from the glass, and was surprised to find that the tincture tasted different, the bitterness of the root slightly masked not only by the usual wine but by something sweet. "Oh," he said. "That's not bad."

"Cook added treacle." He took the empty glass and eased his hand away from Julian's head. "I remembered you had a sweet tooth and suggested that she do something . . ."

"Thank you." Julian tried not to read too much into the gesture. Sugar syrup in one's medicine did not constitute a declaration of love, or even a truce. He lifted a feeble hand to pet the sleeping kitten. It was still at the fragile stage of early kittenhood, all bones and fluff.

"Do you want me to take the cat away?"

"No."

"Good, because the two of you look adorable, and besides, there are two other kittens hiding in the bookcase, waiting for their chance to stake their claim."

Julian squirmed. He knew he didn't look anything close

to adorable. He was sweaty and disheveled and wearing nothing but one of Standish's borrowed nightshirts. He could smell himself, which was never a good sign. Courtenay, meanwhile, was reprehensibly handsome in his evening clothes, even after a night of sitting in a sickroom. Julian thought he'd never get used to the stark fact of Courtenay's beauty. Or, rather, he never would have, in a world where he was given the chance to find out.

"The kitten was probably cold," he said, stroking one of the cat's impossibly tiny ears. "And I'm the warmest thing in the room. It would be mean-spirited for me to send him away."

Courtenay touched Julian's brow. "Not as hot as you were when I brought you here. Perhaps you're recovering?"

"Or perhaps the fever will return tonight, and tomorrow night, and the night after."

"Is that what usually happens?"

"When I was a child, yes. But since coming to England it's been mild." Or, as mild as these things ever were. He remembered entire summers with fevers coming nightly. Then, he had thought it would kill him. Now, he still thought it might kill him, but likely not for decades, perhaps not until he was already old and infirm.

"Do you want me here, Julian?"

"Yes, please," he answered, too quickly, but he didn't care. "You're the only one I want here." *You're the only one I could stand to have here*, he wanted to say.

"Then I'll stay."

Relief washed over Julian. He didn't know whether he was still delirious or whether the illness had weakened his resolve, but he had never before wanted anyone with him when he was sick. He had always tried his hardest to send even Briggs and Eleanor away. He remembered what Courtenay had said about fighting desire being like tethering a balloon, and wondered if he had always wanted a companion, somebody he could turn to when he was at his most miserable, somebody to whom he could expose this most secret part of himself.

"Until you're well," Courtenay added.

That brought Julian crashing back to earth. Courtenay wasn't here out of any affection for Julian, but out of some misguided sense of obligation. "No, damn it, please go if you're going to be a martyr about it. I'd rather have Briggs, in that case." He knew he sounded peevish and ungrateful but that was better than sounding pathetically disappointed.

"Of course I want to be here. When I thought you were . . ." He gestured as if he couldn't come up with the word, but the word was *dying* and they both knew it. "There wasn't anywhere else I could have been."

He didn't say that he wanted to be here. He said that he couldn't have been anywhere else, and Julian didn't know if that was better or worse. Before he could puzzle it out, he shut his eyes and fell asleep.

CHAPTER TWENTY-ONE

Julian woke to the sound of Standish's voice and the bizarre feeling of not knowing where or even when he was. He cracked open an eye just enough to see that he was in Eleanor's drawing room. At some point, Julian couldn't quite be sure when, he had graduated from the sofa in the back parlor to a chair in the drawing room. This was supposed to be a sign of improvement, it was supposed to be heartening. The dangerous part of the episode was over, but now Julian was a wrung-out rag, a dried husk of a man. This was the worst part, the weariness and weakness, the bodily stiffness, the bone-deep sense of bored uselessness. It was in this state of mind that he had written *The Brigand Prince*.

"You're good at this," he heard Standish say.

"I've had practice." It was Courtenay, somewhere behind Julian's chair. Judging by the sounds of silver clinking against china, he was stirring something. Over the last day—two days, three days, however long it had been—the tincture had grown decreasingly noxious. "I like making sick people comfortable."

"He's a terrible patient, though. Once he threw a dish at a wall. Broke the dish and a window." Julian had been ten bloody years old and so fucking tired of being sick in bed.

A pause stretched out. Would Courtenay laugh with Standish about Julian's peevishness, his bad temperament? "But he must have been a child," Courtenay said with a mildness Julian knew to be deceptive.

"I suppose he must have been. It's funny, but I don't remember him being a child. I mean, not a proper child."

Julian wasn't sure if he could actually hear Courtenay grind his teeth or if he just knew that it had to be happening.

"I find it hard to imagine Julian being a less than proper anything," Courtenay said.

"What I mean to say is that he was never climbing trees or stealing sweets from the kitchens."

"You know more about those days than I do, but my understanding is that old Mr. Medlock gave Julian a good deal of responsibility as a way of sticking it to Julian's father. Julian didn't have much opportunity to steal sweets." He paused, and when he spoke again he had resumed his customary charm. "Besides, I have it on good authority that he used to harbor wounded animals in the library. I believe Eleanor specifically told me of a mongoose."

Standish cracked a laugh. "Good God, I had forgotten about that. But even then, he acted as if the mongoose had to be given quarter in the library as a matter of course, and anyone who had the temerity to suggest otherwise was out of line. As if the mongoose had to be in the library, not because

Julian wanted it, but because it was written in some book of household management. He's always been like that."

"And when he negotiated Eleanor's marriage settlements it was in much the same spirit, I gather. Really, Standish. You and Eleanor let yourself get led around like a dog on a string by an actual child. You, I can believe." Julian had to bite the inside of his cheek to stop from laughing. "But Eleanor?"

Standish didn't sound offended. "She always did whatever he said. I think it was because he had been so unwell."

The truth of that left Julian slightly shaken.

"And yet you still didn't understand why she had to go to England?" Courtenay snapped, again seeing things that he wasn't meant to. "Most of us don't enjoy watching our siblings die. She didn't leave you. She was going to lose her brother to death or to England, and she chose to follow him to England. Or—wait now." Julian could almost hear the gears turning in Courtenay's mind. "She probably convinced him that she was going to England for her own purposes and trusted that he would follow her. She didn't expect you to be such an idiot as not to come with her. I hope you apologize to her in grand style."

"I see that now," Standish protested.

"Pair of idiots," Courtenay murmured, but not without fondness. "Really, I'm glad you patched it up. The two of you are too good to be with anyone else." He said good like it was a synonym for daft.

Julian decided that this would be a wise moment to feign waking. "Do I smell Bath buns?" he croaked, raising his arms in a weak approximation of a stretch. It was an effort to get the words out and make them sound like the words of a man who gave a damn about baked goods rather than an invalid trying to stop his brother-in-law and lover—former lover?—from quarrelling in the drawing room.

"I'll tell Eleanor you're awake," Standish said. Julian didn't protest, because he knew Standish was only slipping out to give him and Courtenay time alone. When he left, he shut the door. Julian heard a key turn in the lock.

"He's being very decent, you know," Julian said.

"About what?"

Julian weakly gestured back and forth, to Courtenay and back to himself. "About this."

Courtenay folded his arms across his chest. "You mean he isn't scandalized by our very existence? How kind."

"You know perfectly well most people would be."

"I've been spoiled by only associating with the demi-monde, then."

"You're grumpy." Julian liked grumpy Courtenay.

"I'm fond of Standish. He has the good sense to know Eleanor's worth, so that's something in his favor."

"Are they still quarreling?"

"God help me, no. There they are, nearly thirty, married, but acting like the most incompetently courting couple I've ever seen."

They had never needed to court much the first time around. They might have, if Julian hadn't swept in with his numbers and ledgers. But, he reminded himself, he had been eighteen years old, and he had been trying his damned best to help the one person he had in the world. "That's much better than quarreling."

"You only say that because you haven't had to sit at table with them. Yesterday he presented her with a box of rocks."

"Really?"

"Apparently, he picked up a rock everywhere he went— Shanghai, Lima, New Orleans, and everywhere in between."

"What kind of rocks?" He hoped Standish had the sense not to scoop up handfuls of gravel. There were rocks and there were *specimens*.

"Oh, they all have names, and long complicated ones at that. And he knew every one of them."

"She must have loved that," he managed. Perhaps the illness had left him emotional, because Julian felt tears prickling in his eyes.

It was too much to hope that Courtenay hadn't noticed his tears. "The damnedest thing is that she did. I've spent thousands of pounds on rubies to less effect," he said, not a hint of rancor in his voice.

"That's probably because the lady—or the gentleman— wasn't predisposed to fall in love with you."

"Evidently not! How humbling. But that was never my goal until—" He broke off suddenly with an abashed look.

Had he meant *until you?* "Indeed," was all Julian said. And then, pushing himself more upright, "Are they trusting one another?" He remembered what Courtenay had told him, that love required trust, letting your heart be exposed and vulnerable.

"Yes," Courtenay said, his mouth tightening. Perhaps the mention of trust reminded him of Julian's deception.

"How about one of those buns?" Julian said weakly.

Courtenay reached for the bag.

"First, help me to sit by you." It was pathetic, a transparent effort to have some last bit of closeness before this was done between them. "I think I can get there on my own, but I doubt my pride can take stumbling in front of you." He said this with the consciousness that he had likely done a good deal worse than stumble in front of Courtenay in the last few days. And still, Courtenay was looking at him with unmistakable affection. Maybe even hunger. But not trust. Julian didn't think he would ever earn that.

Courtenay's arm was around him in an instant, though, guiding him the short distance from the chair to the sofa. His arm stayed around Julian even after they sat side by side, and Julian let his head sink onto Courtenay's shoulder, the bun momentarily forgotten as Courtenay traced circles on the sleeve of Julian's dressing gown.

One of the kittens leapt onto Julian's lap. "That creature has adopted you," Courtenay said. "He makes himself agreeable so you'll let him nap by your side."

Indeed, Julian had noticed the sleek black kitten whenever he opened his eyes. "I've named him after you. Dark hair. Insinuating ways."

Courtenay snorted. "Come here," he said, pulling Julian closer.

"I'm already there."

Courtenay put a finger under Julian's chin and tilted it up.

"You can't possibly mean to kiss me. I'm revolting." *Please kiss me.*

"You aren't. And even if you were, you'd be other things too."

It was a gentle kiss, the sort of patient and meandering kiss Courtenay liked and Julian had never understood before. It wasn't a prelude to fucking, it wasn't even a prelude to a more thorough kiss. It was a conversation, without the burden of words. *Please*, Julian wanted to say. *Let me try again.* Julian's heart felt full of something terrifying, something more dangerous than anything he had ever thought possible. And he didn't care. He was throwing himself into an abyss he couldn't even see, and that was fine, at least for the duration of the kiss.

Courtenay kissed the corner of his mouth and pulled back, looking at him with an expression Julian couldn't read.

Then there was the sound of a key in the lock, and the door opened to reveal Eleanor standing on the threshold, an expression of shocked betrayal on her face.

"**I** cannot believe you have the nerve," Eleanor said, slamming the door behind her. Courtenay quickly pulled away from Julian, but she could apparently tell they had just kissed or were about to do so again.

Courtenay was no stranger to being on the receiving end of angry protests. But Eleanor wasn't speaking to him. Her furious gaze was focused entirely on her brother.

"After the way you acted when you thought I was going to bed with Courtenay, I can hardly believe it. You should be ashamed of yourself. I don't expect any better from *you*, Courtenay," she said, sparing him an indifferent glance before turning her wrath back to Julian. "But *you*." She shook her head. "So officious, so eager to tell everyone else when they've stepped out of line. And you're carrying on with Courtenay in my drawing room?" These last words she whispered— more like hissed—but the previous part of her tirade had been loud enough for the entire household to hear.

"Lower your voice, Eleanor," Julian said. His voice was very soft, weak and hoarse from his illness, with none of his usual acerbic edge.

Eleanor opened her mouth to say something but Courtenay held his hand up. "Now is not the time," Courtenay said. "We don't know who is listening." Courtenay had no intention of finding out whether a man as rich as Julian Medlock and a peer of the realm, however dissolute, would actually be tried for sodomy in England, or if instead he and Medlock would only be barred from all decent society. Julian would be devastated. He had worked so damned hard to be accepted. Courtenay wouldn't let him lose that, not on his account. "And besides," he added, "Julian isn't well."

"I'm plenty well," Julian retorted, sitting up straight in a way that pulled him entirely away from Courtenay. Their bodies were no longer touching in even the most innocent way. Courtenay didn't want to think it was a repudiation or a dismissal, but he felt the affront in his bones.

"You didn't even tell me?" Eleanor demanded. "You know I don't object to your liaisons with men."

"Well, given how you're handling yourself, can you blame me?"

Away went one of the last pathetic wisps of hope that he had meant something to Julian, that this had been more than fucking. He hadn't told Eleanor, hadn't meant to ever tell Eleanor, even though she evidently already knew about her brother's preference for men. Indeed, Eleanor's shock had nothing to do with finding out her brother was involved with a man, but rather that he was involved with a man who was beneath contempt.

"Yes! You were so cut up when you thought I was involved with Courtenay. You could have at least let me know you— arbiter of right and wrong—absolved me of that one sin."

More flimsy hope, blown away on the wind. So, going to bed with Courtenay, or kissing him gently in a drawing room, was the worst one could do. Good to know. And Julian wasn't protesting. What a fool Courtenay had been to think that he could have something lasting, something meaningful for once in his life, with a man who thought he was a walking scandal.

"I ought to go," Courtenay said, rising to his feet. Nobody stopped him, although he heard Julian say something that sounded like farewell.

He opened the door to find the butler and a housemaid loitering in the vestibule, the better to pick up the strains of raised voices. He couldn't be sure how much they had overheard, or if any of it was particularly incriminating in the first place. He had been too busy watching his last idiotic particles of hope being crushed beneath Julian's heel.

Damn it. He didn't know whether these two servants were likely to spread tales. Tilbury, for all his distaste for Courtenay, seemed devoted to Julian. But Courtenay knew better than to overestimate a servant's interest in protecting an employer, even less an employer's brother. No, Courtenay would need to do something about this.

Even if Julian didn't care a jot for him, Courtenay wasn't going to let him be besieged by scandal. And Julian was in no condition to solve this problem on his own. Grimly, he knocked on the door to Standish's study.

Chapter Twenty-Two

Julian had seen the dismayed sinking of Courtenay's shoulders, had seen the darkening expression on Courtenay's face, and known the man was hurt. He wanted to go after Courtenay, he wanted to follow him out into the hall and apologize for not having defended him to Eleanor. A better man, a braver man, would do precisely that.

Instead he buried his head in his hands. He hadn't meant to insult Courtenay, hadn't meant to tacitly accept Eleanor's suggestion that being involved with Courtenay would be a terrible thing. But Julian hadn't been thinking of how Courtenay must have felt to have been the subject of that ugly conversation. And Julian knew he ought to have done a better job considering the feelings of a man he cared for. It had only occurred to him what had gone wrong as Courtenay left the room.

Weeks ago, Courtenay had said that what Eleanor needed from Standish was proof of devotion, a display of feeling. Julian hadn't understood then. Now he did, and he also knew that he wasn't able to give that to Courtenay or anyone else.

Julian wasn't capable of gushing sentiment. He was hardly capable of any sentiment at all, he was quite certain. And if he had any feelings he certainly didn't acknowledge them, even to himself. If he did he might have to think about how desperately he already missed Courtenay, how happy he had been each time he opened his eyes and saw Courtenay by his sickbed, how right and good it felt to be in the same room as Courtenay and how awful it felt not to be now. He felt like one of those sea creatures whose soft undersides were protected by spikes.

He rang for Briggs to send for his carriage and pack his bags immediately. The morning's post had brought an invitation to spend a week in Richmond with Lady Montbray. It would be a small house party, entirely suitable for a lady in her last weeks of mourning, she assured him with what he had to assume was a degree of irony. He didn't care very much about propriety at the moment. What he needed was to get away from here. Convalescing in the country with pleasant company seemed about as ideal a situation as he could possibly come up with.

"You're in no state to travel, sir," Briggs ventured tentatively.

"I cannot stay here, and have no interest in holing up at my lodgings." Without company, he would have time to appreciate how truly alone he was. He had ruined things with Eleanor through first his judgment and then his secrecy. Which, now that he thought about it, was precisely how he had ruined things with Courtenay. At least he was consistent.

With as much haste as Briggs's dignity and Julian's weakness would allow, Julian dressed and was bundled into the carriage. Only then did he realize he was somehow still clutching the bag of buns Courtenay had brought, and now the carriage was filled with the scent of butter and cinnamon and incongruous spices, and the memory of the joy and hope he had experienced the last time he had eaten one.

He couldn't bring himself to eat one now. When they arrived at Lady Montbray's house in Richmond, Courtenay handed the crumpled, grubby bag to Miss Sutherland, the companion. "They're very good," he managed. A quarter of an hour later he was asleep in the spare room, still wearing his boots, still thinking of all the things he ought to have said to Courtenay if he were better, braver, and truer.

Courtenay had once told Julian that he was terrible at entrusting his heart to people who would take care of it. It seemed that nothing had changed, because he knew that he loved Julian and he was fairly confident that Julian felt nothing of the sort in return. And still, Courtenay was going to go out of his damned way to protect Julian and shield him from whatever scandal might arise as a result of servants' gossip. He was going to grossly inconvenience himself, and he was going to do it because he couldn't stand any harm coming to a person he cared about. He never could.

Having met with Standish and set their conspiracy in motion, Courtenay now had nowhere to sleep. Staying with Eleanor and Standish was out of the question now that their plan was afoot. He had given up his old lodgings on Flitcroft

Street. There was the Albemarle Street townhouse, but he didn't know if it was still unoccupied. There were, he recalled, other properties scattered across the kingdom, none of which he had any intention of visiting. He could sleep on Norton's sofa or he could take a room at one of London's cheaper hotels.

Or he could sleep at his own damned house.

Carrington Hall was his, and had been the principle seat of his family for more generations than anybody could be expected to remember. It was his and he had every right to sleep there.

He packed his belongings, including that blasted trunk filled with papers, and hired a post chaise heading west.

This time, as the carriage approached the village, he saw what Julian had noticed right away: cottages in need of new roofs, a bridge in need of repair. The road was badly rutted and would likely mire carts in any amount of rain. All these little things were signs of insufficiency. Julian had recognized them as evidence of bad management; Courtenay alone could fix that. Not only was this his house, it was his responsibility. It didn't matter who he let live here—his mother for free or Radnor for rent. This land, this village, the people living here—all depended on him at least to not bollocks it up.

In the weeks since his last visit, spring had settled into the landscape in a way that Courtenay only thought possible in this corner of the English countryside. He had seen every season in a dozen or more countries, but was confident he could identify Carrington in May with his eyes closed. The breeze rustling through trees that were heavy with leaves, the faint sound of the trout stream in the distance, the air fresh with the scent of hollyhocks and pinks. He had a rush of whatever sensation was the opposite of homesickness—homecoming, perhaps—but then it was swept away by the realization that this too was evidence of bad management: money had been poured into the grounds and garden when it ought to have been put into roads and roofs.

It was as if he had Julian by his side, clucking over the stupidity of it all. When he walked into Carrington Hall, he tried to imagine Julian there, wrinkling his nose at the butler's discomfiture. Julian, coming to his defense as he had during their past visit. As Courtenay remembered that day—supper at the inn and then their night in Julian's bed—he thought that Julian couldn't possibly have believed Courtenay beneath reproach. He had to have seen some mote of goodness in Courtenay.

But then Courtenay realized it didn't matter. It didn't matter in the least what Julian thought of him, it didn't matter what anyone else thought of him, all that mattered was what Courtenay thought of himself. He now understood that one of the reasons that he had always been indifferent to general public opinion was that he thought all the foul things said about him were basically true: he was a villain. And this past year without Isabella and Simon—the two people who loved him and to whom he meant anything at all—had done a number on his ability to think of himself as anything worthwhile. Without the people who thought the best of him, he had forgotten how to think the best of himself. Shame had seeped bone deep.

Time with Julian had done something to help that, but he couldn't let his pride rest entirely with one person. Well, he would just have to get himself in the habit of doing things he was proud of, and he would start with Carrington.

It took Julian about a week to realize that Lady Montbray was very carefully sheltering him from any gossip she thought he might find distressing. There were conversations that broke up as soon as Julian entered the room, letters hastily thrown into the fire. He was too preoccupied with his own matters to care.

Julian hadn't told anybody where he was going, so he assumed his own correspondence was collecting dust in London. He wrote to Eleanor, informing her that he was well on the road to recovery and that he wished he had never her questioned her judgment about her choices nor failed to trust her when he ought to have. He didn't mention where he was staying. It was a wholly inadequate letter, and he knew it as he sealed it and gave it to Lady Montbray's footman to post. But there was no adequate letter he could have written, and not sending a letter would have been cruel.

There was no letter at all he could have written Courtenay, at least not without exposing them both to criminal prosecution. If he could, he'd tell Courtenay that the time they had spent together had meant more to him than anything else that had happened in his life, that his greatest regrets were not only writing that book but also ever thinking that Courtenay was anything other than what he was—a thoughtful friend, a generous lover, a man Julian cared for more than he had thought he was capable of.

During his week at Lady Montbray's house, it dawned on him that he had been in love with Courtenay. Or, rather, that he still was and likely would continue on in that state for quite a while. He had spent so long telling himself that he wasn't capable of love that he had started to believe it. But Courtenay had been with him when he was sick and not only had Julian not minded his presence, he had actually wanted it. He wanted Courtenay with him always, even if that meant letting him in past Julian's defenses.

He got into the habit of sleeping late, of walking in the gardens and not doing much of anything. This was a proper convalescence, of the sort Eleanor had always tried to insist on, and which Julian had always rejected as needlessly indulgent. He had always wanted to be doing things, solving problems, being useful. Now he drifted, he meandered, he took up space without feeling like he needed anything to show for his days.

Children were exceedingly good for using up time, and Lady Montbray had no scruples about pressing her houseguest into service as a childminder. Julian didn't protest. Playing knights of the round table with the young Lord Montbray was no less amusing than many tea parties he attended, and he didn't know if this was because this child was particularly droll or because Julian perhaps had never enjoyed tea parties so very much in the first place. Perhaps he had never really enjoyed anything until he had met Courtenay. Perhaps he had never tried to.

He was in the summer house, attempting to whittle an elephant for young William—it had to be an elephant, the child was quite clear on this matter—despite never having whittled anything before in his life, when Lady Montbray approached, waving a piece of paper. Her white muslin dress floated around her like the petals of a flower.

"Quite a to-do over your friend Lord Courtenay," she said carefully.

"Oh?" Julian replied, pretending to interest himself in the misshapen knob of wood he held in his hands. "What's he been up to now?" An affair, presumably. A countess. A diplomat. Could be anyone, he supposed. Julian determinedly did not care.

"Apparently, your brother-in-law called him out."

Julian dropped the knife. "For what?"

"For interfering with Lady Standish's honor."

"But Standish knows perfectly well—" Julian couldn't finish that sentence. Standish knew that Courtenay and Julian were lovers; he knew that Courtenay and Eleanor had never been involved.

"It's taken Anne and me days to piece this together. I suppose we could have asked you but we really wanted to honor the spirit of convalescence and not bring up anything sordid. However, with this latest news we simply have to keep you informed. As hostesses, you see. Apparently, you discovered Courtenay and your sister *in flagrante*."

"I did?" Julian asked, not sure whether to deny or confirm until he knew what the devil was going on.

"Yes," Lady Montbray said. "You did. There was a good

deal of shouting, which the servants overheard. Then, if Anne and I are right, you left your sister's house and came here. Your brother-in-law felt that he had to challenge Courtenay."

"Has this duel taken place?" Julian felt his blood run cold even though logically he found the idea of Ned Standish and Courtenay fighting a duel over Eleanor's honor to be the most preposterous thing he had heard in his life.

"Not yet. But that's what's interesting. Courtenay went to Carrington Hall."

"What?" Julian was on his feet now, still clutching the piece of wood in his hand.

Julian didn't doubt Lady Montbray's intelligence. If her sources said that Courtenay was on the surface of the moon, it meant Courtenay was on the surface of the moon. And even if he were, Julian would find a way to get to him. How long would it take to get to Carrington? One hour? Two? It didn't matter. "May I borrow a horse?"

He needed to go to Courtenay. If Courtenay was cooking up a scheme with Standish, and—if as he suspected—it was for Julian's own benefit, he needed to see Courtenay and find out if there was anything salvageable left between them.

CHAPTER TWENTY-THREE

Only when Julian was within sight of Carrington Hall did he realize he didn't have a plan. He didn't even have the shadow of a plan. After so many years of calculating his every move several steps in advance, he hadn't the faintest idea what to do or say once he saw Courtenay.

He was spared any immediate decision when the butler who answered the door solemnly announced that his lordship was at Nettle Farm.

"What about the mistress of the house? Is Mrs. Blakeley not present?"

"Mr. and Mrs. Blakely have left for their new home in Somerset rather earlier than expected, Mr. Medlock."

"I'm surprised you didn't go with your mistress."

If the butler thought Julian was being rude, he didn't let on. "My duty is to whoever Lord Courtenay chooses to invite to live in his house."

Clever man, to know where his bread was buttered.

Julian nodded approvingly and headed in the direction the butler had indicated.

He found Courtenay in a cluster with other men, one of whom was gesturing at the ground, and then at a spot in the distance. He would have bet that one of the men was a surveyor or an engineer, and the other, some kind of land agent. The part of his brain that longed for something to do—interest to calculate, investments to multiply—wanted to know exactly what they were planning and how much it would cost. But this wasn't his affair, so he slowed his horse to a walk and approached the group.

One of the men noticed Julian's arrival and said something to the other men that caused them to look up. Julian knew the moment Courtenay recognized him because his mouth twitched into a smile that was replaced immediately with a look of confused dismay. He spoke to the men and approached Julian's horse.

Julian dismounted. He opened his mouth to make the expected apology—so sorry to interrupt—but he couldn't cobble the words together. Instead he stood there, gaping, his horse's reins in one hand and his riding crop in the other.

It was Courtenay who spoke first. "You look well."

"It's a new coat."

Courtenay took off his hat and ran a hand through his coal-dark hair. "That's not what I meant. You look healthy."

"Of course I'm healthy." Julian knew he sounded peeved but that was the only note he could manage to hit. It was either silence or irritability. "I've been having those . . . episodes for a while now, and I'm good at recovering."

"I'm glad to hear it." For some reason, Julian's peevishness seemed to amuse Courtenay, because he smiled. "Did you come all this distance to be difficult?"

No, by God. But he wasn't sure he could put into words the reason why he had come. "It wasn't that far," he said, because he was evidently intent on digging his hole deeper. "I'm staying in Richmond." He took a deep breath. "I was surprised to hear that you were here, of all places."

Courtenay cut a glance to where the surveyor and land agent stood, looking at a large sheet of paper. "Drainage ditches," he said, as if that explained it. And it did, come to think, because if Courtenay was attending to drainage ditches then he must be planning to do something with the property other than let it go to waste.

"Are you still going to let the house to Radnor?"

"Yes. I need the money, as you well know. I'll stay in the dower house. Then I'll be near Simon too."

That was a thoroughly sensible plan. Some of Julian's surprise must have shown on his face, because Courtenay said, "I went through the contents of that trunk, and—"

"Did you really?"

"Well, I had Beauchamp's help. He's the land agent. I'm not a total idiot, you know."

"Yes, I do know." He was far from it.

"I just didn't want to think about all that."

"Understandable."

They stood in silence for a moment. "Why did you come here, Julian?"

"I had the most improbable story from London about a duel and thought you might shed some light on the matter." That wasn't why he had come. He could have written to Standish and gotten a fair account. Hell, he didn't even need to do that. All he had to do was think about it for ten seconds and he understood what Courtenay and Standish had planned. There were babies in their cradles who could have figured it out. "Since I know you weren't having an affair with Eleanor, I assume somebody overheard that set-to in the drawing room and wondered if there was another possible pairing of lovers in the house. So you and Standish spread a different rumor to save my neck. In the process, you've cemented your reputation as a scoundrel, Standish is now a cuckold, and Eleanor a wanton woman. I owe you a thanks."

"I don't want to see you pilloried," Courtenay said, so low it was a whisper. "You must know that I'd do more than that to spare you the danger." And Julian did know, so he gave a brief nod of his head. "Besides," Courtenay went on, "you ought to thank Standish. He's the one who has to shoot me next week."

Julian tried not to shudder. "Nonsense. You'll delope. You've educated me on this process already, you recall."

"Indeed. There won't be blood. But," Courtenay said, a gleam of understanding in his eyes, "you already knew that. So why did you come, Julian? I'm not going to ask again." He was giving Julian a chance to . . . to what? Apologize? Declare himself?

"I . . ." His voice faltered, and then he said the only thing he could admit to. "I've come to discuss the terms of that debt you entered into the last time I visited Carrington," he said, in case they were overheard, and also because he knew Courtenay would understand immediately. Indeed, Courtenay's eyes flared. He had promised to fuck Julian, and now Julian thought he had a good chance of collecting.

"Ah. Well, I do make it a point to pay my debts when they come due." He held Julian's gaze for another moment. There was something like disappointment in Courtenay's eyes. "But is that all?"

It wasn't. Not even close. "I . . ." He shook his head. The rest of it would have to wait until they had some privacy.

Courtenay frowned. It likely said nothing favorable about his character that he was abandoning his efforts at a useful life to once again waste his time in bed.

But this time, with great determination and the headache-inducing tallying of funds, he and his bailiff had hired people to do the work that needed to be done on Carrington, and had plans to visit his other properties and do the same. So, Courtenay's momentarily stepping away wasn't abdicating his responsibility.

And fucking Julian was about the farthest thing from a waste of time he could imagine. Even if they never saw one another again, even if Julian truly believed the worst of Courtenay, Courtenay couldn't believe that a moment spent with the man he loved was truly a waste. Some other time he'd figure out how to love more wisely, but for now he loved Julian and that was all there was to it. However long he had with Julian, he'd accept those hours and minutes like a gift from a God who hadn't always been overly generous with him.

If Julian had ridden over an hour for a fucking, then that's what he'd get.

Julian turned his horse over to a stable hand and Courtenay led the way to the dower house, the backs of their hands occasionally brushing together. Courtenay didn't even try to make conversation.

"Here," Courtenay said gruffly when they approached the path that led to the dower house.

"Here?" Julian echoed, in that way Courtenay had once found irritating and now found endearing beyond all belief.

"I've been clearing the cobwebs and making it habitable." It wasn't grand, wasn't nearly as fine as Julian's London lodgings. He held the door open, watching with surely disproportionate anxiety as Julian entered.

Courtenay had pulled the dust covers off the furniture himself, and had assigned a few of the housemaids his mother had left behind the task of making the place reasonably ready. It was spare but tidy, with few furnishings but fresh paint and plenty of light. Although he was still staying at the main house until Radnor arrived, he had his books shelved here, and it felt like a place that could be his home in a future that didn't feel bleak. But for now all that mattered was that it was private: no servants, no chance of anyone intruding on them.

Julian turned around in a slow circle and Courtenay found that he was holding his breath, waiting for a reaction.

"This is the house your mother declined to live in? It's perfectly lovely. I suppose she has terrible taste along with all her other flaws." He looked over his shoulder at Courtenay, an adorably amused expression on his face. "How long did it take for the lot of them to clear out of here after you arrived?"

Courtenay laughed, giddy again with the thrill of Julian's thorns and prickles being used to protect him. "Less than two days." He took hold of the sleeve of Julian's coat and pulled him close so they were chest to chest. "I'm glad you like it."

"I do." He was looking so intently at Courtenay that it seemed he was referring to more than the dower house.

"Now, I have a debt to discharge, it seems."

Julian's gaze cut away. "I wasn't being quite serious about that, you know."

The bulge in his breeches argued otherwise. "Too bad. You rode all this way for my cock and I intend to give it to you."

Julian made a sound low in his throat. "Is that something you'd like to do today? I don't want to presume." He sounded like he was talking about borrowing a book or staying for supper.

Courtenay tried unsuccessfully to suppress a smile. "I'd very much like to fuck you," he said into Julian's hair. "I'd like it excessively." Another helpless hum of interest from Julian. Courtenay turned them both around so the bright spring sun shone on Julian's face and examined him at arm's length.

He really did look well, as if he had never fallen ill. Thank God. He kept one hand on Julian's elbow and brought the other to cup his jaw, then did what he had longed to do since seeing Julian's horse approach. He leaned in and brushed his lips against Julian's, and it felt like the continuation of that tragic kiss in Eleanor's drawing room, gentle and un-demanding, the unhurried touch of two people who had all the time they needed, infinite stores of love, and absolutely no fear.

It was a lie, of course. But it was nice to pretend.

He deepened the kiss, making it into the desperate and urgent embrace that it truly was, the kiss of a man who shouldn't even take this time with his beloved but who would steal it anyway.

Julian pulled away. "Before we do this, I have to tell you something. If I could go back and choose not to write that book, I would."

"I know that," Courtenay said quickly. He tried to pull Julian closer but Julian wouldn't cooperate.

"I never want you to feel any pain or sorrow. Ever." Julian sounded both fierce and sad. "Least of all by my hand. But, Courtenay, I also don't want you ever to believe that I could wish you harm. I want only good things for you—happiness and acceptance and . . ." He waved his hand, as if unable to find the right words. He looked agonized.

"You don't have to do this," Courtenay said, stroking Julian's cheek with his thumb. "I know you regret it."

"You deserve an apology, Courtenay. Even if you don't think you do. Even if you never want to see me again after today, please understand that I wish you only the best and that you deserve the best."

Julian looked like he'd fight to the death any person who thought Courtenay didn't deserve all the finest loveliest things. Courtenay had never seen him so angry and so vulnerable. "I . . ." Courtenay cleared his throat. "Thank you. I accept your apology." Wordlessly, he led the way up the stairs to the room he intended to make his own in the vague future where this was his home. The windows were bare, so the room was bright with unfiltered spring sunlight. The bed was only covered by a plain sheet, but it was large and soft.

He let Julian shove him onto the bed, relishing the show of strength, the proof that he was wanted, maybe even needed, by this man, now, despite everything. Then he returned the favor, tugging Julian down hard on top of him, so they were sprawled together across the bed.

They made a graceless scramble out of their clothes, hungrily devouring one another with their gazes, as if they both knew this would be the last time they could see one another like this. "I love you," Courtenay said, because he might never get another chance to say so.

Julian stared at him, an expression of bewilderment on his face. "Really?" he asked, propping himself up on one elbow but not pulling away.

Courtenay was certain he had ruined the moment, had destroyed his chances of having even this. "Yes, really," he said. "Since you came with me to Carrington the first time." Maybe even before that, but it wasn't as if these things began at obvious moments. Falling in love wasn't like a bird hatching from an egg, for all both events were rather messy and fraught with vulnerability.

"That's what I had suspected," Julian said, his brow wrinkled, as if Courtenay's declaration required him to reorganize the contents of his brilliant mind.

"Had you now?" Courtenay shouldn't be amused when he was worried that at any moment Julian might put his breeches back on and leave him forever, but he couldn't imagine a world where he didn't find all Julian's strangeness amusing and adorable.

"You shouldn't have wanted to be around me after finding out I wrote that book," he said with the air of man mentally calculating sums, "but you stayed with me when I was sick. I . . ." And then, in a totally different voice, "I liked that."

Courtenay's heart started to pound. "Why did you like it?" He didn't need to hear that Julian loved him in return. It wouldn't matter—they'd part company one way or the other, and giving a name to the thing between them wouldn't change that. But Courtenay was used to wanting things that didn't make any sense.

"Because you're my favorite person," Julian said simply.

Courtenay thought his days of being shocked were over and done with. He thought he had heard everything it was possible to hear, in bed or out of it. But at Julian's words, he thought his heart might stop beating. There was no other declaration that could have laid him so bare or pleased him so much.

"I think you might be my favorite person as well," Courtenay said, and felt something like a blush rise to his cheeks, as if this statement cost more than his earlier profession of love. His heart felt near to bursting. "I probably ought to get on with fucking you before you change your mind," he added, wanting to get back to safer, more familiar ground.

"Do you have oil?" Julian asked.

Of course he had oil. Did he think Courtenay intended to fuck him dry? "In that drawer," he said, gesturing.

Julian got the oil and put it within reach and then leaned back down so his body covered Courtenay's, relaxing over him with a sigh.

Courtenay rolled them both over and kissed Julian until he was squirming beneath him. Yes, this was what they both needed. This was what they had, this connection, raw desire and unchecked passion mixed with just enough affection to complicate things badly.

"Yes," Julian breathed, arching his body to meet Courtenay's, desperate and pleading.

Courtenay used his knees to push Julian's legs apart, then bent down to swipe his tongue over the man's rigid cock. Julian nearly sprang off the bed at that, so Courtenay kept going. The last time—the only time—Courtenay had done this to Julian, Julian had used his mouth with a vigor Courtenay hadn't ever expected from the polished and urbane Mr. Medlock. But now he was almost docile, lying prone on Courtenay's bed.

Courtenay understood that. Sometimes it felt right to be the one doing the fucking, the taking, the doing. Other times it was lovely to have all that done to you. For you. He would do anything to, for, or with Julian that the man wanted.

He teased the head of Julian's cock with his tongue, licking around the crown and into the slit before drawing him down deep into his mouth. He slid his finger into his mouth before stroking lower, finding Julian's entrance and pressing in. He paused when he heard Julian's gasp and felt him clench around his finger, but then tasted the salt of his desire and continued on. Everything about this felt right, felt like they ought to have been doing this forever, Julian open and yielding, Courtenay kneeling with something like devotion, both of them giving themselves up to this. To one another.

He added another finger, then curved and twisted them so his fingertips would touch the spot he sought. Julian moaned, and Courtenay pulled his mouth away so he could properly see Julian's face. How had he ever thought Julian ordinary-looking? He was perfect. Looking at him felt like the answer to a question Courtenay had been asking for as long as he could remember, a question that wasn't formed with words.

Still stroking Julian, he reached for the oil and slicked himself up. "How do you want it?" he asked, needing to know exactly what Julian wanted from him so he could deliver precisely that. He knew Julian would have an answer and he wanted to know what it was.

Julian rolled over and tucked his knees under his chest. Courtenay groaned and stroked himself, admiring the sight of that round arse before lining his cock up with Julian's entrance and starting to push in. He felt Julian reflexively tighten around him, so he paused, gritting his teeth and digging his fingers into Julian's hips. Then Julian pushed back and Courtenay sank inside with a groan. "Oh, God, Julian. The way you feel." He stayed still for a moment, savoring the tightness and the heat wrapped around him, appreciating the dip of Julian's spine and the strength of his shoulders and back. Julian was resting his head on his folded arms, and the half of his face that Courtenay could see was a study in agonized pleasure: lips parted, eyelids heavy, beads of sweat forming on his forehead.

"I never want to forget what you look like right now," Courtenay groaned as he started to move. "You look like you belong to me." It was half a lie, because Courtenay knew that he belonged to Julian. Or maybe it was all the same thing.

Julian turned his face into the pillow and said something that might have been "I do," or might have been anything else. He was pushing hard against Courtenay now, encouraging him to go harder, faster, more. Courtenay did. He put one hand on Julian's back, bracing himself but also holding Julian still, and with the other hand he grasped Julian's prick. It was as hard a cock as he'd ever felt in his life, and at the first touch Julian cried out in pleasure, the beginnings of his release spilling against Courtenay's hand.

Courtenay felt the stirrings of his own climax, and gave Julian more, gave them both more, because the two of them were all that he knew to be real and true and important.

Chapter Twenty-Four

Julian lay collapsed on his stomach, Courtenay an unseen weight half on top of him, equally inert. They lay there until Courtenay's breathing became so regular Julian thought he had to be asleep. He tried to slide out from under Courtenay, but Courtenay's arm tightened around his chest.

"Stay here," Courtenay said, his words muffled by Julian's hair.

It would be so easy to say yes, to linger with his back pressed against Courtenay's hard chest, basking in the illusion of safety. "I need to get back."

"Your arse will be in no condition to get on a horse."

"Yes, well, thank you for that," he said, putting some sourness into his voice for no reason at all other than the fear of what lay on the other side of his crumbling defenses.

"That's what you wanted," Courtenay said. "That's what you came for. Tell me."

Julian, besotted idiot that he was, didn't care that a trap had been set for him. Of course he'd reassure Courtenay that the urgent fucking he had given had been exactly what Julian had craved. "You know it was," he admitted. His prick was pulsing again at the memory, and he could feel Courtenay's length hardening behind him. "I want to feel it as I ride home. I want to remember that you were inside me."

Courtenay groaned and buried his face in Julian's neck, and the solid warmth of him was almost enough to make Julian want to stay here.

"I need to leave," he said, wriggling out from Courtenay's grasp.

"Stay here," Courtenay said again. "At Carrington Hall, I mean. There's nothing remarkable about that—a gentleman availing himself of another gentleman's hospitality instead of making a long trip at the end of a day."

"I missed you," Julian said once he was standing firmly on the floor, safely away from the temptation of Courtenay's embrace. The problem was that now he could see Courtenay, beautiful and rumpled, his hair everywhere, his lips swollen from kissing.

"I missed you too," Courtenay said, a smile playing on that wicked mouth. "So stay longer."

If he played his cards right, there would be plenty of time later on for lingering in bed. But he now had to get to work if he wanted to undo some of the mischief Courtenay and Standish had gotten up to. Julian stepped into his breeches, trying to put something, anything between him and Courtenay's body.

"Missing you is profoundly inconvenient, I'll have you know. I have things to do and places to be, and all the while

I'll feel like I've mislaid a piece of my soul and I won't get it back until I see you again. That can't be normal."

Courtenay stared at him with mute astonishment before stepping forward and taking his hands. "That's a lovely thing to say. Didn't think you had it in you, Julian."

"Bollocks." Julian tried to pull his hands away, but Courtenay held fast. "You can't tell me that this is how people always feel when they love one another."

Courtenay pulled him closer, so Julian could feel the warmth coming from his body. "I'm not the seasoned expert you take me for," he murmured into Julian's ear, "but I gather it's a common experience."

"How dreadful." Julian put some sham chilliness into his voice, mainly because he liked when Courtenay tried to cuddle him out of his frosty moods. Indeed, Courtenay's hands were now sliding suspiciously low along Julian's hips and arse.

"It's terrible, isn't it?" Courtenay was doing a bad job of suppressing a smile.

"How can you stand it?"

"There's only one way. By being together."

Much, much later, after they had returned to bed and gotten dressed once again, Julian cleared his throat.

"If you and I are to remain . . . friendly, and carry on with this plan of not missing one another, first I need to clean up the mess you all made about this duel. Eleanor may be a genius about rocks but I wish you'd all leave polite society to me."

Courtenay's arms were around him again. "Gladly. We did what we could to protect you. You have two people—

three if you include Standish, which seems only fair—who love you and don't want to see you die or harmed," he murmured. "That's not a bad thing."

Julian felt his defenses crumbling, his heart scattering into fragments that he'd never collect.

Julian was sitting in the library at Carrington Hall, his hands clasped in front of his mouth, obviously deep in thought. He had insisted that they remove immediately to the main house so his plotting could disguise itself as a normal social call. Courtenay had agreed. Of course he had. He'd like a lifetime of opportunities to acquiesce to Julian's every whim.

Tea was carried in by a curtsying housemaid and Courtenay asked that she also bring up a plate of biscuits or whatever sweets the kitchens could come up with on such short notice, and she returned with a tray heaped with raisin-studded saffron buns and an entire treacle tart, as if the cook had been waiting for an opportunity to send up a feast.

Courtenay had the impression that the staff were doing their best to impress him. On his first day here, he had gone down to the kitchens himself and apologetically requested that a tray of something, anything, be sent up to him. He had been astonished to find that he remembered the cook from when he was a boy. Stranger still, she seemed pleased to see him. "It's right to have the master here," she had said, and he had heard the sentiment echoed repeatedly by people in the village. He belonged here. And while it offended his egalitarian principles that he was welcomed principally by virtue of his being the lord of the manor, he supposed beggars couldn't be choosers, and he was glad for the warm welcome he received, regardless of the cause. He was going to try his damnedest to earn their respect.

He poured out two cups of tea. By now he knew how Julian liked it—sweet beyond all reckoning and nearly as white as milk. He put a thick slice of the tart and a buttery bun on a plate and set it before him. Julian absently picked up the bun and took a bite out of it, making a happy, satisfied sound that Courtenay delighted in.

"How do you find the best pastries?" he said, popping the rest of the bun into his mouth.

"I really don't," he said, although he probably ought to take credit for it. "This is just what the kitchen sent."

"Your cook must be in love with you."

"She's sixty years old and knew me as a baby."

"Well, you must have some talent in inspiring bakers to ply their craft excessively well, because I swear that every morsel I've eaten in your company has been better than anything else I've ever had." And then he paused, a forkful of treacle tart halfway to his mouth, and blushed deeply, as if realizing what Courtenay had known for weeks now. "I suppose it's the company. It's part of your sinister charm, no doubt. Do you still have that pistol?"

Startled by this abrupt change in conversation, Courtenay asked, "Do you mean the one you shot my wall with?"

"Yes, because I know it shoots straight."

Courtenay retrieved the pistol from the drawer where he had decided to keep it—it was a strange thing, distributing two trunks' worth of belongings across a house of this size. He figured he'd find out what Julian was planning soon enough. Meanwhile, Julian had risen from his chair and was pacing the length of the room. The man never looked happier than when he was scheming. "It's loaded," he said, handing it carefully over.

Julian took the pistol and held it, his finger off the trigger, then proceeded to lock the library door. "Now sit in that chair," he said gesturing to the chair he had just vacated.

Courtenay complied, faintly amused by the fact that Julian had a deadly weapon in one hand and a half-eaten saffron bun in the other.

Then Julian raised the pistol and aimed it at him.

Courtenay didn't move a hair but he braced himself. This must have shown on his face because Julian dropped the pistol to his side. "I'm not going to shoot you, you pillock!"

"That's a relief," Courtenay said with feigned nonchalance.

"I needed to know where to aim the bloody thing to make it look right, and it's the whorl in the paneling just next to your left shoulder."

"Quite," Courtenay said, his heart still beating madly.

"You really thought I was going to shoot you and you sat stock-still!"

"I knew you weren't going to actually harm me. Maybe wing me. Draw a bit of blood for whatever fell purpose you're entertaining."

Julian was staring at him. "You trust me that much?"

"You're a terribly good shot, so I knew you wouldn't hit anything vital."

Julian slid the pistol onto the nearest table and crossed the room in three strides. "I wasn't going to shoot you at all."

"Well, I understand that now," Courtenay said, not quite grasping why Julian had that look on his face. But then Julian was sitting astride his lap, kissing him fiercely, and he didn't care anymore.

If Julian had ever thought he understood the faintest, sorriest thing about love, he now knew he was wrong. Love was somebody aiming a pistol at your heart while you sat there and acted like it was perfectly fine because you trusted them. Courtenay perhaps had always known that, had always been open to that kind of love and trust and the danger that came with both.

Julian would learn how to exist alongside such an unreasonable emotion. Somehow.

But first he had a wall to shoot.

"Come over here," he said, extracting himself from the circle of Courtenay's arms and getting to his feet. Courtenay at his side, he turned and aimed at the spot in the paneling he had marked out. He braced himself and fired the pistol, sparing only the briefest of glances to confirm that he had hit his mark. Then he pressed one last kiss to Courtenay's mouth before they'd be interrupted by the servants who would inevitably come running.

"What's our story?" Courtenay asked.

"I tried to shoot you because of the malicious falsehoods I mistakenly believed you spread about my sister. I missed."

"While I was sitting. Unsporting of you."

"I was outraged, you see. And later on, when you forgive me, it will be that much more magnanimous of you. Lord Courtenay, having sowed his wild oats, returned to a quiet life at his ancestral seat. He was accosted in a most vicious manner by the common son of a merchant."

"Why did we have tea before the shooting?"

"I wanted to take you unawares."

"Very unsporting indeed."

"But now I've vented my spleen and I feel the score is even. After your servants come—ah, I hear pounding at the door, so you might as well open it and assure them there isn't a corpse—I'll go back to Lady Montbray and then to London. The duel will be quite unnecessary. Nobody will be firing any pistols anywhere near you, not while I'm still breathing."

Courtenay let in the butler and assured him that all was well and that he and Mr. Medlock had merely settled a dispute in a rash way. Julian took his leave, coolly shaking hands with the man he loved while ten wide-eyed servants looked on.

Chapter Twenty-Five

It turned out that there was nothing like getting shot at to stir up local sympathy. If Courtenay hadn't known what Julian was capable of, he might have thought it a mere coincidence. But since he knew Julian was nothing less than a genius, he understood that this response was exactly what Julian had intended.

The magistrate called on him the very evening of the incident to inquire if Courtenay was in need of any assistance, and then proceeded to enjoy one of the last bottles remaining in the Carrington cellars while bemoaning the sad behavior of today's youth.

"Mr. Medlock had heard some untrue rumors about his sister," Courtenay said mildly, just as Julian had instructed him. "I daresay I'd have done the same."

"Yes, well, in my day we did that sort of thing out-of-doors."

Courtenay couldn't argue with that.

The next morning brought the vicar and his daughter—the redoubtable Miss Chapman who had been his mother's aide de camp—carrying with them a bottle of elderflower cordial and tales of a church steeple that needed replacing. Courtenay was about to commit to financing the repair, because that was plainly what they intended, when inspiration struck. "I daresay we ought to let Mr. Medlock have the honor. He's devilish awkward about what happened yesterday and this would give him a chance to make things right." The vicar and Miss Chapman left, doubtless intending to spread the tale of hapless Mr. Medlock. Courtenay wrote to Julian in London about the steeple, but didn't get a letter in return.

It was a steady stream of callers after that, and Courtenay returned each call in turn. If anything, the neighborhood seemed vaguely disappointed that Courtenay wasn't more obvious a sinner. If you were going to have a reprobate in the neighborhood, it seemed a waste to have but a reformed one, a man who had quite properly left London when his name got mixed up with a married lady's, and then got himself shot at when he was entirely unarmed—truly, you could go into the library at Carrington Hall and see the bullet hole for yourself! But at least the man who had done the shooting—a confused young man, easily swayed by gossip—was replacing the church steeple. That had to count for something, everyone agreed.

In this way, Courtenay was transformed from a wild scoundrel to something tame. The stories told about him were in the past tense. Any village gossips who hoped to see ladies of ill repute being ferried in from London were sadly disappointed; Courtenay didn't host so much as a single orgy nor even a dinner party. He kept country hours and evidently intended to let the house to some relation or connection of his with an even finer title than his own.

Two weeks passed in an orderly progression of morning calls and visits with the bailiff and land agent, without a single word from Julian. Of course he could hardly swan in after firing pistols in the library, but Courtenay had expected something. Every additional day he became less certain of what terms they had parted on. At the time, Courtenay had been certain that they were to build a future together, a future of shared time and shared touches, a future that dazzled Courtenay with a shining brightness he could hold in his hand and keep close.

But now he wasn't so sure. Perhaps he had been confused. Perhaps that wasn't what Julian had intended at all. Perhaps the fact that they loved one another mattered as little as he had feared.

And then Courtenay would be left with the other side of Eleanor's strange rock, not the dizzying crystals but the workaday stone of neighborhood calls and land stewardship, the anticipation of Simon's arrival in a few weeks, the crops that were growing lushly across his land. There was work to do, and he'd get along fine without the dazzling crystal. The gray rock would be enough.

He was walking through the gardens when one of the young stable boys came running. He hadn't had the heart to sack any of the stable hands or grooms, even though there weren't any horses for them to tend to. The stables were empty, his mother having taken the horses with her. Courtenay thought that what he really ought to do was acquire horses for the servants to tend to, even though he could ill afford such an expense. This was likely a backwards way of dealing with things, but this was his property and if he wanted to use his scant available funds to purchase horses and implement some kind of breeding program, then that's what he'd do.

"What's the matter, lad?" he asked the panting stable boy.

"There's a great big black stallion that the man says is yours."

"Mine?" Courtenay echoed. A thought—impossible but lovely—occurred to him. "Does he have any markings?"

"A white sock on his left foreleg, my lord."

Courtenay broke into a run in the direction the boy had arrived from. It was indeed Niccolo, and none the worse for the past few months apart. The horse nickered in recognition, and Courtenay ran his hands all over the animal's glossy coat. "How did this happen?" he asked the man who had brought the horse.

"There's a letter, m'lord," the man said, doffing his cap.

Courtenay took the letter. His name was written across the front in Julian's bold slanted hand. Courtenay broke the seal unsteadily.

My Dear Lord Courtenay,

   Please accept the return of your horse as a token of both my esteem and my earnest desire to apologize for my bad behavior and slanderous accusations earlier this month. I blush to add that I must impose on you even in the making of

amends. During your horse's stay in Wiltshire, he befriended
a chestnut mare. In order to secure your horse's return, I had
to agree to purchase the mare as well. Unfortunately, I have
no way of stabling an additional horse; thus I must depend on
your kindness and understanding to give shelter to this poor
beast whose acquaintance was the one happy outcome of your
own dear horse's exile. She has all the spirit of a chaise longue,
and therefore will admirably suit your nephew or perhaps
your new tenant's secretary, at least until she delivers herself of
the foal she undoubtedly carries.

Since I rode the mare from Wiltshire, she is currently
waiting for you in the stables of the Three Oaks, which is
where I intend to break my journey back to London. If
you hear that I passed through the neighborhood, you'll
understand that I didn't wish to burden you with my
presence and the noisome memories of our last encounter.

> *Yours in most sincere friendship,*
> *Julian Medlock*

Courtenay tried to school his expression into something
other than raucous joy, but that wasn't possible, so he buried
his face in his horse's mane. In one masterstroke, Julian had
restored Courtenay's horse, given him a broodmare, and come
up with an excuse for the two of them to meet.

Courtenay saddled Niccolo himself and rode to the Three
Oaks. For half a second he wondered why Julian hadn't come
to Carrington, but then realized that Julian intended them to
have a public reconciliation. That would be the final genius
of Julian's plan—Courtenay would get to be generous and

decent by forgiving a man who had tried to shoot him in such an unsportsmanlike way. Courtenay was fairly dazzled. If this was what the man was capable of at four and twenty years, what would he be doing ten, twenty, years from now? Courtenay fully intended to be by his side to find out for himself.

Julian assumed an air of ashamed embarrassment when Courtenay walked through the inn's door, when what he really wanted to do was get to his feet and fling himself into Courtenay's arms. It had been a long two weeks. He and Eleanor had apologized to one another profusely and apologetically. Apologies were easy when you were happy, Julian now understood. Gratitude was even easier, and Julian was intensely grateful for his sister and brother-in-law's asinine scheming to save his neck. He even refrained from telling them how they could have gone about it better.

He felt like he had a stockpile of warm sentiments and he could distribute them freely and without restraint. He had spent years being miserly with his affections until he had learned better from Courtenay. Being loved by someone as open and generous as Courtenay filled Julian's coffers, and now he could afford to be less cheap. Maybe it was just knowing that he was capable of loving someone and worthy of being loved in return that did the trick.

Eleanor, herself basking in the affections of a plainly smitten husband, was similarly inclined. Ned's basket of rocks—geodes and fossils and strange things Julian couldn't identify—must have won her over. Or maybe they had loved one another all along and only had to find a way to trust that they were loved in return.

Courtenay was scanning the tap room, plainly seeking Julian out. Julian didn't try to draw attention to himself, partly because he was still playing a role and partly because he wanted to savor this moment of Courtenay searching for him, eyes darting across the room until finally finding Julian and filling with relief.

Yes, that was how it was when your soul was in pieces and somebody else had one of them. Only when you were together would the pieces fit into place and become whole.

Courtenay made his way across the room and slid into the seat across from Julian. Julian needed a moment to figure out how to not reach across the table and clasp his hand, stroke his arm, anything. He shoved the pot of tea across the table.

"You ordered tea," Courtenay said.

"I like tea," Julian responded.

"You like sugary milk." Courtenay, as if to demonstrate the point, poured about an inch of tea into Julian's cup and then added a nearly equal amount of sugar before stirring it and sloshing in some milk. When he slid the cup over to Julian, their knuckles brushed.

"I *love* sugary milk," Julian said, and he was surprised to find that he was a little choked up, his voice thick and his eyes prickling with utterly unnecessary tears. Of course Courtenay had come, there had never been any question. He was reckless and loving and kind and of course he had come to Julian. But the loveliness of it, sitting at a table in a tavern with the person who possessed a stray fragment of his soul, and knowing they could do it again and again, that there were meals and moments stretching out infinitely before them—it was more than he could bear with equanimity. Even the poor inadequacy of the charade—they couldn't touch, couldn't speak freely, had to endure the absurd pantomime of reconciling after a quarrel that they had only staged to prevent the truth being found out—underlined the rare preciousness of what they truly had.

Julian sipped his tea, which Courtenay had doubtless intended as a parody of the tea he preferred but was actually the best tea he'd ever had.

Chapter Twenty-Six

It was July, and Courtenay felt warm to his bones, warmer than he had thought possible in England. He lounged in a cane chair on the bowling green at Carrington, watching Radnor's secretary and Simon attempt to assemble the herd of cats that had come to live here. Eleanor and Standish were spending a week at Carrington Hall before leaving on a voyage. They intended to go around the world and collect a good many rocks and butterflies and whatever else Eleanor fancied. Being joint subjects of a mild scandal had apparently been precisely what they needed to cement their new bond. Standish looked pleased as pie, quite possibly because he had unburdened himself of a half dozen bloody cats, who would now be living at Carrington Hall.

Courtenay had been about to congratulate himself on keeping the dower house serenely free of all feline visitors, when he noticed that Julian, who was deep in conversation with Radnor about the particulars of steeple engineering, was cradling a cat in the crook of his arm. It was the same cat who had taken a fancy to Julian during his illness. Well, that was fine. Courtenay liked cats. And if Julian required a cat, he could have as many cats as he damned well pleased.

Not that Julian—or any number of cats—was precisely living at the dower house. They couldn't share a house—at least not yet. Julian had insisted; they were, for all outward appearances, two men forging an unlikely friendship after the strangest of events. So, Julian had taken a house in the village, ostensibly to supervise the repair of the steeple. In the fall, they would go to Paris for a few weeks and enjoy greater proximity, before returning to Radnor's Cornwall estate for yuletide—Simon had declared Christmas at Penkellis to be a firm tradition, and everyone helplessly agreed. Later Julian and Courtenay would go to London for the season, where Courtenay, if all went as planned, would take up his seat in the House of Lords. If the kingdom wanted to throw the poor to the wolves, Courtenay at least wouldn't be silent about it. If they liked that cycle, they'd repeat it again the following year, a predictable pattern, together. Meanwhile, Courtenay was content to sleep at the dower house and spend his days weaving in and out of Julian's company, while working on his estate and playing with his nephew.

He knew Julian would fall ill again. That would also be part of the pattern, part of the cycle that organized their lives. Julian's attitude toward his illness seemed to be mostly irritation that he was occasionally bedridden. He didn't dread recurrences, so Courtenay decided to follow his lead. No use in being morbid, no sense in grieving losses that might never come to pass. They had laid up a stockpile of tincture and that was the best that could be done. And looking at Julian now, sun-bronzed from time spent out of doors, a crop of freckles on his nose that Courtenay pretended he hadn't noticed, it was easy to believe that his episodes were minor aberrations.

Sometimes when Courtenay came home from calling on tenants or supervising improvements, he found Julian already waiting for him in his study, scribbling something on a loose sheet of paper. When Courtenay had crept up on him and peered over his shoulder, he saw a passage involving Don Lorenzo.

"I thought he had fallen into a ravine," Courtenay had said, startling Julian so he nearly jumped out of his chair.

"People survive these things all the time in gothic novels," Julian had said. "Besides, this isn't for publication."

"Oh? May I read it? When it's done, that is. I did enjoy *The Brigand Prince*, despite everything."

"Oh, you'll read it all right," Julian had said, with a look of intent mischief. Courtenay gathered that this manuscript was something filthy and was dearly looking forward to reading it.

That pleasant line of thought was interrupted when Eleanor started waving at a carriage in the distance.

"Oh, hell," Radnor said. "I thought we'd have until supper at least." He looked rattled, the way he always did when he had to talk to people outside the circle he tolerated—a circle that now, startlingly, included Courtenay and, by extension, Julian. Courtenay watched approvingly as the secretary angled himself so that he was closer to Radnor. Radnor's dog, who Courtenay had previously mistaken for an enormous rolled-up carpet or a sack of laundry, had slept through the cat invasion and the arrival of a carriage, but at his master's mild distress he perked up an ear.

The carriage approached and came to a stop. Out tumbled a towheaded boy in short pants, followed by two ladies who descended more gracefully, one in a sea of pale blue muslin and the other in a gray traveling costume. Courtenay squinted and pushed his hat back to get a better view. It was Lady Montbray and her companion. "We're a bit early," Lady Montbray cried. "But Julian said William could have a cat if we hurried."

William, he assumed, was the child who was presently chasing one of the more spirited animals. "You can have three cats, at the very least," Courtenay said, rising to his feet and kissing the air over Lady Montbray's glove before clasping Miss Sutherland's hand in warm affection. "They come and go in multiples of three."

"You're funning, Uncle Courtenay," Simon said. He was a grave child, but a content one. And about twice as clever as he needed to be. He'd start school again soon enough and then there'd be no telling what he'd become.

"You caught me." Courtenay ran his fingers through Simon's hair, as golden in the sun as his mother's had been. Happier and luckier than Isabella ever had been, surrounded by a small regiment of adults intent on spoiling him silly. Simon would have what Isabella never had, what Courtney himself had to fight to learn—he'd know that he was loved, he'd know that he deserved whatever joy his life would bring him, he'd know his worth and never doubt it.

There came the sound of hoof beats and carriage wheels, and a curricle came into view, being driven at an alarming pace before it stopped short. Two gentlemen descended. One of them, Courtenay immediately recognized as being some relation of Lady Montbray's—same guinea-gold hair, same general air of refined prettiness. And indeed, she threw her arms around the man, greeting him as Oliver. So, this was her brother, the scapegrace. Didn't look like much of a hellion. The other man, though, had none of Oliver Rivington's sunny smiling cheer. He looked like he had been brought to Carrington Hall as a hostage.

Except . . . Courtenay narrowed his eyes. Rivington wasn't touching the dark, scowling fellow. But the way they weren't touching was familiar to Courtenay because it was the way he and Julian didn't touch one another in public. Leaning a bit close, gazing a bit too long, reaching out but pulling back at the last minute. It was as if they were deeply conscious of all the ways they could have been touching but weren't. Well, well. This was shaping up to be a profoundly irregular picnic. Courtenay strolled across the lawn and got a better look at the new arrivals.

At that same moment, Radnor's secretary approached and gripped the scowling man's shoulder. "Jack, I had no idea to expect you. Did you mean to surprise me?" he asked, beaming.

"I'm the one who was surprised," the scowling man, Jack, said. "Oliver put me in his bloody curricle and didn't stop until we got here."

"Well done, Rivington," the secretary said, clapping Rivington on the back. And then to Jack, "I haven't seen you in weeks."

"That's because I'm in London, with everybody and everything a reasonable person could possibly want to see. And where are you? First Cornwall and now frolicking in some kind of fucking glen?"

"I believe it's a bowling green, but I won't stand on particulars."

"Place is crawling with gentlemen." Jack was a larger, rougher version of the secretary. And, sure enough, when Julian introduced Rivington, who then presented Jack to Courtenay, it turned out they were indeed brothers.

And if the secretary hadn't arranged for his brother's visit, that meant Julian must have done so. Courtenay found Julian in the growing crowd and raised a questioning eyebrow. Julian responded with a satisfied little smile. This gathering was his gift to all of them; he had assembled a group of people who were all, Courtenay realized, safe with one another. They all shared the same secret, or could be trusted to keep that secret for their loved ones. Nobody was likely to be free with their affections—servants were always at hand, gossip was always a commodity—but it was worth something to know that one was loved for one's entire self, without any need to hide anything in the shadows.

Courtenay shook hands all around and settled back into his chair, tilting his face up to catch the sun and watching the company from beneath half-lowered eyelids. All around him were the sounds of happy conversation, people who cared about one another sharing a moment of their lives. There would be more like that, moments when he would be dazzled by the joy around him. He must have dozed off for a bit, lulled into a happy stupor. When he opened his eyes, the sun was slightly lower in the sky and he had a kitten resting against his boot. He could hear Eleanor and Radnor engaged in a friendly debate—likely an argument about explosives or something about rocks—and slightly closer he heard Simon trying to teach Lady Montbray's child Italian while the boy's mother and her companion strolled in the distance. Standish and Julian were sitting on the garden steps, the secretary was smoking a cigarillo he had filched from Courtenay's stash while eying Radnor, and Jack Turner's scowl was now replaced with laughter as Rivington tried to persuade him to take home a cat.

Julian caught Courtenay's eye at that moment and flashed him a helpless smile that was just for him. Courtenay grinned lazily back and got to his feet to stand by his beloved and enjoy the gift of this summer afternoon.

AUTHOR'S NOTE

While malaria is an illness that can recur throughout a person's lifetime, Julian's health was especially poor in India because he was repeatedly re-infected. In London, free from the mosquitoes who transmit malaria, he only had to suffer through the recurrences of the original infection. The tincture Eleanor gives him is made from the bark of the South American cinchona tree, which was used to treat malaria beginning in the seventeenth century. Quinine, which was isolated from this bark a few years after this story takes place, is still used as a treatment for malaria.

Have you read all of Cat Sebastian's spellbinding romances? Keep reading for an excerpt from her critically acclaimed debut,

THE SOLDIER'S SCOUNDREL

A scoundrel who lives in the shadows

Jack Turner grew up in the darkness of London's slums, born into a life of crime and willing to do anything to keep his belly full and his siblings safe. Now he uses the tricks and schemes of the underworld to help those who need the kind of assistance only a scoundrel can provide. His distrust of the nobility runs deep and his services do not extend to the gorgeous high-born soldier who personifies everything Jack will never be.

A soldier untarnished by vice

After the chaos of war, Oliver Rivington craves the safe predictability of a gentleman's life—one that doesn't include sparring with a ne'er-do-well who flouts the law at every turn. But Jack tempts Oliver like no other man has before. Soon his yearning for the unapologetic criminal is only matched by Jack's pleasure in watching his genteel polish crumble every time they're together.

Two men meant only for each other

Available now from Avon Impulse!

CHAPTER ONE

Jack absently skimmed his finger along the surface of his desk, tracing a swirl through the sand he had used to blot his notes. Another case was solved and done with, another gentleman too drunk on his own power and consequence to remember to pay servants and tradesmen, too dissipated to bother being faithful to his wife. Nearly every client's problems were variations on that theme. Jack might have been bored if he weren't so angry.

A knock sounded at the door, a welcome distraction. His sister always knocked, as if she didn't want to interrupt whatever depravities Jack was conducting on the other side of the door. She did it out of an excess of consideration, but Jack still felt as if she were waiting for him to do something unspeakable at any moment.

She was right, of course, but still it grated.

"Come in, Sarah."

"There's a gentleman here to see you," she said, packing a world of both disapproval and deference into those few words.

Really, it was a pity she hadn't been born a man, because the world had lost a first-rate butler there. The butlers Jack had served under would have been put fairly to shame.

"Tell him to bugger off." Sarah knew perfectly well he didn't take gentlemen as clients. He tried to keep any trace of impatience out of his voice, but didn't think he quite managed it.

"I have customers downstairs and I don't want a scene." She had pins jammed into the sleeve of her gown, a sign that she had been interrupted in the middle of a fitting. No wonder her lips were pursed.

"And I don't want any gentlemen." Too late, he realized he had set her up for a smart-mouthed response. Now she was going to press her advantage, because that's what older sisters did. But Sarah must have been developing some restraint, or maybe she was only in a hurry, because all she did was raise a single eyebrow as if to say, *Like hell you don't.*

"I'm not your gatekeeper," she said a moment later, her tone deceptively mild. But on her last word Jack could hear a trace of that old accent they had both worked so hard to shed. Sarah had to be driven to distraction if she was letting her accent slip.

"Send him up, then," he conceded. This arrangement of theirs depended on a certain amount of compromise on both sides.

She vanished, her shoes scarcely making any sound on the stairs. A moment later he heard the heavier tread of a man not at all concerned about disturbing the clients below.

This man didn't bother knocking. He simply sailed

through the door Sarah had left ajar as if he had every right in the world to enter whatever place he pleased, at whatever time he wanted.

To hell with that. Jack took his time stacking his cards, pausing a moment to examine one with feigned and hopefully infuriating interest. The gentleman coughed impatiently; Jack mentally awarded himself the first point.

"Yes?" Jack looked up for the first time, as if only now noticing the stranger's presence. He could see why Sarah had pegged him straightaway as a gentleman. Everything about him, from his mahogany walking stick to his snowy white linen, proclaimed his status.

"You're Jack Turner?"

There was something about his voice—the absurd level of polish, perhaps—that made Jack look more carefully at his visitor's face.

Could it—? It couldn't be.

But it was.

"Captain Rivington," Jack said with all the nonchalance he could muster. "What brings you here?"

Jack saw Rivington's eyes go wide for one astonished instant before he gathered his wits. That was faster than most people, and Jack had to give him credit.

"Have we met?" the other man asked, his voice indicating exactly how unlikely it was that he would ever have met the likes of Jack Turner.

"Not exactly," Jack said, holding back the details as a matter of principle.

The truth was that a man would make a poor go of it in

this line of work if he couldn't remember a face like Rivington's. Though the last time Jack had encountered this pretty specimen of the English upper classes, the man had been a few years younger and didn't have that limp.

Nor that murderous look in his eye, for that matter.

What he'd had was his cock in the mouth of some other lazy young fool at his father's house party. That had made Rivington of particular interest to Jack. There were few enough men who shared Jack's preferences—let alone sons of earls—that he certainly wasn't likely to forget a single one. Jack had added that fact to the stockpile of secrets he kept, never knowing when he might need to avail himself of some especially unsavory truth.

Jack kept his gaze fixed expectantly on the other man's face. The fellow was handsome, Jack would hand him that. Fair hair, bright blue eyes, very tall, very thin. Not Jack's type, but nothing to sneeze at either. A pity about that limp.

"May I ask what type of business you run in this establishment?" The brusqueness of Rivington's tone suggested that he expected an answer.

And just for that, Jack decided he wasn't going to give him one. "I'm not taking gentlemen as clients at the moment." It was always an unexpected pleasure when the truth aligned with what he wanted to say.

"What the devil does that mean?" Rivington's hands were clenched into fists.

"My clients are ladies and other sorts of people who need help solving problems. Wealthy gentlemen seldom need the kinds of services I offer." That, and Jack would sooner have gouged out his eyeballs than work for an aristocratic man ever again.

Not to be trusted, that lot.

"Well, I certainly have a problem and you would seem to be the man to fix it," Rivington all but spat. "My sister paid two hundred pounds to someone of your name at this address."

Lady Montbray. Of course. The usual arrangement was for ladies to pay through Sarah's dress shop, so the expense would pass unnoticed by suspicious husbands or fathers. But Lady Montbray had quite a bit of her own money and had been moved to displays of extreme gratitude by the services Jack had rendered. She'd paid Jack directly, not to mention generously.

Not that Jack was going to tell this amusingly irate toff any of that. "Did she now?" he murmured. God, he wished he had someone here to admire how well he was getting this fellow's dander up. The poor sod's pretty face had practically turned red.

"You very well know that she did," Rivington said in tones that were clipped with barely restrained fury. "I'd like to know precisely what services you render, for such a fee."

Jack bet he would. Really, he ought to leave the matter there and refuse to say anything else. He half wanted to see what this fine gentleman would do if he got any angrier. But he also didn't want Rivington talking to magistrates or Bow Street Runners about him. The success of this operation depended on Jack's relative invisibility. He would have no clients at all if his business were exposed in the newspapers.

"As I said, I help people with problems. If a lady is wondering whether her servants are robbing her or whether her husband is playing her false, I find out. And I fix it." There were other situations he helped with, but he certainly wasn't discussing those predicaments today.

Not ever. Not with this man.

"You're saying that Charlotte—Lady Montbray—called upon you to solve some sort of domestic dispute?" Rivington shook his head, plainly incredulous. "I don't believe it. It's a ruse. Two hundred pounds! My God." His face was dark with a degree of anger that Jack guessed did not come readily to him. "I think you're a crook, Turner."

Jack gave the man his due for knowing a crook when he saw one, even though he had been more or less on the right side of the law as of late. "If any of my clients think I've defrauded them or failed to uphold our bargain, they can bring an action against me. But your opinion doesn't enter into it."

That was the whole point. This prig's opinion *didn't* matter. Two years earlier, Jack had set up this business to make himself independent of men like Rivington, and to do something to get other people out from under the thumbs of wealthy, highborn men. And there Rivington stood, carrying a beaver hat that a younger Jack would have pinched just on the principle of the thing. With a curl to his lip, Rivington surveyed Jack's shabby little study like he owned the place. Like he owned Jack.

But then the man helplessly scrubbed a hand through his pale hair. At the same time he shifted his weight onto his walking stick.

Jack stilled. It would never do to feel anything like compassion for this man, but then Jack was a practiced hand at overcoming any stray decent impulses. More worrisome were the decidedly indecent impulses he was feeling towards Captain Rivington. Even after four years, Jack had never quite been able to rid himself of the image of the young gentleman in the throes of passion, all that restraint and hauteur gone up in smoke.

Mercifully, there was a brisk rap on the door. "Come in, Sarah," Jack called.

"And now there's a lady here to see you. I'm sending her up. I have two ladies downstairs for fittings and heaven only knows where Betsy has gotten to," she said, already heading back down to her shop.

"If you'll excuse me, Captain Rivington, I need to meet with a client. I'm sure you'll understand the need for privacy." He could hear the lady's steps coming up the stairs.

Rivington made for the door before hesitating, then turning back to Jack. "No, I think I'll stay," he said, his voice thoughtful, his feet planted firmly on the floor.

"Not possible." There was no time for this nonsense. But Rivington didn't budge. "Good day, sir."

Rivington, blast him, raised a single eyebrow. Worse, his mouth quirked up in the beginnings of a smile. Oh, he knew perfectly well that he had the whip hand in this situation, did he? There was nothing Jack could do to get rid of him without risking a scene that would frighten off Sarah's customers or his own client. He certainly didn't want to turn their landlord's eye more closely to what was occurring on these premises.

Jack sighed, resigned. "Then stay, on the condition that you swear not to breathe a word of anything you see or hear in this room." Besides, if Rivington ever tried to breach a client's confidence it wouldn't take much for Jack to ruin him.

A comforting thought, as always.

Rivington regarded him for a moment. "I swear it."

The earnestness in his face was almost laughable. Ever so honorable, these gentlemen. Always so eager to uphold their oaths, to value their word. It was one of the few things they actually managed to get right, and maybe they ought to be encouraged, but it wouldn't be by Jack.

"Then sit over there." He gestured to an empty chair in a shadowy corner of the room. "And don't speak."

As Rivington sat, a spasm of pain crossed his face. It was brief, just as soon replaced with more bland aristocratic chilliness.

"Are you all right?" Jack asked, before he could remember that his official stance was not to give a damn about Rivington. But how the hell badly was the man's leg injured? Small wonder he had turned up ready for bloodshed after climbing that steep flight of stairs.

Jack wasn't ready for the smile Rivington shot him. *Fuck*. A startled flash of perfect teeth, accompanied by a choked laugh. Was that all it took to dismantle Jack's composure these days?

"Christ," Rivington said, "I must be in bad shape if I have career criminals asking after my welfare."

"Don't get too excited." Jack tried to sound bored. "It's

just that it would be a bloody inconvenience for the Earl of Rutland's son to die in my office."

Those blue eyes were now plainly shining with amusement. "I'll endeavor to keep body and soul together until I reach the street."

Jack bent in a slight, ironic bow. God's balls, was Rivington flirting with him? Was he flirting with Rivington? Before Jack could decide, his client appeared in the doorway.

She was dark, pretty enough, and expensively dressed. Neither plump nor thin, neither tall nor short. There were probably five hundred women like her within two miles of where they stood. About five-and-twenty years old, maybe a bit less. She had circles under her eyes that suggested weeks of insufficient sleep.

She handed Jack a card—ladies always did, as if they had come to take tea. He nearly felt bad for them, so at sea were they in these circumstances. The women of a lower station got right to business, but ladies were at a loss. He gave the card a cursory glance.

"Mrs. Wraxhall, please take a seat," he said with exaggerated courtliness, entirely for the purpose of letting Rivington know that he hadn't merited Jack's best manners. He drew his own chair closer to hers to preserve the illusion of this being a social visit. "I have an associate with me today," he said, gesturing dismissively to Rivington, "but you can pretend he isn't here." Out of the corner of his eye he watched for Rivington's reaction—a fraction of a smile. Not that Jack cared in the slightest. "How may I help you?"

"I . . . well." Her gaze flickered between Jack and her own lap, where she fiddled with the edge of a glove. "Mary said you see all manner of things and nothing I could possibly say would surprise you."

"She was right." He'd ask who this Mary was in due course. "It's best if you just come out with it."

"I lost some letters." She hesitated before continuing, her gaze darting around the room. "They were stolen, rather." Another pause, this one longer. "And in their place I found a note threatening to expose the letters to my husband unless I followed instructions."

Ah, blackmail. That was Jack's favorite. It warmed the very cockles of his heart.

To be fair, he liked any reminder that he was entirely middling when it came to sin and nastiness. He was a veritable baby in a cradle compared to blackmailers. The best part was that very often all it took was a bit of sniffing around and you could turn the situation on its head, blackmailing the would-be blackmailer into silence. And you needn't feel the slightest bit ashamed of it either.

Jack felt like a regular Robin Hood when he could manage that kind of trick.

"Mrs. Wraxhall," he said. "You've come to the right man. Now tell me everything."

**And be sure to check out her second
heart-stoppingly romantic romance,**

THE LAWRENCE BROWNE AFFAIR

An earl hiding from his future . . .

Lawrence Browne, the Earl of Radnor, is mad. At least,
that's what he and most of the village believes. A brilliant
scientist, he hides himself away in his family's crumbling
estate, unwilling to venture into the outside world. When
an annoyingly handsome man arrives at Penkellis, claiming
to be Lawrence's new secretary, his carefully planned world
is turned upside down.

A swindler haunted by his past . . .

Georgie Turner has made his life pretending to be anyone
but himself. A swindler and con man, he can slip into an
identity faster than he can change clothes. But when his
long-dead conscience resurrects and a dangerous associate
is out for blood, Georgie escapes to the wilds of Cornwall.
Pretending to be a secretary should be easy, but he doesn't
expect that the only madness he finds is the one he has for
the gorgeous earl.

Can they find forever in the wreckage of their lives?

Challenging each other at every turn, the two men soon give into the desire that threatens to overwhelm them. But with one man convinced he is at the very brink of madness and the other hiding his real identity, only true love can make this an affair to remember.

Available now from Avon Impulse!

CHAPTER ONE

Cornwall, 1816

All this fuss about a couple of small explosions. As far as Lawrence cared, the explosions were entirely beside the point. He had finished experimenting with fuses weeks ago. More importantly, this was his house to burn to the ground, if that's what he wanted to do with it. Hell, if he blew up the godforsaken place, and himself right along with it, the only person who would even be surprised was the man sitting before him.

"Five servants quit," Halliday said, tapping Lawrence's desk in emphasis. Dust puffed up in tiny clouds around the vicar's fingertips. "Five. And you were woefully understaffed even before then."

Five fewer servants? So that was why the house had been so pleasantly quiet, why his work had been so blissfully undisturbed.

"There was no danger to the servants. You know I keep them away from my work." That was something Lawrence insisted on even when he wasn't exploding things. The very idea of chattering maids underfoot was enough to discompose his mind even further. "And I conducted most of the actual explosions out of doors." Now was probably not the time to mention that he had blown the roof off the conservatory.

"All I'm suggesting is a sort of secretary." Halliday was dangerously unaware of how close he was to witnessing an explosion of the metaphorical variety. "Somebody to keep records of what you've mixed together and whether it's likely to"—he puffed his cheeks out and made a strange noise and an expansive gesture that Lawrence took to represent explosion—"ignite."

The Reverend Arthur Halliday did not know what was good for him. If he did, he would have fled the room as soon as he saw Lawrence reach for the inkwell. Lawrence's fingers closed around the object, preparing to hurl it at the wall behind the vicar's head. Sod the man for even suggesting Lawrence didn't know how to cause an explosion. He hadn't invented Browne's Improved Black Powder or even that bloody safety fuse through blind luck, for God's sake.

"Besides," Halliday went on, "you said you need an extra set of hands for this new device you're working on."

Oh, damn and blast. Lawrence knew he shouldn't have told the vicar. But he had hoped Halliday might volunteer to help with the device himself, not badger Lawrence into hiring some stranger. The vicar was convenient enough, and when he wasn't dead set on sticking his nose where it didn't belong, he wasn't entirely unpleasant company.

"I've had secretaries," Lawrence said from between gritted teeth. "It ends badly."

"Well, obviously, but that's because you go out of your way to terrify them." Halliday glanced pointedly at the inkwell Lawrence still held.

And there again was Halliday missing the point entirely. Lawrence didn't need to go out of his way to frighten anyone. All he had to do was simply exist. Everyone with any sense kept a safe distance from the Mad Earl of Radnor, as surely as they stayed away from rabid dogs and coiled asps. And explosive devices, for that matter.

Except for the vicar, who came to Penkellis Castle three times a week. He likely also called on bedridden old ladies and visited the workhouse. Maybe his other charity cases were grateful, but the notion that he was the vicar's good deed made Lawrence's fingers tighten grimly around the inkwell as he plotted its trajectory through the air.

"I'll take care of the details," Halliday was saying. "I'll write the advertisement and handle the inquiries. A good secretary might even be able to manage the household a bit," the vicar said with the air of a man warming to his topic, "get it into a fit condition for the child—"

"No." Lawrence didn't raise his voice, but he slammed his fist onto the desk, causing ink to splatter all over the blotter and the cuff of his already-inky shirt. A stack of papers slid from the desk onto the floor, leaving a single dustless patch of wood where they had been piled. Out of the corner of his eye, he saw a spider scurry out from under the papers.

"True," Halliday continued, undaunted. "A housekeeper would be more appropriate, but—"

"No." Lawrence felt the already fraying edges of his composure unraveling fast. "Simon is not coming here."

"You can't keep him off forever, you know, now that he's back in England. It's his home, and he'll own it one day."

When Lawrence was safely dead and buried, Simon was welcome to come here and do what he pleased. "I don't want him here." Penkellis was no place for a child, madmen were not fit guardians, and nobody knew those facts better than Lawrence himself, who had been raised under precisely those conditions.

Halliday sighed. "Even so, Radnor, you have to do something about this." He gestured around the room, which Lawrence thought looked much the same as ever. One hardly even noticed the scorch marks unless one knew where to look. "It can't be safe to live in such a way."

Safety was not a priority, but even Lawrence wasn't mad enough to try to explain that to the vicar.

"Villagers won't even walk past the garden wall anymore. And the stories they invent . . ." The vicar wrung his hands. "A secretary. Please. It would ease my mind to know you had someone up here with you."

A keeper, then. Even worse.

But Lawrence did need another set of hands to work on the communication device. If Halliday wouldn't help, then Lawrence had no other options. God knew Halliday had been right about the local people not wanting anything to do with him.

"Fine," he conceded. "You write the advertisement and

tell me when to expect the man." He'd say what he needed to in order to end this tiresome conversation and send the vicar on his way.

It wasn't as if this secretary would last more than a week or two anyway. Lawrence would see to that.

These past months of soft living had rendered Georgie Turner sadly unfit for an evening of dashing through alleys and capering across rooftops. His new Hessians were better suited for a tea party than for climbing up drainpipes and shimmying through attic windows.

Still, he landed lightly on the bare wood floor and soundlessly closed the window behind him, not even daring to breathe until he heard the patter of his pursuers' footsteps on the roof overhead, then receding into the distance. He had lost them.

For now, at least. Georgie had no illusions about evading Mattie Brewster's men for long. Georgie was a traitor, an informer, and the Brewster gang would make an example of him. And rightly so.

Heavy footsteps were coming up the stairs. Familiar ones, Georgie thought, but these days he didn't trust his judgment enough to wager his life on it. The door swung open, and Georgie held his breath, wishing he had a knife, a pistol, anything.

"That had better be you, Georgie," came the rough voice of Georgie's older brother. "Of all the people for you to cross, it had to be Mattie Brewster?"

Georgie let out his breath in a rush that wasn't quite relief. "I don't think I led them here," he said, hoping it was true.

"To hell with that. You think I can't put Mattie off for a bit? He and I were pinching ladies' handkerchiefs before you were even born." Jack lifted a lantern and peered at Georgie's face. "When was the last time you slept?"

"Not since leaving the Packinghams' house." Which somehow was only yesterday. "You know everything?"

"'Course. Mattie came here last night, all friendly like. I told him to bugger off, equally friendly like. He's had a man across the way, watching the house, naturally."

Georgie winced. It wasn't right to bring his troubles to his brother's doorstep. Jack could hold his own, but what if Brewster decided to pay a visit on their sister? A chill trickled down Georgie's spine. "I needed to catch my breath, and this was . . ." He let his voice trail off. This was the only place on earth where he wouldn't be arrested as a housebreaker or murdered as a traitor. He had hardly anywhere else to go, hardly anyone else to turn to. He could have fallen from the rooftop and been equally lost. "I'll leave in a few minutes. As soon as I catch my breath."

"Like hell you will. Come down and have supper with us."

Georgie nearly laughed. "This isn't a social call."

"Oh, were you engaged to dine elsewhere?" Jack paused, as if expecting an answer. "No? Then eat with us, and we'll figure out what to do with you. I doubt your enemies want to murder you badly enough to poison my soup. Oliver will be glad to see you're well."

But then Georgie would need to endure the confused sympathy of Jack's high-minded lover. Which wasn't to say that Georgie objected to Oliver; he was fine enough, in a stiff-upper-lip sort of way. Georgie was in no frame of mind, however, to make conversation with a fellow who likely thought Jack's wayward brother deserved whatever punishment he had coming his way. Hell, Georgie was inclined to agree.

"If it's all the same, I'll stay where I am, thank you." He heard the edge in his own voice. Georgie wasn't used to living off anyone's kindness. He wasn't the sort of man who inspired acts of benevolence, nor the sort to accept anything he hadn't earned—or stolen. He knew he ought to be grateful to Jack, but he was only annoyed—mainly with himself.

He had earned himself a place among London's criminal classes, and he had done it with nothing more than a bit of cunning and a complete disregard for decency. He stole and he cheated, he swindled and he lied. His favorite targets were overbred nobs who were too greedy to look closely at what Georgie offered, too blinded by visions of their own prosperity to ask the right questions. They were begging to be swindled, and Georgie was happy to oblige.

And then he had thrown it all away. He didn't know whether this was what it felt like to have a conscience, but he simply couldn't take that old woman's money. He had tried to persuade Mattie to go after another mark. When Mattie refused, Georgie had taken matters into his own hands, and now Georgie was persona non grata in London, and probably everywhere else that wasn't the bottom of the Thames.

Jack grumbled and disappeared downstairs. When he returned he carried a supper tray, which, Georgie noticed, held enough to feed two people. If Georgie would not go down to dinner, then Jack would take his dinner here in the attic. Georgie tried to muster up the appropriate gratitude but found his gaze shifting to the window he had come through and the darkness of the sky beyond. He wished he hadn't come here.

"I got a letter from a vicar in Cornwall," Jack said, and Georgie gathered that they were to attempt normal conversation. "Or rather Oliver did, and now he wants me to look into why some barmy fellow won't leave his house."

Georgie poked at his meat with a fork. "Vicars and lunatics aren't in your usual line." Jack made a living solving other people's problems, but—as far as Georgie could tell—only if the problem was an aristocrat and solving it involved a fair bit of what Jack liked to think of as retributive justice.

Jack shifted in his seat, drawing Georgie's attention like a hound catching a scent. Georgie had been swindling and stealing since he could walk, and he knew what a man looked like when he had something unpleasant to say. More importantly, so did Jack. There was no such thing as Jack Turner accidentally letting someone get a peek at his cards. If he looked uncomfortable, it was because he wanted Georgie to know it.

"The vicar went to school with Oliver," Jack said, his gaze fixed on some point over Georgie's shoulder. "The fellow who won't leave his house is Lord Radnor."

Now Georgie wasn't a hound catching a familiar scent. He was a shark, and somebody had just dropped a bloody carcass into the water. For the first time in two days, he forgot about his predicament. "The Mad Earl?" Georgie had heard of him. Everybody had. "Tell the vicar the man won't leave his house because he's absolutely crackbrained." And murderous too. There had been a missing courtesan, a dead bride, and so many duels it was nearly tedious. "And then charge your usual fee."

"This fellow isn't the Mad Earl. That was his older brother, who died a few years back. I think the father was mad too, but he wasn't such a nuisance about it. Nobody knows much about the present earl, except that he's nine and twenty and as rich as Croesus. But he can't be as bloodthirsty a bastard as his brother was, or I suppose the vicar would only be relieved that he didn't leave the house."

"And instead the vicar is enlisting the help of his old school chum's *petit ami*."

Jack ignored that. Likely because he didn't speak any French and didn't care about Georgie's barbs anyway.

"Sounds like a matter for a doctor." Georgie's interest was fast slipping. He made a great show of examining his fingernails, which were in a terrible state after the day's mishaps.

"Trouble is how to get the doctor in there without the earl's permission," Jack mused.

"Are you going to take the case?" Georgie couldn't see his brother leaving his snug townhouse long enough to travel to Cornwall to appease meddlesome vicars and investigate aristocratic hermits.

"I was thinking that I might send you, actually." It wasn't every day Jack Turner looked that shifty.

Georgie put down his fork and folded his arms across his chest, almost eager to hear whatever convoluted nonsense Jack was going to say next. "And why would I do that?"

"You could pose as his secretary, just long enough to let me know whether he's right in the head."

"There are a great many things I *could* do." He could step out the front door and wait to be attacked by his old friends and left for dead, for example. Or he could march right over to Bow Street and turn himself in. Georgie's life was a positive cornucopia of bad ideas these days. "What I want to know is why you think I ought to."

"Do you have something better to do?" Jack gestured around the empty attic. "Oliver wants to help his old friend, and I want to keep Oliver happy. Sarah would like to see you far away from anyone who wants to stick a knife between your ribs or a noose around your neck. The recluse needs a secretary. So, you go to Cornwall, and we all win." A pause. "You'd have my fee, of course."

Lurking beneath the surface of Jack's offer was the unpleasant reminder that Georgie's presence in London was putting everyone he loved in danger. "Send Sarah out of London. I don't want Brewster going after her." He scrambled to come up with a reason for flight that his sister wouldn't balk at. "She can fit Oliver's sister for some new frocks."

"Is that a yes?"

He did need to get out of London until this mess died down a bit and he figured out a way to make it up with Brewster, some way to earn back the man's trust and protection, which was the only way he'd be able to keep Jack and Sarah safe.

"Fine," he said, ignoring the look of triumph in his brother's eyes. "But I'll take half the fee in advance."

CAT SEBASTIAN lives in a swampy part of the South with her husband, three kids, and two dogs. Before her kids were born, she practiced law and taught high school and college writing. When she isn't reading or writing, she's doing crossword puzzles, bird watching, and wondering where she put her coffee cup.

Discover great authors, exclusive offers, and more at hc.com.

A LETTER FROM THE EDITOR

Dear Reader,

I hope you liked the latest romance from Avon Impulse! If you're looking for another steamy, fun, emotional read, be sure to check out some of our upcoming titles.

If you're a fan of historical romance, get excited! We have two new novellas from beloved Avon authors coming in August. *JUST ANOTHER VISCOUNT IN LOVE* by Vivienne Lorret is a charming story about an unlucky-in-love Viscount who just wants to find a wife. But every lady he pursues ends up married to another . . . until he meets Miss Gemma Desmond and he vows not to let this woman slip through his fingers! This is a delightful, witty story that will appeal to any/all historical romances fans—even if you've never read Viv before!

We also have a fabulous new story from Lorraine Heath! *GENTLEMEN PREFER HEIRESSES* is a new story in her Scandalous Gentlemen of St. James series. The second son of a Duke has no reason to give up his wild ways and marry, but when an American heiress catches his eye, the prospect of marriage seems much more appealing. As any true #Heathen (a Lorraine Heath superfan!) knows, her books are deeply emotional and always end with a glorious HEA. This novella is no different!

Never fear contemporary romance fans . . . we didn't forget about you! Tracey Livesay is back at the end of August with LOVE WILL ALWAYS REMEMBER, a fun and sexy new novel with a While You Were Sleeping spin! When a woman awakens from a coma with no memories from the past six years, she's delighted to learn a handsome, celebrity chef is her fiancée . . . or is he? Don't miss this wonderful diverse romance that will have you sighing with happiness!

You can purchase any of these titles by clicking the links above or by visiting our website, www.AvonRomance.com. Thank you for loving romance as much as we do . . . enjoy!

Sincerely,
Nicole Fischer
Editorial Director
Avon Impulse